PENGUIN BOOKS

RUN AWAY WITH ME

Praise for *Run Away With Me*

'Bold and romantic, *Run Away With Me* is a road-trip thriller that starts at high speed and doesn't let up'
Erik J. Brown, author of *All That's Left in the World*

'A thrilling, evocative coming-of-age story. I devoured it'
Cynthia Murphy, author of *Win Lose Kill Die*

'*Run Away With Me* is the emotionally – and literally – high-stakes road-trip book I never knew I needed. Buckle up, because you're in for one heck of a ride'
Kayvion Lewis, author of *Thieves' Gambit*

'A thrilling joy ride of unexpected twists and turns'
Benjamin Dean, author of *How to Die Famous*

'Don't start *Run Away With Me* late at night, as you won't be able to stop reading. A sublime debut. A perfectly executed road-trip romance with lots of thrills'
Elle McNicoll, author of *Some Like it Cold*

'What a ride! What a thrilling, soulful, life-affirming ride!'
Simon James Green, author of *Noah Can't Even*

'Jessie and Brooke are a modern-day Thelma and Louise. I raced through this book! The tension, the adventure, the swoon – a brilliant debut!'
Abiola Bello, author of *Love in Winter Wonderland*

'*Run Away With Me* is a high octane coming-of-age YA romantic thriller. A read-in-one-sitting, turbo charged drive across America that will have your heart pounding and your pulse racing right till the very last page'
A. J. Clack, author of *Lie or Die*

RUN AWAY WITH ME

J. L. SIMMONDS

PENGUIN BOOKS

PENGUIN BOOKS

UK | USA | Canada | Ireland | Australia
India | New Zealand | South Africa

Penguin Books is part of the Penguin Random House group of companies
whose addresses can be found at global.penguinrandomhouse.com

www.penguin.co.uk   www.puffin.co.uk   www.ladybird.co.uk

First published 2025

001

Text copyright © J. L. Simmonds, 2025
Cover and map illustration copyright © Gavin Reece, 2025

The moral right of the author and illustrator has been asserted

The brands mentioned in this book are trademarks belonging to third parties.

Penguin Random House values and supports copyright. Copyright fuels creativity, encourages diverse voices, promotes freedom of expression and supports a vibrant culture. Thank you for purchasing an authorized edition of this book and for respecting intellectual property laws by not reproducing, scanning or distributing any part of it by any means without permission. You are supporting authors and enabling Penguin Random House to continue to publish books for everyone. No part of this book may be used or reproduced in any manner for the purpose of training artificial intelligence technologies or systems. In accordance with Article 4(3) of the DSM Directive 2019/790, Penguin Random House expressly reserves this work from the text and data mining exception.

Set in 10.5/15.5pt Sabon LT Std
Typeset by Jouve (UK), Milton Keynes
Printed and bound in Great Britain by Clays Ltd, Elcograf S.p.A.

The authorized representative in the EEA is Penguin Random House Ireland,
Morrison Chambers, 32 Nassau Street, Dublin D02 YH68

A CIP catalogue record for this book is available from the British Library

ISBN: 978–0–241–70814–9

All correspondence to:
Penguin Books
Penguin Random House Children's
One Embassy Gardens, 8 Viaduct Gardens, London SW11 7BW

Penguin Random House is committed to a sustainable future for our business, our readers and our planet. This book is made from Forest Stewardship Council® certified paper.

For Lola and Margo

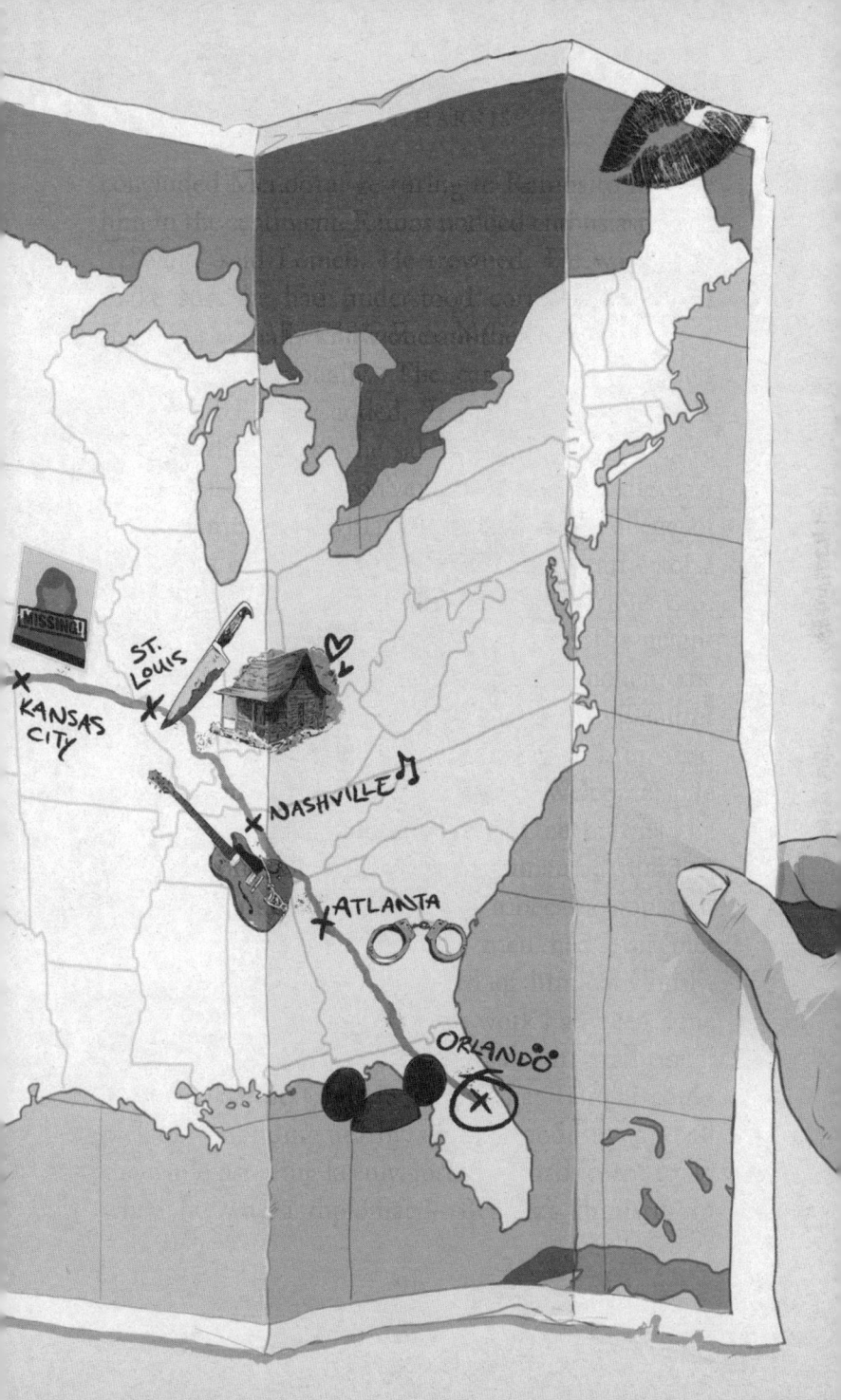

1

Born to Run – Bruce Springsteen

My feet and shoulders were aching, and my breath kept catching in the back of my throat, like the panic was rising up and snatching the air before it could reach my lungs. To distract myself, I repeated the same mantra, over and over.

Get to the bus station. Get on a bus. Go.

It was a comfort as I walked, the words falling into the same rhythm as my footsteps. I needed a distraction, to keep my mind focused on something other than the absolute horror I was leaving behind me.

I glanced up from the sidewalk and wondered how late it was. The sun was starting to set, bathing the city in a peach glow. It couldn't have been that long since I'd gotten off the bus, maybe an hour at most. But in that time, everything had changed.

Night fell slowly as we edged through spring, the city on tenterhooks with winter jackets packed away and bare ankles on display. Over the past few days the famous

Seattle rain had fizzled out and the last of the chilly nights seemed to be behind us.

Get to the bus station.

Get on a bus.

Go.

I had to keep going, had to keep myself distracted, because hot bile kept pushing up from my stomach and the acidity was threatening to spill out of me at any second. I really didn't want to spew on the city streets – partly because that would be so gross, and mostly because I didn't want to draw attention to myself. All this would be for nothing if someone saw me leaving.

My ear and jaw still throbbed from what had happened this morning. I'd gotten up and showered, then braided my hair so it fell to the middle of my back, keeping it out of my way for school.

Then he hit me.

After that, I unpicked the braid so I could let my hair hang loose around my face and hoped no one would notice the mark on my cheek.

Not that anyone ever looked that closely at me anyway.

All day I'd been pressing my tongue to my back tooth to see if it was still loose, and every time I'd tasted blood. Now, my feet hurt from pounding the sidewalk, my shoulders were sore from the combined weight of a backpack and duffel bag, and I had a headache blooming behind my eyes. Luckily, I was good at ignoring pain. I'd take a couple of Tylenol when I got to the bus station.

Get to the bus station. Get on a bus.

I forced down my self-pity, knowing it wouldn't help me.

Go.

And then her car pulled up.

'Mouse?'

Brooke drove a red vintage convertible Mustang. The top was down, and she was leaning out of the window, her face etched with concern. I focused on the car for just a moment too long and my whole body violently contracted – *blood* red, dark and shiny, like the way blood pools on polished tile . . . I forced myself to look at Brooke instead.

'Hey,' I tried to say nonchalantly.

Brooke Summer was the most beautiful girl in our whole school. It wasn't just me who thought it, either – it was a widely agreed-upon opinion. She had deep, dark-brown eyes with tiny gold flecks in the irises and defined cheekbones that made her look elegant and mature. She was still wearing our St. Catherine's uniform, so her lush, dark hair fell in effortless waves over the crisp white shirt she'd unbuttoned at her throat.

In school, she always said hello to me, even though she was one of the popular girls and I was me. She didn't have to be nice, but she was, offering me small smiles when we passed in the hallway or inviting me to sit next to her in Chemistry lab. We were in the school choir together, too, so every week for an hour I got to stand two rows behind her and look at the back of her head.

I liked to admire her from afar.

'Do you need a lift anywhere?' Brooke asked, tapping her fingers on the steering wheel in a distracted pattern.

I hesitated for a moment, because my plan was a good one. But it was going to take me another hour to get to the bus station on foot, and time was against me. I needed to go, *now*.

'Could you take me to the –' I couldn't say *the bus station*, that was too obvious. 'To Chinatown?'

To her credit, she didn't ask me why I was going there with a shoulder full of bags, but it was the closest place to the bus station I could think of under pressure.

'Sure. Get in.'

My duffel bag fit in between my feet and I placed my backpack on my lap, which now felt heavier than it had when I'd been walking. I put my seatbelt on, and Brooke waited until it clicked in place before signaling to pull back out into traffic.

I carefully adjusted my plan, still needing the mantra to keep my head clear of flickering mental images that were trying to barge in.

A broken door.

A broken body.

No! I wouldn't . . . I couldn't . . .

Get in the Mustang. Get to the bus station. Go!

The gorgeous cream leather seat was cool against my arms as I settled in, turning away from Brooke so I didn't have to look at her. It was rude of me, but I was on edge. I could apologize another time.

If there ever was another time.

I only started paying attention to my surroundings when Brooke pulled up outside the bus station twenty minutes later. I looked over at her, alarmed.

She shrugged and gave me a sad smile. 'I know what someone running away looks like, Mouse.'

I stared at her for a second, taken aback and not knowing how to reply. I'd only ever looked at Brooke through the lens of my ridiculous, cringey crush, so it hadn't occurred to me that maybe she was going through something too. I glanced around, searching for the right words to say.

Brooke had a black leather bag on the back seat, next to her school backpack and a large duffel bag. I looked over at her, now even more unsure of what to say. Her dark eyelashes flickered as she blinked a few times.

'So,' she said, 'do you want to come with me?'

My heart started to beat a little faster. 'Where are you going?' I asked.

'I don't know yet. Does it matter?'

'No, not really. But . . . why?' I asked, suddenly desperate to know.

Brooke looked down and pushed her hair behind her ear. 'Okay, here's the deal. You don't ask me why I'm leaving town, and I won't ask you. How does that sound?'

She was prepared to take me with her *and* she wouldn't ask for details? This was a much better plan. I hesitated for a second, wondering if dragging Brooke into the mess I was running away from was a good idea. Or, you know . . . ethical. But leaving with Brooke meant not being alone and, honestly, I wasn't sure how long I would have lasted on my own anyway.

'Deal,' I said quickly. 'Absolutely deal.'

Brooke looked up and grinned, flashing white teeth, a little shark-like.

'Let's go.'

The Mustang growled when she revved the engine, and I couldn't help but run my hand over the side of the seat, letting the buttery-soft leather caress my palm. I knew nothing about cars, but this one was seriously cool, and it was getting me the hell out of Seattle. I was growing fonder of it by the second.

'Do you like music?' Brooke asked as we merged onto the I-5 and headed out of the city.

'Sure.'

'There are cassettes in the glove box.'

'Cassettes?' I replied.

She laughed brightly. 'Yeah, Mouse, cassette tapes. The car came with a cassette deck and it still works. The radio signal is shit once I leave the city.'

I opened the glove box and, sure enough, it was stuffed with a dozen or so shiny clear cases. The first one I picked up was *Born to Run* and that sounded appropriate. I knew Bruce Springsteen. I wasn't a total idiot.

The case opened with a satisfying *click* and I took out the cassette, turning it around to study it.

'Side one needs to be facing up,' Brooke said, watching me from the corner of her eye. 'It should be right at the start.'

I stuck the cassette into the stereo, and after a second the speakers whirred to life. The car might have been old, but the speakers were clearly new. Sound burst out of them, bright and clear, and Brooke turned the volume up.

'I love this album,' she murmured.

I had no idea where we were going, or how long it would take to get there, but those questions all blurred into irrelevance. I was out of Seattle, and in Brooke's car, and everything else could wait.

The city started to fade behind us, and Brooke put her foot down on the gas.

Brooke drove *fast*, and I wasn't used to that. She headed south toward the Oregon border, her fingers lightly tapping the steering wheel like it was a habit. I closed my eyes for a while, content to listen to the music and the sound of the cool night air whizzing past, the scents changing as we moved out of the city, through the suburbs, then into more wide-open space.

As the sky deepened into inky night and Brooke continued to put more distance between me and my house, each of my muscles started to relax, releasing the tension I'd been desperately clinging to. Sitting next to Brooke wasn't awkward. The silence wasn't awkward, either. It was almost . . . *nice* . . . to spend time with someone without being on edge, waiting for the next barbed comment or backhanded slap.

I smothered a yawn and rubbed my fingertips over my eyelids. The mental effort not to let my thoughts wander back to earlier this afternoon was exhausting. I couldn't let myself go there. It had cost me so much to get out.

I didn't realize I'd fallen asleep until I woke up with a start. I glanced over at Brooke, who smiled back at me.

'I didn't want to disturb you,' she said softly.

'That's okay.' I stretched my back and squinted out of the windshield. 'Where are we?'

'About an hour outside of the city.'

'Where are we going tonight?' I'd been too afraid to ask, not sure if this counted in our deal not to ask each other why we were leaving Seattle. I also wasn't sure if I'd like her answer.

'Where do you want to go?'

That made me laugh. 'You're the one driving.'

'We've got the entire continental US to explore,' Brooke replied, and it sounded like a joke and also really not like a joke at the same time. 'Unless you brought your passport, in which case both Mexico and Canada are possibilities.'

'I don't have a passport.'

She didn't comment on that. I hadn't spent my life going on fancy vacations in other countries like she had, and I was almost baiting her – waiting to see if she would turn out to be a Mean Girl after all.

'Have you ever been to Disney World?' she asked, and I grimaced.

'No. I've never –' I decided not to finish that sentence. Brooke didn't need to know I'd only ever visited two other states, and both of them shared a border with Washington.

'I haven't,' I said instead, hoping she hadn't noticed.

She smiled. 'Awesome. That's where we're going, then.'

'Brooke. That's, like, a two-week drive,' I said with a disbelieving laugh.

'Nah, I figure we can do it in ten days. Maybe less.'

'How fast do you drive?' I asked.

'I won't break the speed limit,' she said simply. 'But we'll get there, don't worry about that. Do you have cash on you?'

'Yeah. And a credit card,' I said. Not all the money was mine. The credit card definitely wasn't. It wouldn't take a lot for Brooke to figure that out, but she didn't question it. That almost made it worse. She'd want answers eventually, and I had no idea how to explain what had happened.

'Great,' she said. 'I'm gonna keep going for another hour, then we should probably stop and get a motel room.'

'Sure.'

I was so intimidated by Brooke that going along with her plan was easier than trying to suggest something of my own, something that would probably be stupid in comparison. I never got the impression that she tried to be intimidating, but some girls had this thing about them – an aura, maybe, or an attitude – that made me cower in front of them.

Brooke was tall, which helped with her attitude, and classically beautiful, which doubled it. I frequently got tongue-tied in front of pretty girls and usually ended up mumbling or running away ... or both. Fortunately, I did that in front of girls who I didn't think were pretty, as well as grown women, and *especially* men, so when I got flustered by a girl I liked, no one knew why. Over the years, I'd become good at hiding what I really thought. Or felt. Or wanted.

Brooke seemed lost in her own thoughts, too, or maybe she was just concentrating on driving. It was harder to see the street signs in the dark. Eventually she slowed down and pulled into the parking lot of a motel.

'You should find a space out front,' I said absently.

'Oh, no way. I like to park away from the road.'

I glanced over at her. 'It's easier to get out in the morning if you park at the front.'

When I was younger, I'd stayed in motels with my mom, and she'd always wanted an easy escape in case the landlord she hadn't paid was chasing us out of town. We'd only had someone catch up with us once, but that was enough for her to change her habits.

Brooke shook her head. 'In this car? Do you know how often people try to steal it? I need to keep it out of the way somewhere.'

I opened my mouth to reply, then closed it again. 'Okay.'

I couldn't explain without telling her the whole messy story, and it was late, and it didn't matter.

Brooke pulled into one of the short-stay spaces and killed the engine. 'You want to wait here?'

'I can do that.'

'Great. Thanks,' she said, already pushing the car door open. She got out and walked toward the lobby, her back straight and chin up.

I waited in the dark as the automatic doors of the motel swished open and closed. We'd been on the road for a couple of hours, long enough to get us out of Seattle and past the suburbs, too. Far enough away from home, I hoped, that no one would think to look for us here.

I watched as two businessmen walked into the motel, practically dragging their feet with tiredness. Then I spotted a woman, who could only be here for one reason, following half a step behind a seedy-looking guy.

My brain felt sluggish as I processed all my failures from today.

Get to the bus station. Failed.

Get on a bus. Failed.

But . . .

Go. Done.

2

Rumours – Fleetwood Mac

I woke up to the soft *whoop whoop* of a police car, and sat bolt upright in bed, my heart thundering in my chest. Had the cops caught up with me already?

After a split second I remembered we were in a motel off the interstate, and the police probably drove through here on a regular basis. There was really no reason for me to panic, especially so early in the morning. I pressed the heel of my hand against my breastbone and forced myself to take a deep breath. I glanced over at Brooke, who was sleeping soundly on the bed next to mine, curled up and facing away from the window.

The motel room had two narrow, lumpy beds and a threadbare carpet – far from modern, but it was clean, and I wasn't going to argue about the quality when it had been so cheap.

Brooke had taken care of paying for the room and collecting the keys last night, and we'd driven around the back of the building to hide her car in a dark corner of the parking lot before taking all our bags into the room. Brooke had gone back to put the top up on the Mustang, while I tried not to worry about everything that had happened.

I didn't want to go to sleep right away, but Brooke looked exhausted, so I didn't shower before I got into bed like I usually did. She'd fallen asleep only minutes after crawling under the covers and I hadn't. I'd laid on my back for a couple of hours, staring at the ceiling and listening to Brooke snore. Asleep, I had no control over what memories my subconscious flashed at me. It was easier to stay in control while I was awake.

Brooke's exhaustion had made me even more curious about what she was running away from, but I wasn't going to ask. Not when I knew she would only ask me the same question back.

While I'd been lying awake, I'd been able to hear the cars outside racing up and down the highway. That hadn't bothered me, though. It was nowhere near as bad as some of the apartments I'd lived in with my mom, where I could hear babies crying and adults arguing through the paper-thin walls at all times of day. I guess the sound of the traffic must have eventually lulled me to sleep.

Now, looking over at the thick curtain covering the window, my curiosity got the better of me and I quietly slid out of bed to see what was going on outside. Two police cars were in the parking lot, their red and blue lights flashing, and I watched a female officer get out of the second car and go around the corner to the motel reception.

Oh no.

I'd been here before – well, not *here*, but I knew exactly how this scene played out – and the last thing I wanted was to be directed into the back of a police car to be returned to my mom. I guessed there were two cars because there were two of us, one car each for me and Brooke, and both would be carrying a stony-faced police officer accompanied by a fake-smiling child protection social worker. They always sent the female officers after teenage girl runaways.

I wasn't going back. Not this time.

'Brooke,' I said, stumbling across the room to urgently shake her awake. 'We have to go. Get up.'

'What the hell?' she grumbled.

'The police are outside.'

'Police?' She sounded more alert now.

'Yeah. We have to go. Right now.'

'Shit,' she groaned.

She sat up quickly then, and I pulled on a sweater and my sneakers while shoving everything else into my backpack. I was shaking and I couldn't do anything to stop it. It took three attempts for me to tie my shoelaces. My fingers kept slipping.

'Where's the room key?' I asked in a panic.

I turned around and noticed Brooke had put her jeans on over the top of her pajama shorts.

'Just leave it.'

'Leave it here?'

'Yeah, housekeeping will find it when they come by later,' she replied.

Not having to check out with the front desk would cut down on how long it would take to get out of here, which was fine by me. I swung my backpack onto my shoulder and took a few quick steps toward the door.

'You're sure they're here for us, Mouse?' she asked, and I nodded frantically.

'There are two cars, both with police officers and what look like child protection social workers. We have to leave *now*, unless you want a police escort home.' I forced myself to unclench my jaw. 'But I might be wrong. Do you want to hang around and find out?'

She stared at me for a moment, then shook her head. 'Let's go.'

We left the room as quietly as possible and tried to act casual, like regular people who had decided, *Hey, let's get up super early and leave, rather than waiting for the free breakfast buffet.*

'There's a back staircase. I noticed it last night,' Brooke said. 'It goes straight down to the parking lot.'

'Let's do that,' I said, my words coming out more blunt than I intended. I just wanted to be out of here, away from the two police cars that were such a threat.

It would take a moment, I was sure, for the officers to get the information they needed from the front desk and then find our room. What I was more worried about was Brooke's incredibly ostentatious car. If someone decided to go poking around the parking lot, it wouldn't take them long to find it. At least Brooke had insisted on parking at the back of the motel, out of sight of the road. That would buy us a few more minutes.

We scrambled down the narrow staircase and then fell into step alongside each other as we crossed the lot to the car. I didn't dare say anything as Brooke got into the driver's side and turned the engine on. I slid into the seat next to her and fixed my eyes firmly on the windshield.

'Can you see anyone?' she asked.

I swallowed hard and forced myself to look around. 'No. We're good.'

'You better be fucking sure about this,' she muttered, and followed the signs for the exit.

There was a single officer left in one of the police cars – the others must have joined the first at the front desk – and she barely looked up as we pulled around the building and onto the highway.

I looked down at my hands, surprised to see that they were still shaking, then flicked my eyes to the rearview mirror, watching for when the police cars would surely appear. Meanwhile, Brooke put distance between us and the motel.

I was breathing too hard, but I couldn't slow down my rapid-fire heartbeat. I wasn't going to get away with this. Someone was going to catch me, and then I'd go on trial for murder, and, worst of all, I was dragging Brooke into all of this too.

Brooke reached across me and fumbled for the glove box.

'What are you doing?' I asked.

'I need another cassette,' Brooke said. 'I hate driving in silence. It stresses me out.'

'Jesus, it's not the time, Brooke! Just drive!' I said, my voice rising with panic.

'I'll drive better if we're not sitting here in silence.'

'Fine! I'll do it,' I said, slapping her hand away. 'You just . . . watch the road.'

'I'm watching it,' she grumbled.

I picked a cassette at random, pushing the button to eject *Born to Run* and replacing it in its case. It was good to have a task to focus on. Something to distract me.

'This is Fleetwood Mac,' I said, sliding the cassette into the slot.

'A classic.'

'You have eclectic taste in music, Brooke Summer,' I said, trying to lighten the mood.

She shrugged one shoulder. 'I like good music. You must, too, if you're in the choir.'

'Eh. I'm only in the choir because –'

'Because?' she prompted.

'Never mind.'

I didn't want to go into all the excuses I had for not coming home straight after school. I could sense she was curious, but I wasn't going to tell her anything. Not at six in the morning, anyway. My ear was still throbbing from what had happened yesterday, the pain right there if I wanted to tune into it. I did my best to tune out again.

'Where do you even find cassette tapes?' I asked, changing the subject.

Brooke didn't take her eyes off the road, but I could see her quick smile. 'Thrift stores, mostly,' she said. 'There's rules, though.'

'Rules? Tell me.'

I was distracting both of us now, and Brooke seemed to realize that.

'They have to be original albums, not recordings,' she said. 'You can find lots of mixtapes at Goodwill, but most of them totally suck, recorded off the radio or whatever. Or the start of the song is cut off because the person recording it didn't know what they were doing.'

'Okay.'

'And you can't pay more than five bucks per album.'

'How much do they cost?' I asked.

'It depends,' she said. 'Some places you can pick them up really cheap, like a dollar or less. But there's some music stores in Seattle where people are betting that cassette tapes will make a comeback like vinyl did, and then people will want the originals. So the Goodwill on Rainier Avenue is starting to hike up their prices. You have to be careful where you buy them from, otherwise you'll get ripped off.'

'Does it matter who the artist is?'

'Yes,' she said emphatically. 'I'm not playing terrible music in my car, Mouse.'

The way she said it made me laugh, but I wished she wouldn't call me Mouse. I hadn't figured out how to ask her not to. After all, it's what everyone called me, whether I liked it or not.

'No eBay, either,' she said, and it took me a moment to catch up with her.

'Huh?'

'The tapes. You can't get them on eBay. That's cheating.'

This was the longest conversation I'd ever had with Brooke – a conversation that wasn't about running away, at least – and I realized I was only just starting to scratch the surface of getting to know her.

'All right,' I said. 'Do you have a list of albums you want? Or do you buy whatever you find and like?'

'Bit of both. I'm still trying to find Paul Simon's *Graceland*.'

I glanced in the rearview mirror again, and this time Brooke caught me.

'Mouse?' she asked.

'I can't see anyone,' I said quietly.

Yesterday I had been ready to leave Seattle, even if that meant being on my own, but now I was here with Brooke, I wasn't going to jeopardize the company by telling her why the police were after me.

'Do you think we've been reported missing?' Brooke asked. 'It's not even been twenty-four hours since we left.'

'Yeah, but we're seventeen. Did something happen to you?' I asked, deflecting hard.

'No! You?'

I shook my head, not trusting myself to come up with the right words to convince her.

'And how the hell did they find us so quickly?'

I'd been thinking about that, too. 'Did you use a credit card to check in last night?' I suggested, and Brooke groaned.

'Shit. You're right.'

'Or our cell phones. Is yours still on?'

'It's on airplane mode,' she said. 'Do you think that's enough?'

I'd turned mine off completely. 'I don't know,' I said honestly.

'I'm gonna turn it off now,' she said, fumbling in her pocket.

'I can do it,' I said quickly, wanting her to keep her focus on the road.

'Thanks,' she murmured and handed it over. 'I'm going to take a detour,' Brooke said after a few moments. 'Get off the main drag. Just in case they're following us.'

'Sure. Good idea.'

'I need coffee,' she added, her words stretched out by a yawn. 'And I want to get dressed. I don't have a bra on.'

I really didn't want to think about what underwear Brooke Summer was or was not wearing. It was way too early for that kind of existential angst.

Thankfully, it took less than ten minutes for us to find a Starbucks, and Brooke pulled into a parking space rather than the drive-thru, which had a huge line anyway. There didn't seem to be many people inside.

'I'll order and you can go get dressed, then we can swap?' Brooke said, and I nodded. 'What do you drink?'

'A caramel latte?' I asked it as a question, like this was something I could get wrong.

'Hot or iced?'

'Hot, please.'

She nodded and edged into the line, looking slightly more human in jeans and a sweater than I did in pajama pants. Then again, no one looked at me twice, and I got the impression I wasn't the worst-dressed person the baristas had ever seen.

The restroom was impressively clean, and I double-checked the lock on the door before stripping out of my pajamas and putting on clean underwear and jeans. I was grateful I'd packed long pajama pants because they covered the ugly scar at the top of my thigh that I really didn't want Brooke to see, and I didn't like looking at either.

Checking my body in the mirror for bruises was second nature and I twisted uncomfortably to see how the one on my back was fading. It had turned yellow-green, which was good news. It would be gone in a few more days.

I threw on an old but clean T-shirt and washed my face, smoothed down my eyebrows, and felt almost normal again. My hair was a mess. It had gone greasy around my hairline, turning the light brown darker, but I couldn't do much about that, so I pulled it all into a messy bun on the top of my head and decided I would try to pretend that was my intention all along.

I stared at myself in the bleary mirror, pulling strands of my hair loose from the bun so I didn't look like I'd tried too hard, then applied a tiny dot of foundation over the faint mark on my cheek. Brooke hadn't mentioned the mark, and I wasn't sure if she was being kind or discreet or if she just hadn't noticed it. Either way, it was easier to hide it than to answer questions.

It had been a while since my last encounter with Child Protective Services, which put me on edge. When I was younger, I had been on their radar for a whole host of reasons, most of them related to my mom's terrible taste in men, but as I'd edged through my teenage years, they seemed less and less interested in me. Knowing someone was looking for me put a different spin on the road trip. It was more important than ever that we put distance between us and Seattle . . . for my own freedom, and so I could protect Brooke from the mess I was leaving behind.

A knock on the restroom door startled me.

'Mouse?'

'Coming,' I said, quickly shoving everything back into my backpack.

Brooke was waiting outside when I opened the door. 'Sorry, I need to use the restroom. I ordered and paid, but they haven't made the drinks yet.'

'Thanks. I'll give you some money,' I said, already feeling embarrassed that she'd paid for everything so far.

'It's fine,' she said, waving my embarrassment away and dashing into the stall.

I went over to the end of the bar to wait for our order.

'Summer?'

It took me a moment to realize Brooke had given a fake name, which was *smart*. I should have thought of that. I muttered my thanks and took the two takeout cups the barista had set on the counter, then went to a table near the front so I could watch who was coming into the parking lot.

The sharp-sweet smell of coffee and the familiar, generic environment of Starbucks was the permission I needed to relax. Everything here was as it should be, from the menu to the noise of orders being tossed back and forth between customers and baristas, and the gentle background music that I didn't need to listen to.

When Brooke came back out, I couldn't even tell that she'd gotten ready in a Starbucks restroom. She looked as effortlessly perfect as she always did, and something in my belly fizzed with want. My crush on Brooke had been simmering for a while now, at least since the beginning of the school year, when we had started having classes together for the first time.

She slid into the seat opposite me and took the first sip of her coffee, clearly not noticing me staring at her.

'Do you really think they were child protection people?' Brooke asked, both hands wrapped around her cup.

I thought carefully about my answer, wanting to show her that I wasn't just freaking out like some little kid.

'Honestly? Yeah.'

She nodded quietly and looked back out the window. 'Okay.'

'I don't know why else they would've sent two cars and all female officers. That's what they do.'

'Do you –' she paused for a moment, still not looking at me, clearly trying to figure out a polite way to ask her question. 'Have . . . first-hand experience? Of that?'

I huffed a laugh. 'Yeah, Brooke. We're old friends with CPS in our house.'

'Oh.'

'It's not what you think.' Or maybe it was. I didn't know her well enough to guess what she was thinking. 'It's better now. We just had a few issues with my dad when I was younger.'

'I see,' she said, her voice totally neutral.

'It's okay, though.' I'd learned that lie by repeating it so many times it had become true. 'We worked it out.'

'Okay,' she said, nodding, wincing a little in sympathy. 'So, the cell phones have to go.'

'Fine by me.'

No one ever texted me. I mostly used my phone to keep up with K-pop news on Twitter and stalk celebrities on Instagram. Those were habits that I probably needed to break, anyway.

'Credit cards too?' she said, and it took me a moment to realize she was asking for my opinion.

'Well, I don't have a huge amount of cash,' I said. 'Maybe we should get some money out near here, then ditch them?'

'There's cameras at ATMs, though.'

'Does it matter? Once we have the cash, it's not traceable. All they'll know is that we took it out.'

Brooke stared at me, and I wondered whether she had put mascara on. Her eyelashes were so dark, and so long, showing off her beautiful eyes. Then her lips stretched into a smirk.

'You're outrageous.'

'I'm not,' I said quickly. No one had ever called me outrageous. I liked it, even though she was wrong.

'Audacious.'

'Definitely not that.'

Brooke laughed brightly. 'Okay. We should drive somewhere, go to an ATM and draw out a shitload of cash, then double back and keep heading down to Disney World.'

'Why Disney World?'

'Why not? You've never been.'

'It's a long way from Seattle,' I murmured.

'Exactly.' Brooke leaned back in her seat, like that settled it.

Maybe it did.

We got back in the Mustang and Brooke drove around until she found a strip mall with multiple ATMs in the parking lot. I got out of the car and walked in one direction, toward CVS because I'd left my toothbrush behind in the motel bathroom and I needed a new one, and Brooke went in the other direction, to the grocery store.

Just walking across a parking lot made me feel like a felon on the run, like every pair of eyes was on me, even though I was under no illusions. Actually, I was a nondescript teenage girl giving no one a reason to look at her. That didn't stop my heart beating up into my throat, like it had yesterday when I was walking to the bus station.

Only yesterday? Time moved fast.

The drugstore was relatively empty in the middle of the day, and I tried to act normal. What did normal girls do in CVS? Look at makeup? I only ever wore makeup to cover up bruises, scars or zits, and I always felt conspicuous when I tried on my mom's bright lipstick, so I never bothered with it. I browsed the aisles under the fake fluorescent glow of bright white lights, threw powder and concealer into my basket, then went looking for toothbrushes. At the checkout line I picked up two Snapples and a bag of chips and waited for the woman in front of me to be finished.

'Hey,' the cashier said as I walked up to her counter.

'Hi.'

I looked around as she scanned and packed my stuff, checking out where the CCTV cameras were. They'd already caught me, I was sure of that, so there was no point in trying to hide now.

'Forty-two twenty-six is your total.'

'Thanks.' I swiped the card and watched the screen on the card reader for it to clear.

The machine beeped.

My stomach dropped and I swallowed hard, hoping my famously bad lying wouldn't expose me now. We had only just crossed the border into Oregon. If the cashier called for security, then the Seattle police would be able to get here in no time.

'Can I see it?' the girl asked, and I couldn't find any reason to tell her no.

'It's my stepdad's card,' I said with a shrug, playing it cool.

The Creep wasn't my stepdad, he was just my mom's scummy boyfriend who liked to smack me around. Explaining all that took time, and was way too personal, so 'stepdad' was a useful shortcut, even though I hated giving him that title.

'Huh. It's coming up with a code I don't know and saying to call your card provider. You wanna call him?'

'He's at work,' I said apologetically. The lie was far preferable to the cold reality that I was avoiding thinking about. 'He'll get pissed if I call him now. I've got cash . . .' I didn't want to spend it, though, not when I'd picked up a bunch of junk I didn't really want or need.

'You want me to run it one more time?'

'Sure. Thanks.'

She did, swiping it her side this time. 'Try the PIN?'

I hit the numbers I'd memorized months ago, my fingers tingling with pins and needles. They were icy cold, and I wanted to rub them against my jeans to push the feeling back into them again, but I held off. No point in making my nerves even more blatantly obvious.

The till beeped.

'All good,' she said, passing me the card back. I felt like I was going to throw up, like the stress that had curdled in my stomach was desperate to be purged.

'Great, thank you so much.' I took the plastic bag from her with a forced smile.

'Have a nice day.'

'Thanks, you too.' The words left my mouth by habit. My brain had stopped working.

Outside, it had started to drizzle, the cold biting my fingertips.

The ATM was next to the exit doors and no one was around now – no people, only cameras, to witness this.

I slid the card into the machine and punched in the PIN again, absolutely sure that the card would be swallowed and I'd fail. I was going to fail.

The next screen flashed up and I pressed the button for cash.

$250 was the maximum I could withdraw in one transaction.

Fine.

Receipt?

What was the point? I hit the button for No.

It took a second, then the machine whirred and spit out the cash and the card. I rolled the bills up and stuffed them into my bra, then slid the card back in again.

Cash.

$250.

No.

The next wad of bills went into the pocket of my hoodie.

Cash.

$250.

No.

Back pocket.

This was Brooke's plan – break up the cash into smaller amounts instead of putting it all in one place in case we lost a bag or got robbed.

Cash.

$250.

No.

Other side of my bra.

Cash.

$250.

No.

And the ATM did nothing for a few long seconds, longer than it had taken the other four times. So a thousand dollars in cash was the limit for the card?

That wasn't enough ... That wasn't going to get us all the way to Florida. I smacked my hand on the screen and waited, fingers still twitching, until it displayed a new message telling me to contact my card provider.

The machine hummed for a second, then went back to the holding screen. It had swallowed the card.

Shit.

I rubbed my hands together, trying to get blood flowing into them again, and turned to head to the Mustang.

I hadn't noticed the man coming up behind me.

I hadn't noticed anything that was going on when I'd been withdrawing the cash, too focused on what I was doing, and it took me until that moment to realize how epically stupid that had been.

He was probably in his mid-twenties, with a scruffy beard and dirty hair that hung around his ears. He was wearing a hoodie and jeans, like me. Nondescript. Blending in. And he was leaning against the wall a few feet to my right, out of sight of the security cameras.

Clever.

Unlike me.

'Yeah, I'm gonna need you to give me the cash,' he drawled.

The laugh burst out of me. Not humor, but incredulity, maybe. An *I can't believe this* emotion making itself known. I'd finally gotten out of Seattle and now this asshole wanted all my money?

Seriously?

I should have been scared – I should have been fucking *terrified* – but instead my blood boiled with an unfamiliar fury.

His eyebrows drew together. 'I'm not fucking joking.'

'I didn't think you were,' I said slowly. I was already full of adrenaline, and I'd normally give him the money and deal with the consequences later, but we needed this money. My sickly nerves were overlaid with a new energy, an *angry* energy. I was stalling for time, trying to figure out how to get away, and he knew it.

'Look, just give me the money, sweetheart.'

It was the *sweetheart* that changed everything.

I wasn't his *sweetheart*. I wasn't anyone's goddamn sweetheart. And I was sick of gross men calling me that.

'I could scream,' I said, forcing nonchalance I didn't feel into my voice. Still, I was sure it shook a little.

His expression morphed from shock to amusement way too quickly. 'I bet I can stab you faster than you can scream. You really want a knife in the gut instead of a couple hundred bucks?'

So he had a knife, and he didn't know how much money was currently hidden on me, which meant he couldn't have been watching me for long. I glanced over my shoulder, and when I looked back, he was even closer. I could smell the sharp, sour stench of his clothes, the sweat that was baked into the fabric.

'I can also run faster than you, sweetheart. Give me the fucking money.'

Years ago, during a self-defense class that had been scheduled during our usual gym period, me and a group of other eighth-graders had been told, if we ever got mugged, to throw our wallet or phone as far as we could and run in the other direction. Most of the time that was what the muggers wanted – something of value – and they didn't care much about the person they stole it from. A bundle of cash was harder to throw a distance than a wallet or phone, though. But if I threw a handful of bills up in the air, he'd have to scrabble to pick them all up, and I could run . . .

He pulled a flip knife out of the waistband of his jeans.

'Okay!' I said quickly, really, really not prepared to find out what it felt like to get stabbed. I could handle pain, but that was . . . *oh God*, a pain I really didn't want to experience. 'Okay. Just let me –'

The Mustang screeched to a stop a few yards away, and Brooke leaned out of the driver's side window, a handgun pointed in the man's direction.

'All right, asshole, leave her alone.'

While he was gaping at her, I dashed for the car, the plastic CVS bag knocking against my leg. The asshole yelled something, but there was too much blood rushing through my ears, blocking up my brain, and all I could think was *thank God . . . thank God* for Brooke being here to save me. *Again.*

'Go, go, go,' I said, shoving the bag next to my feet and pulling the door closed at the same time.

I pressed the heel of my hand to my sternum, hoping to hold back the sick, terrified feeling and settle my rapid heartbeat. I still felt a little stunned, like I couldn't really believe this was happening, that this was actually my life now.

The man was still yelling something as Brooke pulled away, revving the engine so hard I felt the vibrations through my entire body.

3

Get a Grip – Aerosmith

Brooke drove out of the town in stony silence, her jaw clenched and her knuckles white on the steering wheel. After a few minutes I bent over and put my head between my knees, sure I was going to puke, and she still didn't say anything.

Then she snapped at me.

'Put some *fucking* music on, Mouse. You know I hate driving in silence.'

I grabbed another cassette out of the glove box and shoved it into the player without looking. This time the speakers blasted angry rock music.

It looked like this road trip was going to be over before it had even begun. The plan had been so simple ... get cash out and get back to the car. But no. I'd screwed up, like I always screwed up, and Brooke had had to do something *illegal* to save me.

I couldn't blame her for being angry. I was angry at me, too.

Hopefully I could convince her to drop me off at the next bus station, or a city with good public transport links. I had a thousand dollars in cash on me now, plus what I'd stashed away before leaving home. That was enough to get me . . . somewhere. I'd be on my own again, but at least I had a plan, right? *Get to a bus station. Get on a bus. Go . . .*

My stomach lurched and I held back the instinct to throw up, knowing if I did that in Brooke's car it would only make her angrier. I'd originally planned to run away on my own, so I didn't know why being without Brooke was suddenly such a terrifying idea.

I barely noticed when the car stopped. I did notice when the music cut out.

I forced myself to sit up, my stomach still churning. 'I'm sorry.'

'Jesus Christ, what are you sorry for?' Brooke said irritably.

'For screwing everything up!'

'It was such a simple plan, Mouse. Get some fucking cash and go. You do realize I was probably caught on security cameras waving a gun at someone?'

'I know,' I whispered. 'I'm sorry.'

Brooke closed her eyes and shook her head. 'It's all right. We'll handle it. Are you okay?'

'I . . . Not really.' I couldn't lie – my brain was too scrambled. Even though it was pathetic, and I was probably going to make Brooke hate me even more, I didn't have it in me to pretend.

She reached over and squeezed my arm, either not noticing or choosing to ignore it when I flinched.

'Come on,' Brooke said, opening the car door and getting out.

We were in a small parking lot next to a nature park that had pretty picnic benches angled so they'd be in the shade of the trees. It was raining a little, but not enough to deter me from getting out of the car. Brooke didn't seem to be bothered by the rain, either.

I followed her in silence as we walked over to a picnic bench. I sat down on the table with my feet resting on the bench part, and Brooke straddled the bench so she could look at me from a right angle. I didn't have to look at her at all if I didn't want to.

'What happened?' she asked, more gently this time.

'I . . . I don't know. I got the cash out of the ATM, and when I turned around, he was there. Then you showed up with a gun.'

Brooke had a gun. I hadn't really processed that. She had been driving around this whole time with a *gun*, and that was how she'd managed to save me.

'I'm sorry I didn't tell you,' she said, her voice still a little defiant.

'It's fine.' It wasn't fine, but what else could I say? It had all been my fault anyway, so I couldn't be mad at her for coming to my rescue.

'Really?' she said, prodding just a little now.

'I don't think he would've let me go so easily if you hadn't had it.'

'It's not loaded,' she confessed, and I almost laughed. That felt like a metaphor. The illusion of power, but none of the reality.

We fell into an uneasy silence, and Brooke started picking up leaves and shredding them into tiny pieces.

'Are you going to leave me here?' I murmured.

Brooke's head snapped up. 'What? No. Of course not.'

'Oh. Good.' I forced myself to sit up straight. 'I don't mind where you drop me off. Wherever's easiest is fine.'

'What are you talking about, Mouse?' She sounded irritated again, and my shoulders hunched as I tried to make myself smaller.

'You're . . .' I wasn't sure how to finish the sentence. 'You want to get rid of me, right? I'm a liability.'

She laughed then, shattering the tension. 'You're a liability all right, but I don't want to get rid of you.'

'Oh.' It took a second for that to sink in. I didn't fully believe her. 'Really?'

'Yeah. I'm mad about what happened, but I'm not mad at *you*.'

She should have been mad at me, though, because there was a lot I wasn't telling her, about my house and the Creep and all the blood. Jesus, so much blood.

It had seemed like such a good idea last night to get in Brooke's car and go wherever she wanted to take me. Now, though, I had to face the truth that I'd dragged her into a whole tangle of messes that I'd made. Brooke was on the run with a girl the police wanted for murder. And she didn't even know it. But when I tried to shape my mouth around the words – around the truth – nothing came out.

'What happened with you? Did you get the cash?' I asked, deflecting from my inner turmoil.

She nodded. 'I managed to empty two cards. I got a grand out of one, and eight hundred bucks from the other.'

'Mine had a thousand,' I said. 'But I only had the one card.'

It wasn't exactly a shock that Brooke had access to more cash than I did. She was from a wealthy, prominent family, and I came from a single mom who was well known to CPS. We weren't equals.

'That's okay,' she said quickly. 'We should probably divide it up and stash it in different places. Just in case, you know?'

'Yeah. I've got another couple hundred bucks in cash, too. From home.'

I ran my hands across the surface of the bench, liking the way the grooves of the wood felt as they dug into my palms. Far away from other people, I felt safer out here than I had anywhere else since we'd left Seattle.

'Right, I've got –' she tipped her head to the side – 'about the same? A little more, maybe.'

I did a quick mental calculation. 'That's, like, three and a half thousand dollars!'

'Holy crap!'

'Should get us to Disney World, right?'

Brooke collapsed into laughter, and after a moment, I joined her.

I'd seen her laugh like this before, with her friends at school. She had a way of commanding attention in the hallways or in classes, and I often watched her when I was sure no one was looking at me. Now I was the one making her laugh, and a warm feeling curled in my chest.

'Maybe you can get a job as a princess,' I said. I straightened up, planting my hands on the tabletop so I could tip my face up to the sky. The rain felt nice on my hot cheeks.

'We'll get you a blonde wig and you can be Tinker Bell,' she replied.

I snorted. 'Nah, I can be one of the people they hide inside those giant suits. Like Mickey Mouse.' No one wanted to see me on a parade float. Not compared to Brooke.

'No,' she said emphatically. 'They need girls like you to play the little characters.'

'Because I'm short?' I said with a laugh.

'Short and cute,' she replied, and, while I was still reeling, trying to figure out what that meant, she changed the subject. 'We should get rid of our phones now.'

'Do you need to call anyone before we do that?' I asked, wanting to check, just in case. 'Your mom or anyone?'

'No,' Brooke said sharply.

I dared to glance at her. She didn't look angry, but she clearly wasn't happy.

It was none of my business. I wouldn't pry.

I trailed after her as she followed a dirt path, muddy and overgrown with plants. A few steps along it and suddenly we were enveloped by trees, the branches thick overhead and the clean, loamy smell of the soil filling the air. If I lived somewhere other than the city, I would go for hikes all the time. I loved the feeling of isolation, of being so far away from other people that I didn't have to be constantly on high alert, wondering if I needed to watch my words or actions in case someone lashed out. Places like this felt like magic to me.

We emerged by the side of a lake in a burst of light, and apart from the pattering rain rippling the surface of the water, it was still and peaceful out here.

'There,' Brooke said with a suddenly intense look on her face. 'We'll throw them in the lake.'

'Isn't that a bit . . . dramatic?'

Brooke grinned and shrugged. 'I don't mind a little drama.'

That made me smile as I pulled my phone out of my pocket. The screen was cracked in one corner, but I hadn't had the cash to replace it.

I held up my phone and she did the same. 'On three?'

She nodded.

'One.'

'Two.'

'Three,' we said together, and hurled the phones out into the water. Mine landed first, Brooke's half a second later, both making huge *splosh*es as they sank.

It only occurred to me then that I didn't have my mom's phone number saved anywhere. It was stored in my phone, which was now at the bottom of this lake. I couldn't call her, even if I wanted to. I forced myself to ignore the sudden nausea.

Deep down, though, I knew I wasn't ready to face her or the judgment that would follow. Our relationship had been complicated recently, but she was still my mom. I had no idea if she would ever forgive me for what had happened.

I looked back at Brooke. She seemed to be breathing a little harder than usual.

'You okay?' I asked.

She nodded sharply. 'It's, like . . . really gone.'

'It really is. Unless you want to go for a swim.'

Her laugh sounded more startled than amused. 'And happen to have a really big bag of rice in the trunk of the car.'

'Do you?' I asked.

'No, I left it at home this time.'

I shook my head, hiding my smile. 'Big mistake.'

Brooke kept staring out at the surface of the water. I didn't know what she was running from, but we'd entwined our fates now. Maybe she was thinking about the fact she wouldn't be able to call her mom, either. Maybe, like for me, that was both absolutely terrifying and an enormous relief.

I didn't look at her, but tentatively reached out to brush my fingertips against hers.

After a moment, she nudged mine back.

And my heart skipped a beat.

It had stopped raining when we got back to the car, but Brooke didn't want to take the Mustang's top down again until she was sure her leather seats wouldn't get rained on.

When she started the car, the music came on automatically. We were still in the middle of the album.

'I want to try to get as far across Oregon as we can before we stop for the night,' Brooke said. 'Then tomorrow we can cut into Idaho.'

'Sounds good to me.'

'Mostly I know the way. We just need to follow the signs for Salt Lake City, then Denver, then Kansas City . . .'

'St. Louis?' I asked, and Brooke nodded.

'Yeah. Then Nashville, Atlanta and Orlando.'

'You make it sound easy.'

She grinned. 'I like driving. And road trips.'

I decided on the spot that I liked road trips, too. I hadn't known that about myself, and now I did.

'Me too.'

It felt good to say it out loud.

'Look.'

I pointed at a sign on the side of the road. It was nearly five p.m.; time had passed quickly since we'd gotten back in the car and started making real progress across the state.

THRIFT & ANTIQUE SUPER STORE. OPEN L8. NEXT EXIT – 2 MILES.

'You wanna go?' Brooke asked. 'I could use a break, actually.'

'Yeah, let's do it.'

Brooke seemed brighter this afternoon, lighter now that we'd put Washington firmly behind us and we hadn't seen any more police cars. But I couldn't relax yet. It felt like

Seattle and all the blood and pain and bone-deep fear were still hovering in the rearview mirror. I hadn't fully escaped what had happened – not when my brain decided to flash gruesome images at me as soon as I closed my eyes. I tried my best to shake it off.

When Brooke pulled into the parking lot, her shiny red Mustang was the only car there. The whole complex looked abandoned, apart from the thrift store and a hardware store on the other side of the lot.

My mom had shopped in thrift stores for most of my clothes when I was a kid, so stepping into one again felt like a nostalgic blast from the past. The smell of the clothes, the rows of jeans packed in tight against each other, the brightly colored kids' T-shirts over in the corner. Mom always said I grew too fast to buy new clothes for me regularly. She wasn't one of those eco-conscious hippies buying second-hand to save the environment, we were just dirt poor.

We split up, Brooke disappearing to go look for music, while I found myself browsing the aisles, brushing aside frumpy dresses and plaid shirts.

I'd never really had a sense of style. I wore whatever was cheap, whatever fit or whatever my mom bought for me. That meant jeans I'd picked up at the supermarket and baggy T-shirts that could be worn year-round, either with the sleeves rolled up or underneath sweaters in the winter. Buying nice clothes cost money, and I always handed a chunk of whatever I earned from my part-time jobs over to my mom, so there wasn't much left over for fashion.

'That would look great on you,' Brooke said from behind me, and I almost jumped out of my skin.

'Holy crap, Brooke.'

'Sorry.' She laughed. 'It would, though.'

'I don't think so.' I set the dress back on the rail, not wanting to spend money on clothes when we were trying to save it for gas and food and motel rooms.

'Try it on,' she said eagerly.

The dress was black, knee-length, with tiny white and yellow flowers and a square neckline. It was pretty – unassuming, but pretty.

Brooke reached around me and pulled out the tag. 'It's, like, ten bucks, Mouse. Try it on.'

'Fine,' I sighed.

But I was secretly pleased. I'd never had this before – a girl friend to go shopping for clothes with.

A friend who was a girl.

Not a girlfriend.

I'd never had one of those, either. Although I might have had a few fantasies during our Chemistry lessons about Brooke being my girlfriend, of walking through the school holding hands, jumping apart when we spotted any of our Catholic high-school teachers. Fantasies of hiding in supply closets to kiss between classes, of getting a prime spot to watch her play soccer for the school team.

I followed Brooke to the changing rooms that were an alcove with a scrap of fabric stapled over it to act as a curtain. I hated changing rooms, but no one was around except Brooke, and she'd already seen me in my pajamas.

'What do you think?' I asked, pulling back the curtain dramatically to show off the black dress.

There wasn't a mirror inside the changing room, so I had to step out to see myself. Brooke held a finger in the air and twirled it. I obligingly turned a quick circle, the skirt of the dress flaring out around my thighs.

'It's super cute.' She was leaning against the wall, chewing on the arm of her sunglasses. 'Get it.'

'Maybe.'

The girl in the mirror looked like me ... almost. I recognized myself, even if putting a dress on felt like stepping into someone else's life.

Brooke smiled, like she could read my thoughts. 'You look really nice, Mouse.'

'Thanks,' I said, staring at myself in the mirror instead of at her, for once.

I couldn't think of a time I'd ever felt *really nice*, and I was super bad at taking compliments, so I didn't want to look Brooke in the eye.

'Come on, get changed. My turn.'

I hadn't noticed the monster pile of clothes she'd collected. 'You have to be kidding me.'

'I won't buy all of it,' she protested. 'Probably.'

I shook my head and ducked into the changing room to put my jeans and T-shirt back on.

'Do you have space in the car for all that?' I asked through the curtain.

That made her laugh. 'I told you, I'm not getting it all. But I didn't exactly leave with my entire wardrobe. I need a few more essentials.'

How the hell bright pink Lycra leggings counted as essentials, I had no idea.

I swished the curtain back open again.

'Plus,' she said in a hushed whisper, 'we have *three and a half thousand dollars*.'

I snorted with laughter. 'Fine. I'm going to look at jeans.'

'You're not going to stay for my fashion show?'

'Okay. I can do that.' It sounded much better than browsing jeans.

Brooke wriggled excitedly before ducking behind the curtain.

'Do you need anything else while we're here?' she asked.

'No, I don't think so. I brought enough clothes with me.'

I hadn't exactly been thinking straight when I'd stuffed underwear and jeans and T-shirts into my duffel bag. I realized then that I'd probably never see anything I'd left in my bedroom again. That was the first thing I'd felt sad about since I'd left, which made me shallow, and maybe pathetic. It wasn't like I owned a lot.

I folded my arms across my chest and swallowed hard, trying to keep all the messy emotions inside.

Brooke saved me from my own thoughts by stepping out wearing the pink leggings, a white tank top with sunflowers on it and a black leather jacket slung over her arm.

'Try this. It's too small for me,' she said, thrusting the jacket out.

'Are you sure?'

'Absolutely.'

I set my dress down on a chair and shrugged into the jacket. I could tell it was real leather – like the seats in the Mustang, it was silky smooth, worn in just the right way.

'That makes you look so badass,' Brooke said, so seriously I had to laugh.

'I'm the least badass person on the planet.'

'Not anymore you're not.'

'Those leggings make you look like eighties Barbie,' I said, hoping to make her smile.

'They make my butt look incredible,' she said, twisting around to check it in the mirror.

'I can't argue with that,' I murmured. I'd thought her butt looked incredible for some time now. But being given permission to look felt different. I pushed my hot, squirmy attraction for her aside. Brooke didn't need another person leching over her, she got enough of that from the boys – and male teachers – at school.

She laughed brightly. 'Okay, the leggings are out. You should try this, though.'

She passed something around the curtain. I couldn't tell what it was at first. It was like someone had taken a dozen bright yellow feather boas and sewn them together.

'Is that . . . a skirt?'

'Yeah. Isn't it amazing?'

'Brooke.'

'Just pull it on over your jeans.'

I was sure even the slightest movement would cause the skirt to explode, but I did it anyway, unable to keep in my giggles. At least the waistband was elastic so I could get the stupid thing on.

Brooke came back out again, now wearing a black denim skirt and an oversized New York Giants T-shirt tied up at her waist.

'That's better,' I said.

'Yeah, I like it. And your skirt.'

I turned to the mirror and cracked up again. 'I look like I plucked Big Bird.'

Brooke snorted, then doubled over laughing. 'All right, all right. You can leave the skirt.'

I wriggled out of it. 'Thank God. I'm going to have a look at the music.'

'They don't have *Graceland* – I already checked,' Brooke said over her shoulder as she went to change back into her regular clothes.

I folded the black dress and left it with the rest of my discarded pile before heading for the music section. Brooke could get whatever she wanted, but buying stuff for myself felt stupid. I didn't need it.

We were still the only people in the thrift store apart from the single clerk behind the counter, who seemed mildly bemused by us. She was older than me, and way cooler, wearing vintage or second-hand clothes in a way that looked intensely fashionable. She looked down at her book when I glanced her way.

The back corner of the store was filled with CDs and DVDs and battered paperbacks that had clearly been well read. I ran my fingertips over the deeply creased spines, past the dozens of Dan Brown novels and crime titles, and plucked a copy of *Jurassic Park* from the shelf. I'd never read the book, and it was only fifty cents.

The Harlequin Romances were a quarter, so I picked up three, choosing the ones with the most outrageous titles or swooning heroines on the front. My mom would intensely disapprove of my choices, which only made me more determined to buy them. Then I picked a few cassettes at random, going off album artwork and band names I recognized.

Brooke was already at the cash register when I finally made my way over to her, and I was relieved that the pink leggings hadn't made it into her final pile.

'I'm being good,' she said, gesturing at the small stack of clothes that the clerk was folding. 'Look.'

'I believe you. I found some music.'

She looked the cassettes over and grinned. 'Nice. And books?'

I spread them out on the counter, and she laughed brightly. 'That's quite a swing in genres you have there.'

'That's thirteen seventy-five,' the clerk said, interrupting us.

'What a bargain,' Brooke said pointedly, handing over a twenty.

'I didn't say a word,' I murmured. She elbowed me in the ribs. I held back the temptation to start laughing again and wondered when I'd become comfortable with her touching me. A week ago I would have combusted into a million pieces if she'd done that.

'If you're nice to me, I might let you borrow my new wolf-howling-at-the-moon T-shirt.'

'What?' I exclaimed, playing along with the joke. 'How did I miss that?'

The clerk's lips twitched, just the tiniest amount, and I thought she might be trying to smile. 'We have a whole section of wolves-howling-at-moons T-shirts, if you're interested.'

'It's okay, she said she'd share.'

I pushed my haul over the counter so the clerk could ring me up.

'Five dollars.'

'Even more of a bargain,' I said to Brooke. 'And I managed to pick up some classic literature too.'

By the time we left the store, I was absolutely certain the clerk was laughing at us. And I really didn't care at all.

We dumped everything in the trunk of the car, and I stretched my arms over my head for just a moment, wanting to ease out all the aches before I got back into the passenger seat. It had stopped raining now so Brooke put the Mustang's roof down.

'Shit,' she mumbled. 'I left my sunglasses on the counter. I'll be right back.'

'Sure,' I said.

'Enjoy your sun salutations,' she replied, and I grinned.

'They're not –' I started, but she'd already disappeared.

I went back into the trunk to extract the cassette tapes from the bag so I could put them in the glove box with the others.

'I can't believe you fell for that,' Brooke said, hopping into her seat over the top of the closed driver's side door.

She dumped a package on my lap. It was the dress.

'Brooke.'

'Shut up,' she said, pushing her sunglasses back down on her nose as she turned on the engine. 'We have three and a half thousand dollars and it cost ten bucks. Totally worth it.'

'Brooke,' I murmured again, but my fingers were already caressing the soft cotton fabric. No one had ever done something like this for me – something nice, just to be nice – and any more protests I had faded away.

4

Lady Sings the Blues – Billie Holiday

After a crazy first two days on the road, we decided to spend the third day putting serious distance between us and Seattle. The weather was starting to clear up as we headed into Idaho, with more blue skies and fewer clouds, and that seemed to put Brooke in a good mood.

We were on a stretch of two-lane highway that was full of truckers and tankers and not that many cars like Brooke's. We went for miles at a time without seeing anything, then a cluster of billboards would appear on the horizon, accompanied by a cracked parking lot and another strip mall. Then they'd disappear in the rearview mirror, and we were back to looking at wide-open nothing.

I was worried that the Mustang would get us noticed far more than if we were traveling in some boring beige car, though I knew there was less than no chance of Brooke giving it up, so I didn't say anything to her. Not when we were getting along so well.

We'd stopped the night before in another nondescript motel a few miles from the state border and eaten Chinese food on the bed while watching reruns of *30 Rock*. Brooke had let me choose the TV channel, and comedy was better for me at the moment than dramas – there was less chance of seeing a body covered in blood and having another intense flashback.

I didn't want to wreck this fun, easy thing we had going. Not with my baggage, or my crush on her, or by asking for too much. She'd let me pick the music again, though, and I'd gone for wailing jazz this time, just because it was so different from everything we'd been listening to so far.

'What's your real name, Mouse?' Brooke asked.

I had my feet on the dash of the Mustang, something Brooke only let me do when I took my shoes off. I swallowed the mouthful of Twizzler I'd been gnawing on before answering her.

'Jessie. Jessie Violet Swift.'

'That's pretty. Short for Jessica?'

'No. Just Jessie.'

'Why do people call you Mouse, then?'

'Oh, God, that's a long story.'

'It's a long road,' she said without apology.

'Maybe it's not so long. I guess it started in ninth grade.' Had I really been dragging around the nickname for three years? Holy crap. 'I was the new kid, and I was short and pale and weird.'

I also had light-brown hair and pale-gray eyes, and I jumped whenever anyone spoke to me. I was the new kid in my first year of Catholic high school, and I had to navigate wearing a uniform and rules that definitely weren't part of my last non-religious school. On top of that, I was a scholarship kid, which made me super insecure. I felt like everyone would be able to tell just by looking at me that I didn't really belong.

'You're not pale and weird anymore.'

She had to be joking, right? I was *definitely* still both of those things.

'You're still short, though,' she said, offering me a tiny smirk.

I tucked that smile away, sure I'd want to think about it more later.

'You're not wrong,' I said. 'So, yeah, the kids called me "the mouse", and I guess it stuck.'

'Since you started at St. Catherine's?'

'Yup.'

'Does it bother you?'

'Yeah,' I said honestly. 'That time in my life wasn't the best.'

Almost as soon as we'd settled in Seattle, my mom had a new boyfriend – not the Creep, a guy called Simon – and she immediately became obsessed with him, like she did with every new boyfriend. Simon was okay. He could be weird sometimes, and he was fanatical about hockey, so I learned quickly to be somewhere else if he wanted to watch it at our house.

Simon wasn't around for long. When he broke up with my mom, she would swing between crying for hours and a furious rage, and I never knew what mood she'd be in when I got home from school. That was my strongest memory of starting high school. My mom getting dumped.

'Didn't your parents do anything about it?' Brooke asked.

'No, not really,' I said. 'I never really bothered my mom about stuff that was happening at school. She was too busy with work for things like parent–teacher conferences, and my dad was long gone by then.'

I only had vague memories of my dad. My mom rarely spoke about him, keeping only a handful of photos of him in a battered envelope that I often had to dig through old boxes to find, since we moved so much and I never knew where anything was.

All through grade school I'd missed having a dad, though I'd never really spent much time with *my* dad, even before he left us. He became this great, unknowable figure, and I filled in all the gaps in my knowledge with my imagination, turning him into an ideal that the real man almost certainly wasn't.

'I'm sorry,' Brooke said gently, like she meant it. 'When did he leave?'

'When I was . . . four, maybe five?' Like the Mouse thing, I didn't want to dig into this with Brooke. I didn't want her to know all the dirty secrets of my life.

'Do you ever see him?'

'No, not anymore. My mom knows where he is, just, like, on a general basis. I think he went to New Mexico and worked in construction for a while. She might be able to get ahold of him if she wanted to, but I don't know.'

My mom had been the one to cut ties, and I didn't really know how to bypass her and reconnect with him, or what I'd say if I found him.

'Are you an only child?' Brooke asked.

'Yeah. I mean, I might have half-brothers or -sisters out there somewhere, I suppose, but if I do, no one's ever told me about them.'

'You're not curious about that? Sorry if I'm being too nosy.'

I laughed, even though it sounded a little forced. 'It's fine. I guess I might look into it one day.'

'What about your mom? Are you close?' Brooke pressed.

'We used to be.' That was true. 'She works a lot now.' Also true. 'Sometimes it feels like . . .'

'Like?' Brooke prompted.

'It's . . . whatever,' I said, waving away her concern. 'I got a job last year, so I can go out and do that now and she doesn't have to worry about me.'

'What do you do?'

'Babysitting. Some tutoring. Over Thanksgiving and Christmas last year I worked at the mall on the weekends, too, in one of those stores selling fancy soap.'

I'd never minded working. My mom appreciated me helping out with extra cash and it took off some of the pressure on our relationship. Plus, I got to work with people who called me Jessie, not Mouse, and treated me like a normal person.

'I never got paid for babysitting,' Brooke said, sounding put out. 'My extended family just expects it.'

I grinned. 'That's where being part of the church comes in useful. There's a pretty big network of families, and they all know me, so there's always someone around who wants me to watch their kids for a few hours.'

'That's clever. I should've thought of that.' She paused and pushed her sunglasses back down on her nose. 'What about your stepdad?'

I froze. 'He's not my stepdad, he's my mom's boyfriend,' I said, trying to make my voice sound normal.

Brooke glanced over and raised an eyebrow at me. I'd clearly failed.

'Sorry. Didn't realize it was a sore subject.'

I forced myself to relax. 'It's all right. I just don't like him. People think he's a really great guy, and he's not.'

'Okay.' She dropped it, and I was grateful for that.

'What about your family?' I asked, hoping to turn the spotlight off me for a moment.

Brooke groaned. 'We are . . . dysfunctional.'

'Dysfunctional how?'

'My brother, Daniel, is at Harvard Law. He's also vice president of the tennis club and clerks for Senator Duval in his spare time.'

'He has spare time?' I joked, hoping to cover my weird reaction at her mention of the Creep.

'Apparently. My older sister, Julianne, is studying medicine at NYU. Back last year there was a moment where it looked like she was going to specialize in family medicine or general practice, but my parents staged an intervention and now she's back in cardiology. What a relief,' Brooke said sarcastically.

Her tone had shifted into something that sounded like the *Real Housewives*, gossipy and obsessive. She flicked her fingers at me dramatically.

'And my younger sister, Hope, is a music prodigy. Cello and violin. She'll be going to Juilliard in a few years.'

'How old is she?'

'Thirteen.'

'And you already know she's going to Juilliard?'

'My parents do,' Brooke said, with a twisted smile I didn't think was genuine.

'So what about you?'

A muscle in Brooke's jaw twitched. 'Well,' she said, switching back into her *Real Housewives* voice. 'Brooke was all set to join Julianne at NYU and be a doctor, but she's recently shown a real interest in politics. And you know how much we love to encourage the girls, so it looks like she'll be going to study at Stanford or Berkeley. A real woman-in-government triumph for the Summers.' Her words soured at the end, turning into something awful and bitter.

'That sounds like someone else's idea, not yours,' I said softly.

'That's because it is.'

'They really plan everything out for you like that?'

'Mouse, you have no idea,' she sighed.

'Maybe they just . . . care?' I suggested.

'I wish they wouldn't.'

She was wrong about that, but I didn't correct her.

'So your older brother and sister are already in college?' I asked instead. 'Do you see them very often?'

'Julianne comes home for Thanksgiving and Christmas. She stays in New York during the summer, and I usually go stay with her for a couple weeks. Daniel hardly ever comes home.'

'You'll be the only one staying on the west coast for college, then,' I said, ripping apart another Twizzler, more for something to do with my hands than because I was hungry.

'They need to keep an eye on me,' she said darkly.

I didn't get why. Brooke was practically the perfect daughter. She was in so many extracurricular clubs and teams, not just choir, but the debate team, soccer, the Shakespeare society, French club . . . all while maintaining some of the highest grades in our class.

She didn't seem to appreciate, or even acknowledge, what she had. To have parents who cared about you so much was something I literally couldn't get my head around, and, sure, they sounded like a lot, but I'd spent years wishing someone would care about me just a little bit. My mom was always more interested in the next guy than she was in me. She wanted to get married, to settle down and have the big, happy family that had never been possible when she was a single mom towing around a shy kid. The Creep had promised her that. He wanted a whole bunch of kids running around, and I could see the stars dancing in my mom's eyes every time he mentioned it. He didn't need to spell it out that having me around didn't feature in his plans.

The music cut off with a click, and I reached for the glove box to pick the next album. I was getting good at reading Brooke's mood and matching it to my music choices.

'I hate this part of Idaho,' she muttered.

'Really?' I thought there was something bleakly beautiful in the dirt and scrubby grass and the endless blue sky.

'It's depressing as hell.'

I laughed and put my feet back up on the dash. 'Where do you want to stop tonight?'

'Somewhere outside of Salt Lake City. It'll get too expensive if we go into the city. It's better to find somewhere on the outskirts.'

'That makes sense. Have you ever been to Salt Lake?'

Brooke shook her head. 'No. My cousin Meredith came here once to check out one of the colleges. God only knows why.'

'Did she get in?' I asked, suddenly panicked. I didn't want anyone to know where we were, and if Brooke called her cousin, we could have the police breathing down our necks in no time.

'No, she went to Denver in the end. Do you want to go to college?'

What was I supposed to tell her? That no college in the country – in the *world* – would accept me after everything that had happened. The feeling of having no way out was crushing, and I pushed it down to deal with later.

'I guess it depends on whether I get in anywhere,' I said vaguely.

Brooke glanced at me, frowning. 'I thought you get good grades.'

'I do. Most of the time. I'm not an academic genius, though. And I'd need a decent scholarship to be able to afford it.'

'You're smart,' Brooke said with a confidence I was sure I'd never feel. 'You'll get an academic scholarship.'

'Maybe,' I said, because I couldn't bear to think that far ahead.

If I was honest with myself, I couldn't think much past tomorrow.

5

Fast Car – Tracy Chapman

I was watching the cars whizzing past on the I-15 outside Salt Lake from my vantage point in the Mustang parked by our latest motel. Brooke had been driving for almost six hours before we stopped for the night, and I could tell she was tired. She got irritable when she was tired – not obnoxiously so, but the tension made her eyebrows pinch together in a frustrated frown.

I still couldn't believe I was here with her.

Brooke.

Brooke Summer.

The girl I'd had a crush on for almost a *year*. The girl who used to make my stomach flutter when she smiled at me in school, and now got irritable with me when her blood sugar dropped.

Whenever I offered to drive, she shot me down, so there wasn't much I could do about that. I had my driver's license, but that didn't seem to matter to her. To be fair, if I owned a vintage Mustang, I wouldn't let other people drive it, either.

'All good?' I asked as Brooke got back into the car. She handed me the fake ID she'd been using to check into the motels – since we were both seventeen and some places were funny about that – and I slipped it back into the glove box for safekeeping.

'Yeah. We're on the second floor at the back.'

'Perfect.'

The afternoon was hot, hotter still now that we weren't whizzing down the highway with the top down. Brooke parked in the shade of some tall trees and worked to get the roof back on and secured while I grabbed our bags.

We headed for the stairs, since last night we'd found a dead rat in the elevator and Brooke had turned very green at the sight of it. I'd had to calm her down for a solid twenty minutes before she'd agreed to stay in that motel. This one seemed nicer, but I still wasn't taking any chances.

'We're two-ten,' Brooke said from behind me. 'Should be just down here.'

The room was dim, with heavy blackout curtains and weird floral wallpaper. The dresser was dark wood and held a TV that was *super* 3D. It was probably older than me.

'Ugh.'

'I know,' Brooke said. 'But it was cheap, Mouse.'

'Yeah, it's fine. It's only for tonight.'

'You want to order pizza?' she asked, holding up a leaflet that had been left on the desk.

'Sure. I'll eat anything.'

'They've got some good deals.'

I let her call the order through using the phone on the nightstand while I started separating out everything from my bags. I organized stuff into piles on the bed: clean clothes, dirty clothes, wash bag, cash.

Three and a half thousand dollars had felt like a lot of money, but between gas, food and motel rooms, we were spending it quicker than I had expected. I grabbed all the bills from the different hidey-holes and started bundling it in ways that made sense, a hundred dollars at a time.

Brooke flopped onto the second bed and covered her eyes with her arm. 'I'm going to sleep for a thousand years tonight.'

'That would be one hell of an achievement.'

She snorted with laughter, then fell silent again. After a few minutes, I decided she had fallen asleep. Or a-snooze, at least.

Every now and then it hit me that I had actually escaped. Freedom tasted sweet. But also like something I hadn't earned . . . the sour that went with the sweet was guilt. It swirled in my stomach uncomfortably, forcing me to ignore the emotions that wanted to bubble up. I couldn't start thinking about my mom, or her now dead boyfriend, or how my mom was going to make rent this month without my usual contribution and after everything that had happened. I knew from painful experience that once I opened those floodgates, it was almost impossible to close them again.

'I don't want to stay in the room tonight,' Brooke said, sitting up suddenly. I hadn't realized she was awake again.

'Okay. What do you want to do?'

'I don't know. Go out. We can go out, you know, Mouse.'

'I know,' I said, trying to placate her. 'You're tired, though. You shouldn't push yourself to be sociable in the evenings, too.'

'Let's go down to the bar.'

'They won't serve us, Brooke.'

She rolled her eyes. 'I know. I don't want alcohol, I want company.'

I knew what she meant and tried not to be upset that my company wasn't enough. But Brooke was always with a group of people at school, and she had siblings at home, and I guessed she wasn't used to spending time just one on one.

'I'm gonna get changed, then,' I said. 'We can go downstairs after we've eaten?'

'Yes,' she said emphatically.

The pizza guy turned up while I was in the bathroom trying to do something with eyeliner that didn't make me look like a kid playing in her mom's makeup bag. It was stupid, but I wanted to wear my new dress, and I felt like the dress deserved eyeliner, or some kind of effort not to look like the most boring person in the room. That was difficult when I was traveling with Brooke. She looked like a supermodel in jeans and sneakers.

I let my hair down and tried to arrange it in effortless waves around my shoulders, like Brooke's hair, but it hung limply and had big dents in it from where I'd had it tied up all day. I heaved a sigh of frustration and pulled it back up into a messy bun again.

'Mouse!'

'I'm coming,' I called.

'You look cute,' she said as I sat down opposite her at the small table.

'Thanks.' I tried not to let her see how much her offhand comment affected me. I pushed the fizzy, excited feeling down, down, into the box with all my other emotions, and slammed it shut.

Brooke had ordered a large sausage-and-mushroom pizza with garlic knots and a huge soda and had it all spread out on the table. It smelled incredible.

'Hungry?' I asked, and she looked up at me, her mouth already full. I laughed and took a slice for myself, letting the hot pizza soothe my frazzled nerves.

The bar in the motel was next to the lobby. Brooke walked right up to it like she'd done it a hundred times and slid onto one of the tall barstools.

'Do you want a Coke?' Brooke asked as I awkwardly climbed onto the stool next to her.

'Sure.'

There was a baseball game showing on the TV behind the bar, and my eyes flicked to it automatically. At home, there was often baseball on the TV, and I'd gotten used to having no say in whether or not we watched it.

'Good evening,' the bartender said. 'Do you have ID?'

'Yeah, but neither of us want a drink,' Brooke said easily. 'We have to get up early in the morning.'

'Okay. What can I get you?'

I made a point to close my mouth, sure that it was hanging open watching Brooke navigate the awkward situation with an ease and grace I was certain I'd never possess. And she could lie!

Like, oh my God, she could lie.

The bartender put down two little paper napkins and set a glass of Coke on each of them. Brooke handed him a ten-dollar bill with a smile and waved away the change.

The bar wasn't too busy. It seemed like there was a decent mix of couples, single men in uncomfortable-looking suits, and a group of women who could have been part of a bachelorette party.

I spotted the weirdo before Brooke. *Long* before Brooke.

He was in his early twenties, drinking from a bottle of Bud Light, staring at us as he pretended to watch the game. He was blonde and pale, with a stupid little goatee beard and expensive jeans. The type of guy who paid attention to two teenage girls who looked like they were on their own. And were therefore vulnerable.

I knew his type.

He waited until my glass was empty before sidling over.

'Can I get you girls another drink?'

'Oh, thanks!' Brooke said, beaming at him before I could give him the brush-off. 'We're just drinking Coke, though. We have an early start in the morning.'

I resisted – *just* – the urge to slap my hand over my face.

A few days ago, when Brooke had stopped to pick me up, I'd thought it was because we knew each other, sort of, and she was looking out for me. Now, I was rapidly reassessing that opinion, because it looked like she was maybe just a dumbass with no sense of self-preservation who would stop and pick up a serial killer, given the opportunity.

'I'm Chris,' he said, extending his hand in a way that would make it rude to refuse to shake it.

'Summer,' Brooke said, and thank *God* she had the common sense not to give him her actual name. 'And this is my cousin Jenna.'

Jenna? It wasn't terrible. I could be a Jenna. It was better than Mouse, at least.

'Hi.' I gave him a little wave rather than offering a handshake.

'What brings you to this corner of Utah?'

I could hear the twang of his accent, which gave away that he was local, to the state if not the city, and that was weird, right? Why would he be staying in a motel in Utah if he was *from* Utah?

All my alarm bells were ringing, the red flags waving, Spidey-senses tingling, and Brooke flashed her shiny, happy smile at him. She was just so goddamn *friendly*, and something I usually admired about her turned into a trait that was now incredibly frustrating.

'We're heading down for our Grandpa Jim's funeral,' she said. 'It's going to be a big family thing, but Jenna doesn't like flying, so . . .'

'Don't like heights?' he said, leaning around Brooke to give me a theatrical wink. 'Me neither.'

'I'm not scared of flying. I'm scared of crashing,' I told him, deadpan.

Brooke gave me a subtle kick on the ankle. I took that as my cue to shut up. She was clearly enjoying herself.

Chris waved over the bartender and ordered two more Cokes, another beer and a basket of fries. I was glad we'd already eaten. I didn't want him ordering food for us as well as drinks.

I turned my attention back to the TV and sipped my drink while Brooke fell into a deep conversation with Chris. He seemed charming and personable, and was letting Brooke do a lot of the talking. We'd outlined the bare bones of a story about going to Grandpa Jim's funeral in case we were asked at any point, but Brooke was doing a lot of elaborating. And lying. Whenever I lied, I turned red and started to stutter, which was somewhat of a giveaway.

It took almost forty minutes before I saw him do it.

He was slick, and that scared me. While Brooke was gesticulating wildly and asking something about Rocky Mountain elk, Chris checked his phone, put it back in his pocket, then, while he was shuffling to get comfortable on the barstool again, he reached out and plucked Brooke's room key from her jacket pocket.

If I hadn't been watching for it, I wouldn't have spotted the move. He was good.

Which meant he'd practiced.

Which meant we were in trouble.

I leaned around Brooke, cutting off her conversation, and looked right at Chris.

'Sorry. Do you know where the restrooms are?' I asked, pushing down my nerves.

'Uh, in the lobby, I think.'

'Thanks.' I gave him a big, toothy smile.

I didn't want to leave Brooke alone with him, but I couldn't see how else I could get us out of this stupid situation.

The lobby was busier now with people waiting for a table in the bar, which made me slightly more confident to go to the restroom. If Chris tried anything with Brooke, there would be plenty of witnesses. Just in case he was watching, I went and washed my hands twice, then headed back to the front desk. A man stepped away as I approached, giving me the perfect opportunity to slip in.

'How can I help?' The receptionist's nametag said SUSAN and she had a friendly smile on her face.

'Hi,' I said. 'I'm so sorry, but my cousin has lost her room key and it was still in the wallet with the room number written on it. We're worried someone might pick it up and . . .'

Lying was easier, I found, when I had a clear objective. Susan nodded, already tapping her keyboard.

'What's the room number?'

'Two-ten. It should be in the name Summer.'

'I've got you,' she said. 'Give me a second. I'm going to cancel both keys and give you new ones.'

'Thank you so much.'

After a few minutes, Brooke glanced out into the lobby and noticed me waiting. She frowned, and I shook my head at her, trying to silently tell her it was fine.

'Here you go.' The receptionist slid two new key cards across the counter to me. 'The old ones have been wiped.'

'Great, thank you.'

I put both cards into my wallet and tucked it securely into my purse. Chris wasn't going to get his hands on these.

'Everything okay?' Brooke asked as I took my seat at the bar again.

'Yeah, fine. I just wanted to check what time breakfast is available tomorrow. Since we're leaving early and all.'

She nodded but still looked confused. We had confirmed that at check-in.

'So, Chris, what do you do?' I asked, and Brooke looked even more confused that I was suddenly taking an interest in him.

'I'm in shipping,' he said.

'Chris spends a lot of time in South America,' Brooke added.

I was *delighted* to hear they'd been getting to know each other so well.

'What do you ship?' I asked, ignoring Brooke's glare that was clearly telling me I was being rude.

'Nothing exciting, I'm afraid. Mostly avocados and other fruit and vegetables. Produce that has a fairly short shelf life. There are lots of logistics involved to make sure we've got the right people at either end so they're delivered on time.' He laughed, too high and definitely fake. 'I'm boring you.'

'Not at all,' I said with a sweet smile.

For the next hour I got progressively more snarky, cutting off Chris mid-sentence and earning increasingly furious death glares from Brooke. I didn't want to sit with him anymore, but I couldn't tip him off that I'd seen him taking our room key. And, unlike me, Brooke didn't seem to want to get up to use the restroom. I had no way of telling her what he'd done, other than pissing her off to the point where she wanted to leave.

'We should get going,' Brooke said eventually, and I felt my shoulders slump with relief.

'Right,' I said.

'It was really nice to meet you,' Brooke enthused at Chris, and I forced myself to smile at him.

'You too. Have a safe trip, Summer. Jenna.'

I nodded at him and wrapped my hand around Brooke's arm to drag her out of the bar.

'You were so rude tonight,' she hissed. 'What is *wrong* with you?'

'I'll tell you in a minute.'

'You have to make an effort, Mouse. You can't just go through life not talking to people. He was a nice guy, you could have –'

'I'll tell you,' I said tightly, 'in a minute.'

'Fine,' she huffed.

She sulked all the way back to our room. I stopped outside the door and folded my arms.

'Go on,' I said, gesturing to the door.

Brooke put her hands in her pockets. 'Shit. I must have dropped the key.'

'No, you didn't.' I tried to fight back my frustration and instead pulled one of the new keys out of my wallet and let us into the room, then I put the chain across the door and flipped the deadbolt, too. 'Chris pickpocketed you.'

'What? No, I must have dropped it earlier,' she said, patting her pockets.

'I saw him, Brooke!' I said, my voice rising. 'I literally watched him take the key from your pocket. He was good at it, too, so he's probably done it before. I knew he looked like trouble.'

She gaped at me. 'Are you serious?'

'Yes!'

'Oh my God! And you didn't tell me?'

My fingers curled and I clenched my jaw. 'I'm telling you now.'

'You could've told me earlier! You let me talk to that creep for *hours*!'

'So you would've believed me if I'd told you downstairs?' I said, challenging her.

Brooke opened her mouth to argue, then shut it again.

'And what do you think he would've done if I'd confronted him?'

'I don't know,' she murmured.

'Me neither. I tried to get you out of there as soon as I could, but you wanted to keep *talking*.'

'Ugh. I feel dirty.' Brooke sat down heavily on the end of the bed.

'He's probably still going to try to get in here,' I said, leaning against the dresser.

'You think?' she looked up at me with worried eyes.

'Yeah. He doesn't know I got the key wiped.'

'Should we switch rooms?' Brooke asked.

'I don't know.' I paced over to the window and glanced at the dark parking lot. 'Probably not. That would be even more obvious now.'

'Okay.' Brooke stared at me for a long moment, jiggling her knee with what I assumed was nervous energy. 'I'm sorry,' she whispered.

'You trust people too easily,' I replied, and went to wash the eyeliner off my face before bed.

I got the gun out of Brooke's duffel bag and left it on the table next to the locked door, strangely comforted that we had it. Not that I was sure I could ever use it. I'd never fired a gun, and just the thought of pointing it at a person was terrifying. Tonight, though, it would be another layer of defense.

I tried to move the dresser in front of the door, too, but it seemed to be screwed into the wall, so that plan went out the window. I checked the door bolts once, twice, then a third time, and still decided to stay awake.

Brooke took the bed closest to the bathroom. That was fine by me. I wanted to be closer to the door in case something happened. Brooke had protected me from the last creepy guy. Now it was my turn.

I decided to read one of my vintage romance novels as Brooke slept, mostly to keep myself distracted. Reading about other people's success in their love lives was a much-needed antidote to my own romantic failures.

It was after midnight when I heard footsteps on the walkway outside and sat up a little straighter. I glanced over at Brooke, who was sleeping deeply. The footsteps paused outside our door, and suddenly my heart was thundering in my throat.

I was wearing pajamas.

Of all the things to suddenly be anxious about, wearing pajamas shouldn't have been top of the list, but it was. I felt exposed, and cold.

The door handle shifted, just a fraction.

As silently as I could, I slipped out of bed and walked on the balls of my feet over to the door, trying not to be too loud or obvious.

The person – people – outside weren't doing the same.

'Are you sure this is the right room?' A woman's voice.

'It's written on the fucking card.' Chris.

There were two of them.

Shit.

I pressed my back to the door and this time felt it when they held the card against the reader. I licked my lips, scared, *terrified*, but determined to stay quiet.

A subtle pressure. Then again, a little harder. They tried the handle, and I felt that too. The movement rattled my bones, and with it my nerves.

'It's been disabled,' the woman said. 'For fuck's sake, Chris.'

'Don't blame me! The ratty one must have done something.'

My anger flared. The ratty one was *me*.

I was pissed off now, rather than scared, and so I dared to lean in to the peephole.

Chris was instantly recognizable, though I hadn't seen the woman before. I was good at noticing people, and I definitely hadn't seen her around. She was tall, statuesque, like Brooke, but blonde, with a very slim, pointy nose.

'All right. Let's go.'

For some reason, I was more scared of her than I was of Chris. He was creepy and probably wanted to rob and/or rape us. Those were known things. I had no idea what she wanted, and that was infinitely scarier.

I kept watching as they went back to the parking lot and crossed over to a black van that I could barely make out in the shadows. Chris threw something into the back, then they both disappeared.

They could still come back here tonight.

So I'd stay awake.

Just in case.

It wasn't like I'd be able to sleep anyway, with all the adrenaline rushing through my veins.

6

(What's the Story) Morning Glory? – Oasis

'Well, you look like shit.'

'Thanks, Brooke.' I glanced at the clock on the nightstand. I'd seen the red lights blink 5:00 a.m., but nothing after that. I must have fallen asleep after all. It was a little past eight now, and I'd sort of heard Brooke get up and brush her teeth before she came back into the room and opened the curtains.

'No, seriously. Do you want to go back to sleep?'

I shook my head and rubbed my fingertips into my eyelids, trying to dislodge the dry, gritty feeling. 'I'll be fine.'

She went over to the little fridge and got the leftovers out. 'Pizza for breakfast?'

That made me smile. 'Sure.'

'I thought that might cheer you up.'

Brooke sat down on the end of my bed and opened the box between us. I was suddenly starving. She clicked on the TV, giving us some background noise, and I decided then not to tell her about Chris and the blonde lady. Brooke had made me work so damn hard last night to get Chris off our backs, and even after all that, he'd shown up in the middle of the night.

Brooke didn't need to know.

I wanted to move on, to keep moving, and I would just put last night behind me and forget about it, like all the other stuff that I was trying really hard to forget.

'Do you want to go into the city today?' Brooke asked.

I swallowed my bite of pizza. 'Do you?'

She rolled her eyes at me. 'I'm asking you.'

'I don't mind. Sure.'

'You say that a lot.'

'What?'

'*I don't mind*. And *sure*. And *okay*.'

'That's because I don't mind.' I was happy to let Brooke take the lead.

She licked a spot of sauce off her thumb. 'Okay. I want to go into the city today. All the driving is giving me a headache and I want to have a day of walking around and not concentrating.'

'That sounds really good. Listen, I was thinking last night –' I'd done a lot of thinking last night – 'do you think we stand out because we don't have phones? Like, everyone our age has a phone.'

'Huh.' Brooke tossed her pizza crust back in the box and reached for another slice. 'I hadn't thought about it.'

'No, me neither, but last night Chris was checking his phone all the time. If we're going into the city, we could maybe look for one of those second-hand electronics stores, see if we can pick up a couple.'

Brooke nodded. 'That would make it easier to plan a route.'

'Exactly,' I said, relieved.

I had ulterior motives. I'd never cared about having the latest shiny new phone, but everything that had happened last night had highlighted how vulnerable we were. Even though the last thing I wanted to do was call the cops, if we ever got into a bad situation and needed help, we would be stuck. Or if we broke down. Or got lost. Or whatever.

While Brooke was in the shower, I fell back asleep, and she didn't wake me until almost check-out time, so we didn't leave the motel until later than we usually would.

Before we left the parking lot, I glanced around for the black van, and reassured myself that it was gone. I couldn't decide who Chris and the blonde lady were, which was turning into an annoying itch in the back of my consciousness. Brooke's parents were wealthy, so it definitely wasn't outside of the realm of possibility that they'd paid for a private investigator to find her.

Or maybe Chris was an undercover cop who was specifically looking for us. Well, looking for *me*. I'd stopped checking over my shoulder every other minute, but maybe I'd become complacent as we'd gotten farther away from home. It was possible – *probable* – that the police were looking for me.

Or they could be career criminals – who knew? The whole thing was slightly ridiculous.

The most boring option was usually the truth, so I decided they were petty thieves, looking to rob us because we seemed vulnerable. That was scary, but we would be out of Utah soon, and we'd never see them again.

With that decision made, it was a relief not to worry about them anymore.

Neither of us knew much about the city or where was good to hang out, so Brooke followed the signs for downtown and parked in a multistory lot. It didn't seem that busy, but I had no frame of reference for how busy downtown Salt Lake City got. The whole city was so freaking *clean*. It made me nervous. Like someone was going to sweep down at any second and give me a ticket for looking a mess.

'What day is it today?' I asked as we got out of the car.

Brooke counted on her fingers. 'Thursday.'

She had picked me up on Monday night, and it felt like we'd been on the road for both a year and ten minutes. One moment it felt like things were easier, especially now that we were almost friends. And the next moment I was panicking about who Chris and the blonde lady were, and why they'd wanted to get into our room.

After walking for a few blocks, we found an outdoor mall with a stream running through it and plenty of chain stores where people were hanging out. We stopped to go into a bookstore to poke around and soak up the vibes, then into a few stores to look at expensive clothes neither of us was going to buy. Not having the pressure of somewhere to be or people to impress made me relax in a way that really highlighted how on edge I'd been since we left Seattle.

Here, it just felt like we were two girls out shopping, but after a few hours I started to wilt.

'I need to stop,' I groaned. 'My feet are killing me.'

'We haven't even walked that far!'

'I know, but they still hurt. Coffee?'

'Fine,' Brooke said with a laugh. 'We can get coffee.'

We only had to walk another block to find a Starbucks, and Brooke went to the counter to order for us both while I found a spot at a long, shared table. Someone had left a newspaper behind, so I pulled it over and scanned the headlines.

It was clearly a slow news day.

'Here,' Brooke said, holding out an iced caramel latte. 'Don't say I never get you anything.'

I usually drank my coffee hot, but as soon as I took a sip, I decided I'd been converted.

'Thank you,' I said emphatically.

Apparently my taste in coffee was the latest thing I'd learned about myself. Brooke took a seat opposite me and gently shook her cup, the ice clacking against itself, and I felt myself smile.

'What?' she asked.

'Nothing.'

Brooke was just so stupidly perfect, and I couldn't quite believe that we were sitting together in Starbucks like it was nothing. This would never have happened in Seattle. I wouldn't have ever been able to work up the courage to ask her out for coffee, and even though this wasn't a *date*, it felt like one. Almost. I smiled at her again and she laughed this time.

'You're so goofy, Mouse,' she mumbled, ducking her head like she was embarrassed.

Like, maybe, she was flirting with me . . .

I let that thought wrap around me like a warm balm, and I was about to try flirting back to see how it would be received, when I spotted the blonde woman out of the corner of my eye and a switch flipped. I immediately went on high alert.

She'd done something different with her hair, and I forced myself to glance her way a few times rather than staring, in case that made her notice me. Instead of wearing her distinctive hair long and loose, she'd pulled it into a sleek bun and was wearing a blazer over skinny jeans and heels. But I'd recognize her however she dressed, even after only seeing her once through the distortion of a motel peephole.

'Mouse?' Brooke asked, clearly sensing something was up.

'Give me a second,' I murmured.

My heart was pounding again as I watched the blonde lady pick up her coffee and go back to the front of the store. Instead of leaving, she sat on one of the tall bar stools that ran along the front window and pulled out her phone.

She was blocking our exit.

I wished we'd already bought the phones. All I wanted to do was silently text Brooke with the details rather than tell her out loud and have someone overhear. I had to tell her, though. I'd wanted to protect her from that uncomfortable, sick feeling that came with knowing Chris had come back for us last night, and the questions I knew she would have. Questions that I really didn't have answers to.

I drummed my fingers on the table for a moment, then grabbed the newspaper and spun it around to point at a random paragraph.

'Don't look up,' I said to Brooke as soon as her attention was focused on the paper.

'Okay.'

'I'm serious. Don't look up until I tell you. There's a woman sitting in the window: blonde, white shirt, blue jeans, black heels. Pointy nose. Look now.'

Brooke scanned the front of the store, then nodded and looked back at me. I turned the page and pointed at something else.

'What about her?' Brooke asked.

'Last night, she was with Chris. They tried to get into our room.'

She looked up at me, startled. 'What?'

'Last night,' I repeated, pointing emphatically at the paper to direct her attention. 'When you were asleep. They tried the key card Chris pickpocketed from you to get into the room.'

'You should've woken me up,' Brooke hissed.

'Why? They didn't get in and they left after. I didn't think –'

'That they'd follow us here?'

'It might just be a coincidence.'

Brooke muttered something under her breath that I couldn't quite catch. She put her elbow on the table and her chin in her hand, subtly angling herself toward the door.

'How are we going to get out?' she murmured.

'She doesn't know that I recognize her,' I said, then sipped my coffee again. 'And they don't know that I caught them trying to get in last night.'

'Okay,' Brooke said.

'But if we walk right past her, she's only going to follow us.'

'There's only one door in and out, Mouse.'

I shook my head. 'No way. There will be another door somewhere, for emergencies.'

'Will it set off an alarm?'

'Maybe.'

'Shit.'

We waited in silence for another minute, watching to see if the woman would look up at us or make a move. But she didn't. She drank her coffee and scrolled on her phone, like she was waiting. Like she had all the time in the world for us to move first.

Brooke kept drumming her fingers against the table in a nervous rhythm. I reached out and covered her hand with mine, squeezing it briefly. Brooke looked at me, a little desperate, and my breath caught in my throat.

'It's okay. Stay here,' I said to her, standing up.

Her expression turned panicked. 'Don't leave me.'

'I won't. I'm just going to the restroom.'

'Mouse. Seriously.'

'It'll be fine,' I said calmly.

Starbucks stores were predictable. There would be restrooms tucked away somewhere, probably next to a storeroom or break room. I found what I was looking for quickly, in a hallway running at a right angle to the main part of the cafe, next to two gender-neutral restrooms.

Another woman was waiting for the restroom, so I joined the line behind her, leaning against the wall to look around. The STAFF ONLY sign on the door at the end of the hallway most likely led to the break room, but opposite the last restroom was a fire exit.

And just as someone left the restroom and held the door open to let me use it next, a worker came in through the fire exit, giving me a glimpse of a smoking area behind and a long alleyway.

'Thanks,' I murmured as a girl my age held the door to the restroom for me.

We'd have to move carefully to not tip off blonde lady, but it was a route out that meant we didn't have to walk past her. I had no idea where the alley would dump us out, and our opportunity to keep wandering leisurely around the city was dead in the water, but I couldn't care about that now.

I washed my hands and went back to the table.

'You took ages,' Brooke grumbled as I slid back into my seat.

'I found a way out.'

'Are you sure?' she asked, her eyes clearly telling me she was freaked out. 'Are you absolutely sure about all of this, Mouse?'

I instinctively flinched hearing her call me Mouse, but I hadn't mustered the courage to ask her to call me anything else.

'Yes.'

Brooke glanced at me, then looked over at the blonde woman, then back at me.

'Go to the restroom and wait for me in that hallway. I'll be with you in a minute,' I said.

'Okay,' she replied, blowing out a hard breath and pushing back from her seat to walk away.

I forced myself to count to a hundred, flicking through the pages of the paper and watching a group of girls my age order drinks. This wasn't the time to start freaking out. I didn't want Brooke to panic and draw attention to us, and I wanted her to think I actually had control of the situation, for once.

One last time, I chanced a look over at the blonde lady.

She looked up at me at the same time.

And I froze.

Her eyes met mine, and for a long second, my heart stopped beating. Just stopped dead in my chest.

Then she smirked at me, a tiny little twitch of her lips, and my heart went back to pounding racehorse-fast.

I had to move. The girls waiting for their orders made a good cover, so when they went to the end of the counter, I moved with them and didn't look back to see if I was being followed.

Brooke was waiting for me, leaning against the wall and drinking her coffee.

'It's not alarmed,' she said.

'Good.'

'Don't run. We need to look like we're supposed to be there.'

That was easy for her to say. She was smart and pretty and a good liar, so she could get away with stuff like this. I wasn't any of those things, and I always got caught.

We ducked out of the fire exit and into the smoking area. The light from the afternoon sun didn't reach over the top of the buildings, making the alley suitably dim. I followed Brooke's lead, picking my way through the piles of trash and hoping the murky puddles of water didn't stain my white sneakers.

'This way,' she said, turning sharply right at the mouth of the alley and taking off at a brisk pace.

I had no idea where we were going, though I didn't mind that Brooke was taking over my expertly conceived escape plan. It was almost a relief to have someone else be in charge.

After a minute, I noticed someone was following us, and I was filled with an overwhelming need to cry. We needed a break. Just one little break.

'You've seen the cops, right?' Brooke murmured as we waited to cross the street.

I made a show of looking both ways, watching traffic, and caught glimpses of the two uniformed officers walking up the street toward us. They weren't running, clearly not in a rush, but they hadn't been far behind us since we'd left Starbucks.

'This can't be real,' I said, my voice cracking.

'Don't start,' she said sharply. 'We just need to keep going. Don't run.'

The cops were getting closer, then finally, *finally*, the lights changed, and we could cross the street.

The police officers crossed, too, still strolling easily. I glanced back over my shoulder and one of them caught my eye. He turned to his colleague and said something I couldn't hear. Then they started walking faster.

The coffee turned sour in my stomach.

They were definitely following us.

Did they think we'd stolen something? Or were we in trouble for sneaking out of the Starbucks? I couldn't think why that would be a problem, not unless the blonde lady had called the cops on us.

Even if the police following us was a total coincidence, I didn't like the idea that they could recognize me later from police reports about a teenage murder suspect from Seattle and tell someone I'd been in Salt Lake City. They might think we were planning to keep going south to Las Vegas or Phoenix, or maybe Mexico. The panic hitched in my throat. I didn't want anyone tracking us – that was why we'd thrown our phones in the damn lake in the first place.

The route back to the parking lot was an almost straight line, meaning we didn't have many chances to take a side street and get out of their line of sight. I was desperate to run, even though Brooke had told me not to. I wasn't sure I could run, either – my heart was beating so fast and I didn't think I would be able to take a deep enough breath.

All of a sudden, we were back at the parking lot.

I followed Brooke silently to the car, wanting to check over my shoulder every thirty seconds to see if the cops were still behind us, but instead forcing myself to relax.

Calm down, Jessie.

We pulled out of the lot in silence, passing the police who were still on foot but clearly heading in the direction of the parking lot.

'Did they see us?' Brooke asked.

'I don't know. I don't think so.'

Traffic was heavy until we got onto the I-70, then Brooke pulled her hair loose from its ponytail and stepped on the gas.

'This is messed up, Mouse,' Brooke said as she merged into the outside lane and picked up speed. 'How the hell did they find us here?'

'I don't know,' I said, my voice rising into a desperate sob. 'Maybe Chris really is an undercover cop.'

'Shit,' she muttered. 'I still don't understand why you didn't tell me about last night.'

I wasn't surprised Brooke was upset. It was a big thing to have kept from her.

'I thought it wouldn't be an issue once we left the motel.'

Brooke sighed and pushed her fingers through her hair. 'All right. Just don't keep stuff from me in the future, okay?'

'Okay,' I said, knowing it was a lie. I was keeping a lot from her.

I picked a new cassette and shoved it into the player, still obsessively watching the road behind us, waiting for sirens or flashing lights.

'I don't know if I can go far today,' Brooke said as we finally exited the city. 'Maybe a couple more hours.'

'Don't worry,' I said. 'We can do a longer stretch tomorrow, if you like.'

'Yeah, maybe.'

To the south of us, Utah's mountains loomed in the distance, still snow-capped at this time of year, even though it felt warm down at our level. Well, the air was warm. The mood in the Mustang was positively chilly.

7

Middle of Nowhere – Hanson

I noticed the black van within thirty minutes of leaving Salt Lake City and silently panicked for the next few miles. How the hell had they found us again? And so quickly? I really thought we'd managed to escape without anyone noticing.

The car stereo was playing nineties pop music, and I couldn't tell whether Brooke's continuing sour mood was because of me, or because of what had happened. I didn't know if telling her about the van would make things worse, and, in the end, I did the only thing I could, and watched it weaving in and out of traffic. It never got too close to us, just hovered in the rearview mirror a few cars back.

I couldn't stop thinking about the blonde lady smiling at me. Except it didn't feel right to call it 'smiling', there had been no emotion behind her expression other than pure malice. She knew me, she knew why I was in Salt Lake City, and she knew I was watching her. Just the thought of her sent ice crawling down my spine.

'Are you hungry?'

I jumped when Brooke spoke to me. We'd barely said anything since leaving the city.

'I could eat.' We'd skipped lunch after our leftover pizza breakfast, and my stomach was starting to notice.

'I want a burrito bowl or something,' she said in that decisive way I envied.

'Sure. Sounds good,' I said, going along with her preferences like I always did. I didn't mind. It was more important to me that she was happy than that I got what I wanted, and, anyway, I didn't have a better suggestion than burrito bowls.

We drove for another fifteen minutes before spotting a sign for a Tex-Mex place, and I waited in the car, looking out for the black van while Brooke went inside and ordered.

I couldn't see it, and for a moment, I let myself believe we'd finally lost them.

When she came back outside, I followed her to a seating area set back far enough from the road that the sound of cars mellowed into a low hum, and the day had softened into a beautiful afternoon with fluffy white clouds floating across the endless blue sky.

I waited until she had finished eating to tell her about the van.

'Oh my God, Mouse,' Brooke said, putting both her hands over her face. 'I don't know what to do with you anymore.'

'What?'

She scraped her chair back to stand up and pace. 'First it was Chris supposedly stealing my room key, which I didn't see happen. Then it's Chris and some woman trying to break into our room in the middle of the night when I was asleep. Then this random woman is *somehow* in the exact same Starbucks as us.'

I opened my mouth to protest, then shut it again. She was on a roll.

'Now,' Brooke said, throwing her hands in the air, 'there's a black van that's been following us since Salt Lake goddamn City. A van that I've never seen before, but you're *convinced* was in the parking lot at the motel last night.'

'What are you trying to say? That I'm making it all up?'

Hot anxiety tightened in my throat. I hated this. Hated arguing, hated conflict. But I especially hated being the one who was making Brooke angry.

'I don't know!' she exclaimed. 'I don't know, Mouse. Are you?'

'No!'

I swallowed hard, begging myself not to cry. I didn't know how to make Brooke trust me, and it stung that she clearly didn't.

'But you don't tell me anything until it's happening, or after it's happened,' Brooke said, more gently now. 'Do you see where I'm coming from? All of a sudden there's this new thing that we have to worry about.'

'That's because you don't pay attention,' I snapped, feeling hurt. I immediately regretted it.

'Well, I think you're paranoid,' she snapped back.

'I'm paranoid because you don't pay attention,' I countered.

Brooke slumped down to sit on the grass in one heavy movement, then laid back, crossing her arms over her face. After a second, I got up from the picnic bench and sat down next to her, cross-legged.

The grass was softer than I had expected it to be. I plucked a single blade and ran it between my thumb and finger to smooth it out. Sometimes I was good at smoothing things out, like with my mom. I'd learned how to placate her over the years, and most of the time now I could avoid arguments altogether. But Brooke was different. She bit back, and I actually liked that about her. She wasn't a pushover, and sometimes being snarky with her was fun . . . it almost felt like flirting. I had a feeling this argument was about something deeper, though. Something bigger. If we were going to stay together, we needed to trust each other.

I knew the obvious solution to the current problem – it was the same one I'd been sitting on since Brooke had picked me up.

'I can –'

'If you're about to suggest that I drop you off somewhere, just stop now,' she said, her voice muffled by her arms. 'I'm not going to ditch you.'

An emotion I didn't know how to name flared in my chest, and all of a sudden I wanted to scream.

'You don't trust me,' I whined. I could tell I was whining, but I couldn't stop myself.

'It's not that I don't trust you, Mouse,' she said, propping herself up on her elbows to look at me. 'I don't think you trust yourself. Your instincts are good, but you never want to share them with me, and I don't know why.'

'Because . . .' I sighed.

'Because?' she prompted. 'People haven't believed you in the past?'

That was a little too close to home.

'Yeah.'

'And so now you think it's better not to say anything at all, rather than say what's bothering you and have someone tell you you're being stupid.'

Partly that, and partly wanting to protect her. Brooke saw me in a way no one had before, and that was scary and exhilarating, and I didn't want to lose it.

'All right,' I grumbled. 'When did you turn into a therapist?'

'Not a therapist,' she said easily. 'But I have been told I'm a pretty good friend.'

That stopped me short. I didn't really have friends that I could talk to about these kinds of things. Things that worried me.

'I don't have a therapist. Or many friends.'

That made her laugh. 'I'm your friend, Mouse.'

'Because you're stuck with me and have no other choice?'

'Yeah,' she said, but I could tell she was joking. 'Obviously.'

We fell into a comfortable silence for a while, watching the clouds float past. Before this week, I'd never have thought Brooke would want to be friends with me. I'd never have thought I'd be friends with her, too. That was . . . good.

It was *real*. Not a wild fantasy about a girl I liked, but something messy and imperfect, and real, and that was so much better.

'Go on, then,' Brooke said after a few minutes. 'Tell me about the van.'

'There isn't much to tell,' I said, still smoothing out the blade of grass. 'I saw it last night, and then I've seen it a few times in the rearview mirror since we've been driving.'

'Is it just a generic black van?' she asked, and I nodded. 'So how do you know it's the same one?'

I didn't, not 100 percent, but I was certain Chris was trouble and I didn't want to take a risk. The van was following us, which meant they had some way of keeping track of either us or the Mustang.

'Because it is,' I said. 'If there was a tracker on the car, would you be able to find it?'

'Good God, Mouse,' Brooke groaned.

'Would you?' I pressed.

'Yeah. I restored that car from a rusted chunk of metal. If someone messed with it, I'd notice.'

I didn't say anything to that, letting her stew in the silence.

'Fine!' she exclaimed, after a far shorter period of time than I'd expected. 'I want to check it out myself, though.'

She sulked all the way to the next garage.

We passed garages periodically. Most of them were attached to gas stations and well advertised. I guessed plenty of people had car trouble on these long stretches of highway. Even though it was after four, the garage was buzzing when Brooke pulled in.

The lot was infused with the sharp, bright smell of rubber tires, overlaid with a funky fuel perfume. It was dirty and messy and there were pictures of almost-naked women on the wall, and Brooke looked like she was in heaven.

I had no idea how we'd be received – two teenage girls in a vintage Mustang – but Brooke had a confidence around her car that was completely unflappable, even in the face of dirty men in overalls staring at her like she didn't have a clue.

'I just need you to hitch it up for me,' she said, her hands firmly planted on her hips. As we'd driven south, it had gotten progressively warmer, so Brooke was now wearing denim shorts and a loose white T-shirt tied in a knot, exposing a flash of her belly. She looked *gorgeous*, and I had to wrap my arms around my waist to keep my feelings to myself. This wasn't the time to make things weird between us, not when we were right on the precipice of starting to trust each other.

'What's wrong? We can take a look.'

One of the men stepped forward. He was wearing a white tank tucked into his overalls, which were open to the waist with the arms tied up. With his close-cropped hair and scruffy beard, he was almost too perfect. He looked exactly how I expected a mechanic to look.

'I don't need you to look at it,' Brooke said sweetly. 'I just need you to hitch it up so I can check something.'

Two more guys in the back of the shop exchanged glances.

'Okay,' the first mechanic said, holding up his hands. 'You know what you're doing?'

'Yes,' she said emphatically, already pulling her thick hair back into a ponytail.

In that moment, I didn't feel like I could keep my feelings for Brooke hidden, so I went to the vending machine in the little waiting room and got myself a Sprite, coaxing a wrinkled dollar bill into the slot until it was finally accepted.

One of the other mechanics came in while the machine was spitting out my can.

'Hi,' I said, trying out being friendly.

'Hey. So ... your friend?' he asked, jerking his chin toward Brooke.

'My cousin? What about her?'

I cracked open the can, gunshot-loud in the confined space.

'She knows cars?'

I grinned and sipped the soda. 'She built that thing.'

'She *built* it?'

'Yeah. Well, she stripped it down and rebuilt the engine from scratch. All the interiors. It was a total wreck and she turned it into ...'

I gestured out the dirty waiting room window at the Mustang. I knew nothing about cars, but even I could tell this one was something special. It had been a big thing at school, that first day Brooke had pulled up in her new car. She had the top down, sunglasses on and her hair loose, and every single person in the parking lot stared at her. It was like a scene in a movie. It hadn't taken long for the news to spread that Brooke hadn't gotten the car from her parents or as a gift – she'd actually done the work to restore it herself. According to the boys in my class, that was hot. I thought it was hot, too.

My new mechanic friend went to the vending machine and punched in a code for a drink of his own.

'Luca, the guy who's helping her – he's a total junkie for vintage cars.'

I grinned at him. 'This should be fun, then.'

He held out his hand and I shook it. 'I'm Mikey.'

'Jenna,' I said, tripping a little on the name I wasn't used to yet. Mikey didn't notice.

'Pick a song, Jenna,' Mikey said, gesturing to an iPad mounted on the wall with a handmade sign above it saying JUKEBOX.

They had a music subscription, so I had access to pretty much every pop song ever made. It took me a moment of scrolling to find what I was looking for, then I hit play on 'Graceland'.

'Nice,' Mikey said with a nod. He propped the door of the waiting room open so the music spilled out, gestured for me to follow him into the main part of the garage and hoisted himself up to sit on a long workbench. I put my can down before copying him.

Brooke looked over at me, noticing the music, and grinned.

My stomach fluttered in response, and I knew I was going to chase this feeling – doing things to make her smile, to make her happy.

'Where are you headed?' Mikey asked, which was an innocent enough question. It wasn't his fault it put my hackles up.

'Denver. For a funeral.'

'Ah. I'm sorry.'

'Thanks.'

Our fake funeral cover story didn't invite people to ask more questions, and while Mikey seemed nice, I wasn't going to take the risk.

From across the open space I could hear Brooke arguing with Luca as he raised the Mustang up on one of the car lifts.

'What's she looking for?' Mikey asked.

'I have no idea.' That was almost the truth. 'Honestly, I don't know anything about cars. That's her department.'

He nodded slowly. 'Don't see many girls working on cars. Not around here, anyway.'

'She's ... special,' I said, hoping he didn't see straight through me.

That made him laugh. He gave me a long look out of the corner of his eye. 'She ain't your cousin, is she?' he asked with a gently teasing smile.

I felt myself immediately blush deep red, my cheeks tingling. 'What are you talking about?'

He laughed again. Not in a mean way. 'Hey, I don't look at my cousin the way you look at her. No Midwest jokes. I've heard them all.'

'She's ... not my cousin,' I admitted, sure that I was still bright red. I could feel the embarrassment crawling up my throat, making me hot and itchy.

He grinned. 'Oh, you don't say?'

'I'm not good with . . .' I waved my hand in her direction in a way I hoped would explain everything.

'Girls?'

'I'm better with girls than I am with boys.'

That made him laugh again, showing off a gold tooth. I liked Mikey. He was all right.

'Boys ain't shit. You're doing good with her.'

'I'm not doing anything with her.' He didn't need to know how often I *daydreamed* about doing something with Brooke. That wasn't relevant right now.

'For real? Man, that's a shame,' he said, sounding sincere.

'She's way out of my league. And probably straight.'

'Only probably?' he asked with a raised eyebrow.

'Almost certainly.'

'Ah, well. She's a pretty girl. So are you, for what it's worth.'

'Now you're being a creep.' I barely kept the laughter out of my voice.

'Nah. Just stating a fact.'

'Creepy,' I muttered, and sipped my Sprite to hide my smile. Mikey still noticed, though.

'Hey, I'm an engaged man,' he started, then stopped to pull his phone out of his pocket. It lit up with a picture of a beautiful woman with dark, curly hair and freckles, holding a tiny dog. The dog was licking the end of her nose, and she was laughing.

'Congratulations,' I said. 'She's very pretty.'

'I agree.' Mikey finished his soda and burped loudly.

'Gotta get back to work.' He hopped down off the workbench. 'Shoot your shot, Jenna.'

That was easy for him to say. He was a decent-looking straight guy who could shoot his shot at a pretty straight girl. My situation wasn't quite so straightforward.

Ha. Pun intended.

I slid to the floor and picked up my can before wandering over to where Brooke and Luca were arguing loudly. And flirting loudly. I didn't know you could flirt while arguing, but they were doing a very good job of it.

'What's up?'

They both stopped mid-sentence and whipped around to look at me. I sipped my Sprite.

'Luca is insulting my car,' Brooke said, putting her hands back on her hips.

I was starting to learn that was Brooke's argument mode.

'I'm just *saying*,' he started. 'If you wanted to build for speed, you should've taken out the –'

'Did you find the thing?' I asked, before Luca could build up a full head of steam.

'Not yet,' Brooke said.

She clicked on a flashlight and started scanning the underside of the car again.

'Did you check the engine?' They both looked at me. I shrugged. 'It could be in the engine.'

Luca raised his eyebrows. 'If you told me what you were looking for, I could help.'

'I *told* you,' Brooke said. 'I won't know what I'm looking for until I find it.'

He huffed at her. 'All right. Step back.'

We moved out of the way of the lift and Luca brought the car back down. Before he could step in, Brooke popped the hood and surveyed the engine.

Luca whistled between his teeth. 'Good work.'

How he could tell from just looking at it, I had no idea. I did get the feeling Brooke was enjoying showing off her car, though. I couldn't blame her for that.

'There,' she said, and reached for a small black box, about the size of a credit card.

It took one hard yank to get it off, and Brooke held it up to the light to get a better look at it.

'Motherfuckers,' she murmured.

'A tracker?' Luca asked.

'Her ex-boyfriend is following us,' I said quickly. My heart started beating a little faster, but I didn't think I was blushing too much. 'We couldn't figure out how he knew where we were.'

Luca raised his eyebrows. 'Do you want me to call the local cops?'

'No,' Brooke said, still examining the tracker. It had two metal circles on the back, which I guessed were magnets. 'We'll figure this out.'

'Don't break it,' I said quickly, sensing that Brooke was about to let out all her frustration and smash it to pieces. I took it off her, and when Luca held his hand out for it, I gave it to him.

'Why?' she asked tightly.

'Because then he'll know we found it.'

It took Brooke a moment to process that, then she nodded. 'Okay. What do you think we should do?'

I glanced over at Luca, wondering if we could trust him. They seemed like decent guys here.

'If a man comes in . . .'

He nodded, picking up where I was going. 'What does he look like?' he asked, turning the tracker over in his hands.

I ran down the basic description of Chris, not sure if I was feeling vindicated or scared to death.

'He might be traveling with his sister,' Brooke added.

I nodded. 'Right. There could be two of them.'

'We mostly take care of locals here, or pick up breakdowns along this stretch of highway. If they stop, we'll notice them.'

'Thanks,' Brooke said. 'Could you tell them . . . ?'

She looked at me and I shrugged, feeling helpless.

'A lot of folks,' Luca said casually, 'head south from here. Through the Navajo reservation, heading toward Albuquerque.'

I glanced at Brooke. 'We *could* be going that way. Heading south.'

'That tracks,' she agreed.

'Where are you going?' Luca asked. 'I don't want to accidentally screw you over.'

'Denver,' Brooke said, and I guessed that she'd learned enough about him to trust him.

'Okay. If your ex comes in, I'll send him south. And I'll get rid of this, too, in a couple days.'

'That would be great. Thank you so much,' she replied.

Brooke reached up to drop the hood back down and stepped away from the car.

'Thank you,' I echoed. 'Really.'

'What do I owe you?' Brooke asked. Luca waved her question away.

'We didn't do anything.' He cocked his head to the side. 'You wouldn't *let* us do anything.'

She snorted with laughter. 'I don't let just anyone touch my car.'

'Well, if you ever want a job, I don't care about the gender of my mechanics.'

I watched the shutters slam down behind Brooke's eyes, and suddenly she was frosty and reserved. I could already tell it was going to take me a moment to open her back up again. Something was definitely going on with her and the Mustang, and I wished I knew her well enough to be able to ask outright.

'Thanks,' Brooke said tightly as she climbed into the car.

I lifted my hand in a wave and waited for her to drive out of the garage before getting into the passenger seat.

'You ready to go?' Brooke asked, nudging her sunglasses down onto her nose.

'Yeah. Let's get moving before they catch up with us.'

8

Butterfly – Mariah Carey

We stopped again not long after we'd crossed into Wyoming, in a two-stoplight town nestled at the foot of mountains that had snow on their peaks.

I could fall in love with towns like these. The air was soaked with the deep smell of pine, making everything feel fresh and clean. This one had just one motel, a Mom-and-Pop place with a golden-yellow exterior. I felt safer out here, especially now that we'd left the tracker behind with Luca. It was calm, and quiet, and strangely wholesome.

Before we got into the motel room and unpacked, we needed to stock up on some essentials: gas, snacks, toiletries. Brooke checked in, then gave me printed directions from the front desk that would take us to a supermarket on the edge of town.

'Can I throw some stuff in the laundry before we go back out?' I asked as we walked into the afternoon sun.

'Ooh, good idea.'

We found the tiny laundry room that smelled like clean linen just off the parking lot. I had a handful of quarters in my pocket, and it didn't take long to shove our dirty clothes in one of the washers. I checked the time so I'd know when to go back and move it over to the dryer.

Brooke hooked her arm in mine as we walked toward the car, and I tried not to be affected by that. She was just being friendly. That was all.

'The supermarket is actually back the way we came in,' I said, studying the directions when I was settled in the passenger seat. 'Just off the highway.'

'Great,' Brooke said.

After a few minutes of using the directions to navigate, I tapped her on the arm.

'Can we pull over?' I asked.

'Sure.'

The town had signs directing us to a nature park with a walking trail, and though it was too late in the day to go for a hike, I wanted to get out of the car, off the road and near a tree for a minute. I wanted to smell some flowers, not road dust and gas fumes.

Brooke grabbed our last bag of chips from the trunk and followed me, not saying anything when I laid on the grass in the late afternoon sunshine, my arms and legs splayed wide. She took the picnic bench instead.

'You okay down there?' Brooke asked after a few minutes.

'Yeah.' I had my eyes closed. 'I'm reconnecting with nature.'

I heard her snort with laughter, then crunch on a handful of chips.

The sun was low in the sky, but still warm enough that my skin could feel it. On impulse, I pulled my sneakers and socks off and buried my toes in the scratchy grass.

'Do you think anyone is looking for us?' Brooke asked.

'Like Chris?'

'No, not that asshole. I'm not worried about him anymore.'

'Really? I am,' I muttered.

I propped myself up on an elbow to look at her, shielding my eyes from the sun with my other hand.

Brooke shook her head. 'If we spend our time freaking out about every rude, slimy asshole of a man we come across, we'll never get anywhere.'

I laughed, and Brooke grinned.

'Forget him,' she said decisively.

I wasn't convinced, but I'd go along with her, for now. 'Do *you* think someone's looking for us?' I asked.

Brooke shrugged. 'I don't know.'

'I think someone is looking for you,' I said, pushing away thoughts of my own issues.

'No,' she replied quickly.

'Why not?'

'I left a note.'

I resisted the urge to roll my eyes and laid back in my nice patch of grass. 'Oh, that's all right, then,' I said, letting a little sarcasm creep in. 'You left a *note*.'

Brooke frowned. 'What's that supposed to mean?'

'Have you ever done this? Run off and just left a note?'

'No.'

'Then they'll be looking for you,' I said, stretching my arms over my head.

'Why will they be looking for me and not you? I'm almost eighteen. I can do what I want.' She sounded annoyed.

'Because people care about you, Brooke, and they don't care about me.'

'I'm sure that's not true, Mouse. Your mom and your friends will wonder where you are.'

'I don't have friends,' I said simply, because it was true.

'Have you ever run away before?'

'Yeah,' I said. 'And I didn't leave a note.'

'What happened?'

'I got a flag on my file to say I'm a flight risk.'

'That's it?' she said incredulously.

'Yeah.'

'Jesus Christ.'

I put my palms down on the grass, then moved my arms back and forth like I was making a snow angel. The movement sent the smell of grass and pine into the air, and I took deep, greedy lungfuls of it.

A white butterfly danced by, a few yards away from me, and I watched it for a long moment. I was twelve the first time I ran away, and I didn't get far – I was picked up by mall security when my mom told the cops that was where I sometimes hung out. I couldn't remember exactly why I'd run off that first time. It had probably been some stupid argument, and I was feeling too boxed in, too smothered and suffocated, and I had decided to just go.

Since then, I'd taken off a few more times, never getting very far on my own. If Brooke hadn't picked me up, I probably wouldn't have made it far this time, either. I owed her so much. Without her, I'd almost certainly be rotting in a jail cell back in Seattle.

'Do you want someone to be looking for you?' I asked.

'No,' Brooke said quickly. 'No. I want . . . *this*.'

I nodded. 'Me too. This is better than I thought it was going to be.'

That was the understatement of the century. In all the daydreams I'd concocted during Chemistry or Algebra, I'd never thought I would actually end up hanging out with Brooke Summer. None of those daydreams had come close to the reality of her, either. When she smiled at me, or laughed when we were talking about something inconsequential, it felt like things clicked into place. I knew who I was now, a hundred times more than I had when we left Seattle. I couldn't believe it had only been four days. So much had happened already.

I sat back up and started pulling pine needles out of my hair.

'Do you ever do anything with your hair?' Brooke asked.

'I hate it,' I said immediately.

'Why?'

'It's just . . . fragile and gross and horrible. I have to wash it every day otherwise it gets really greasy, and because I wash it every day it gets super frizzy.'

'You could cut it.'

'So I could look more like a twelve-year-old boy? No, thank you, Brooke.'

'What if you didn't look like a twelve-year-old boy, though?' Brooke asked. 'You need to cut it really straight at the bottom, and shorter, so it doesn't get so tangled.'

'You sound like you know what you're talking about,' I muttered.

'I cut my own hair all the time. And Kendall's and Madison's.'

Kendall and Madison were the other popular girls at St. Catherine's, like Brooke. Madison was in my Chemistry class and was okay, but Kendall could be a bitch, especially when the others weren't around to keep her in line. I'd always wondered why the three of them were friends. They'd seemed to go everywhere together for a few years, though recently I'd seen Brooke with other people more often.

'Why?' I asked.

'Why did we cut each other's hair?'

'Yeah.'

'I started doing it a few years ago, mostly just putting box dye on my friends' hair and styling them in updos, you know, for homecoming or whatever.'

I'd never gone to homecoming or any *whatever*, because I'd never owned a nice-enough dress or had anyone to go with, and I didn't want to stand around looking awkward while my classmates danced. I'd seen photos, though, so I knew what she was talking about.

'I can't do fancy cuts,' Brooke said. 'Only simple things, trimming bangs, you know.'

I nodded like this was normal. Maybe it was.

'So,' she said decisively, 'do you want me to?'

'Oh, I don't know, Brooke. We probably shouldn't be wasting money on things like hair dye.' I never spent money on myself like that. Especially not on my appearance.

'Don't worry about that.' She waved away my concerns. 'I want . . . I don't know. I want to help give you a lift.'

I laughed. 'Like your car?'

'Exactly! Let me boost you up and fix you.'

I wasn't sure how easy that would be, but the idea was tempting. More than a little tempting.

'Okay,' I said.

'Great. I'm going to go to the supermarket. Do you want to wait here?'

My knee-jerk reaction was to say no. I didn't want Brooke to abandon me. I didn't want to be left on my own in a strange town where I didn't know anyone.

Brooke rolled her eyes, clearly reading my thoughts. 'I'll be, like, twenty minutes, tops. I don't want to interrupt your moment.'

'Okay.' I lurched to my feet. 'I'll grab my bag.'

The sun was starting to set, and it was beautiful out here, so I didn't mind staying behind, really. While Brooke was gone, I finished the bag of chips and read a few chapters of my novel.

Even though Brooke was teasing me about being obsessed with these vintage romances, I unironically loved them.

Sure, they danced a line between desperate longing and stalking sometimes, and there was a vague whiff of misogyny hanging over some characters, which totally tracked with when they were written. But they were also swoon-worthy, heart-stoppingly romantic, with characters who knew they couldn't possibly live without each other.

I related to that feeling.

She beeped the horn at me, and I jumped before my brain caught up and reminded me who it was.

'That was quick,' I said, letting myself into the passenger seat.

'I was gone thirty minutes.'

'Really?' I asked incredulously.

'Really,' she said with a laugh. She pulled out of the parking lot and headed back toward the motel. 'I thought you were going to be freaking out.'

Two bags stuffed full of non-perishables were in the footwell, to top up the supplies we kept in the trunk, plus two different types of dye and a pair of decent hairdressing scissors.

'Where did you get all that?'

'Don't worry about it, Mouse.'

'Seriously, Brooke, that stuff is expensive.'

'Mouse,' she said, grinning wickedly. 'I didn't pay for it.'

My jaw dropped. 'You *stole* it? Brooke!'

'*Steal* is a strong word. I . . . acquired a few things, at the expense of one of the wealthiest families in America. It's not like they can't afford to share.'

'You're not Robin freaking Hood!'

'Nah, I'm much better-looking.' She winked. She actually winked at me, and my blood suddenly turned fizzy, and I had no idea how to deal with that. 'There's more in the bottom of the bag.'

'More?' I groaned. 'Oh no, Brooke.'

'I paid for most of it, you know,' she said, still grinning like a Cheshire cat. 'Just not the expensive stuff.'

She'd picked up three more romance novels for me. All had been marked down, so I couldn't be mad at her for spending too much, and it was a sweet gesture. I wasn't used to people doing nice things for me. She must have noticed I had almost finished the last book from the thrift store.

'I was going to get phones, too,' she said casually. 'Since we didn't end up buying them in Salt Lake. But they were all security-tagged.'

'You definitely would've gotten caught if you'd tried to steal two phones,' I said, my stomach lurching at the thought.

'Maybe,' she said, turning to me and grinning. She was clearly riding an adrenaline high, and I didn't want to drag her down. Brooke was fun when she was hyped like this.

She left the music playing loud for the quick ride back to the motel, and then we picked up our bags and dragged them to our room.

'Come on, sit down.'

Brooke pulled the desk chair out into the space between the two beds and wrapped a clean towel around my shoulders. She combed through my hair with her fingers first, then a comb. I closed my eyes, not wanting her to see how that made me feel. I was sure my thoughts about her were written right across my face.

'Any requests?' she asked.

'You know what?' I said, twisting around to look at her. I didn't know where the feeling had come from, but suddenly I was *so* ready for something different. To *be* something different. 'Cut it off. Cut it all off. I'm done with it.'

Brooke laughed. 'We don't have to cut it *all* off.'

'I don't care. I don't want to feel blah anymore.'

'Well, I can de-blah you. Un-blah?'

'Either,' I said. 'Both.' I straightened up and closed my eyes.

If I was being honest with Brooke – and myself – I didn't have a huge attachment to my hair. It was waist-length these days, because I couldn't stand the idea of going to a salon and having other people touch me, and an unobtrusive light-brown color people called *mousey*. I kept it long because my mom liked it that way, and I'd spent years trying to please her. Having long hair was standard at St. Catherine's. The other girls didn't dare cut theirs too short otherwise they'd get accused of being lesbians, even if they were the popular girls.

Heaven forbid.

I didn't need to conform to that anymore, though. Chances were, I'd never set foot inside St. Catherine's again, and I was done with letting my mom make decisions about my life.

'Find something on TV,' Brooke said.

The TV was ancient, like all the TVs we'd encountered so far, but it was pretty big. I found a channel that was showing back-to-back nineties sitcoms: *Friends*, *The King of Queens*, *Frasier*, *The Fresh Prince of Bel-Air*, *Everybody Loves Raymond*. I couldn't remember watching any of the shows, but all the sets seemed familiar, and I knew the characters' names. Joey. Uncle Phil. Niles.

Brooke hummed as she worked, often coming around to study me from the front. Her eyebrows pinched together in a frown as she concentrated, and I sat still and tried to live up to her expectations.

Having Brooke this close to me, touching my hair, occasionally tipping my head to the side or angling my chin, was almost too much. More than once I decided I couldn't handle it anymore and put my hands on the seat to push myself off and away from her. Each time, Brooke seemed to catch me before I could move and shushed me gently, pressing down on my shoulders to keep me in place.

I didn't know how to explain to her that I wasn't used to this. No one touched me casually or played with my hair or put me under this much intense scrutiny. To have that coming from the girl I thought was really, really pretty had set a fire in my belly that I didn't know how to put out.

'Have you ever been to New York?' I asked, to distract both of us, as the show switched to a wide shot of Central Park in the fall.

'Hmm? Yeah. Have you?'

'No.'

'New York is a hell of a diversion, Mouse.'

'I didn't mean we should go. I was just curious.'

'We could. We'd just turn left instead of right at St. Louis.'

'But then we'd miss Nashville.'

'You want to go to Nashville?' she asked.

'Yeah.' A lot.

The reason why was embarrassing.

After my dad left, while it was still me and my mom on our own, she worked a lot. Mostly waitressing, mostly in diners. For a while she had a job in an Italian restaurant, but the owner kept making a move on her, so she quit. The one diner where she worked for the longest was called the 4th Street Diner in a small town in Idaho. It was themed like Nashville, and was famous for fried chicken. I remembered it well because I went there every day after school to sit in one of the booths at the back, or at the bar if it was busy, and either did my homework or colored while my mom worked.

The owner was an older guy, Sam, who had a huge white beard like Santa Claus and an equally huge round belly. He seemed to like me, or at least he tolerated my presence. Sam worked in the kitchen, fiercely guarding his fried chicken recipe and churning out pancakes and eggs and burgers and waffles for the families and truckers and high-school kids who were always coming and going.

When I was eight, 4th Street was the most fun place in the whole world. They had an honest-to-God jukebox that played country music classics, and pictures on the walls of country music legends. One of the pictures was a woman carrying a guitar, wearing white cowboy boots and a red dress, and she was the prettiest lady I'd ever seen in my life. Back then I would never have categorized it as a romantic feeling – more like a quiet obsession that made looking at any of the other pictures incredibly difficult – but I guess that's what it was.

Because of the diner, I'd wanted to go to Nashville more than anywhere else in the world. My mom said no, of course. Nashville might as well have been the moon with how far away it was and how much it would cost to get there.

So, my biggest dream was to go to a place that I'd been introduced to by a cheap diner in Idaho. Not to see the Pyramids in Egypt, or the beaches of Hawaii, or Paris, or Rome, or London. I didn't dream of the great wide world, because even Nashville, goddamn Nashville, felt like an unobtainable fantasy.

There was no way in hell I could tell Brooke that.

'Okay, you're ready for dye,' Brooke said, startling me out of my memories.

'Oh, God.'

'Don't worry,' she said, her voice easy and soothing. 'I'm practically a professional.'

I'd already seen the outside of the box, so I wasn't concerned she was secretly going to try to dye my hair bright pink. Though maybe bright pink was the change I needed. But at this point, I was happy to go along with whatever Brooke had in mind.

She moved us into the bathroom so I could sit on the edge of the tub and she didn't have to bend over to work the color through my hair. My butt hurt from the edge of the porcelain digging in. I took deep breaths and made sure not to complain.

'It says we should leave it for thirty to forty-five minutes,' Brooke said.

When I looked around, she was at the sink, stripping off the gloves from the box dye and washing her hands.

'Okay.'

'Then you can shampoo it out.'

I nodded, not wanting to say 'okay' again. I knew Brooke didn't like it when I went along with plans instead of giving an opinion, and I was getting better at it, I really was, but right now I felt picked apart and raw with nerves.

'Come watch TV with me,' she said, wandering out of the bathroom.

The hair dye smelled so strongly of chemicals that it made my eyes water. I didn't want to complain about that, either, or confess that this was the first time someone had dyed my hair. That was a normal thing, at seventeen, right? To dye your hair? Or get a nose piercing, or something dramatic to piss off your parents? My mom seemed pissed off with me most of the time anyway, so normal routes to teenage rebellion felt mostly pointless.

We watched an episode and a half of *Friends*, then Brooke ushered me into the bathroom again to wash my hair.

'Shampoo it twice, then condition it.'

'I know how to wash my hair, Brooke,' I said lightly.

'I know you know. Just do what you're told,' she said with a laugh.

'Get out, then,' I said, already shoving her through the door and pulling it closed.

The water pressure in this particular motel was terrible, the water spluttering out from a well-rusted showerhead. I tried really hard not to think of all the people who had used this shower before me, and how well it had been cleaned in between reservations.

When I was done, I wrapped my hair in a towel and dressed again in pajama pants and a loose T-shirt. Even though I was desperate to wipe the steam off the mirror and look at the results, I had a feeling Brooke might kill me if I tried.

'Are you finished?' she yelled through the bathroom door.

'Yeah.'

'I'm going to blow-dry it for you,' she said when I opened the door. She was waiting for me, her hands on her hips: business mode.

'I usually just let it air-dry.'

'I know you do. But I'm going to dry it so you can see the color.'

Brooke led me back to the chair in the bedroom and ran her fingers through my hair, her fingernails gently picking out the knots and tugging at my scalp. At every tiny movement I had to fight a shiver. This time I wasn't going to run away, though. I'd decided I liked this, and if Brooke was happy to do it, I was going to let her.

It was a typical *falling in love with a straight girl* story, one I'd read a hundred times. She was the classic beauty, I was the plainest of boring, plain Janes, and only in the hearts and imaginations of queer teenagers did we end up together.

I was a queer teenager. With a very active heart and imagination. Neither of those things were exactly revelations.

But . . . I didn't care. I couldn't make myself care that it was going nowhere. I didn't want Brooke to stop touching me, to stop smiling at me or laughing at my bad jokes. Because, actually, she was starting to become my closest friend.

God knew, I needed a friend more than I needed a girlfriend. One who didn't care about my tragic family situation and my inability to open up to people. I could keep admiring her from afar, and be her friend up close. That worked for me.

I would make it work.

Brooke shut off the hairdryer. 'Are you ready to look at it?'

'No,' I said, suddenly terrified in case it looked bad. How could I tell Brooke I hated it when she'd spent so much time and effort helping me?

She laughed. 'Well, you have to.'

She tugged me to my feet, then took one of my hands and covered my eyes with the other.

'This is very unnecessary, you know,' I muttered.

'I don't care.'

We hobbled to the bathroom and Brooke positioned me in front of the mirror. Then she dropped her hands.

I kept my eyes closed.

'Mouse!' she laughed. 'Open your eyes.'

'No.'

'Please?'

It was the *please* that did it.

I opened my eyes.

And watched my face in the mirror as my jaw dropped.

She'd cut off a *lot* of hair. She had warned me that she was going to do that, but even so . . .

Brooke had done what she'd promised, creating a sharp edge along my shoulders that looked, well, *edgy*. But the color was what threw me, because I wasn't mousey brown anymore. She'd cut through all the blah with different shades of golden streaks, not that much lighter than my natural color in some places and brighter around my face.

'What do you think?' she asked.

I met her eyes in the mirror.

'Holy shit, Brooke.'

'Do you hate it?' She looked genuinely nervous.

'I don't hate it. I don't know . . . but holy shit.'

She reached up to fuss with the strands of hair falling on my cheek, tucking some of them behind my ear. Then she rested her chin on my shoulder and looked at me in the mirror. My heart thudded in my throat, and I wanted to pull away – it was too much, having her this close to me. It was all too much.

It occurred to me then that if I turned my head to the side even the slightest bit, it'd be the perfect angle to kiss her, and my fight or flight mode flared.

'Mouse . . . I don't think I can call you Mouse anymore.'

'You can call me Jessie,' I said absently, still distracted by how close she was.

I reached up to run my fingers through my hair, finding it lighter in weight as well as color.

'Okay, Jessie,' Brooke said with a smile.

Maybe this was what Jessie looked like.

I could live with that.

9

Sticky Fingers – Rolling Stones

I wanted to stay in the little town in Wyoming for one more night, but Brooke said no. I was on the verge of getting fired up to argue with her, wanting to linger in the place where I'd finally found Jessie, when she reached out and brushed my hair back, and all my arguments withered up and died on my tongue.

There would be more two-stoplight towns, more cute nature parks, if we looked out for them.

It didn't feel so much like we were running anymore. It felt like we were just moving.

I liked that.

We'd already decided we were going to Denver next, so we got an early start, not wanting to hit rush-hour traffic. Brooke seemed happier now than she had at any point since we'd left Seattle. It could have been because we were about to head into a city, and she was much chirpier when she was surrounded by people, but she sometimes looked at me and smiled in a way I hadn't seen her smile at anyone else. I almost didn't want to *consider* what that could mean. The disappointment of finding out she was 100 percent straight would crush me.

'We should stay in the city tonight,' Brooke said, turning down the music so I could hear her.

'Won't that be expensive?' I asked.

'Yeah, but we need supplies,' she said, and I wasn't sure what that meant. We'd stocked up at the grocery store in Wyoming.

'Supplies?'

'Yeah,' she said cryptically. 'Trust me. I have a plan.'

We found a huge hotel, which I definitely didn't think was in our budget, but Brooke pulled into the parking lot like she knew exactly where she wanted to go. The other cars were expensive. Like, Mustang-level expensive. It was also pretty full.

We rode up in the elevator to the main lobby with two men in suits. Another thirty or so of them milled around the lobby bar. I suddenly felt self-conscious of my ripped jeans and baggy T-shirt. At least my hair looked good.

'There must be a convention happening,' Brooke murmured, looking around casually.

'That's good?' I asked.

'That's excellent,' she corrected.

We waited in a short line for check-in, and I quietly scanned the room, quickly building an impression of the suited, obnoxious men who were talking in loud voices near us.

'Hi,' Brooke said when we were called up to the desk. She slouched and stuck her thumbnail in her mouth to chew on it, making her look and sound like a stupid, bored teenager – something she definitely was not. 'We need a room for tonight. My phone and credit card got stolen, so I need to pay in cash.'

'I'm sorry to hear that.'

This woman wasn't like the other receptionists we'd encountered in the shabby motels on our way here. She was dressed in a blue silk shirt with a scarf tied around her neck, and an extremely tight pinstriped skirt. She tapped at her keyboard for a really long time – like, a *really* long time, to the point where I started to think she'd forgotten about us – and then nodded.

'I can offer you our saver rate of one-eighty a night, plus tax. That doesn't include breakfast.'

I wanted to wince – a hundred and eighty dollars was a lot more than what we usually paid for a room. I was starting to get annoyed. Brooke had better have a good reason for this.

'Great,' Brooke said. 'Thank you.'

I let her take care of paying, counting out the twenties from our stash and slapping the dirty bills down on the counter. The receptionist took the money and counted it again before handing Brooke the change and two key cards.

I still didn't say anything as we went up to the room, dodging the suits. We got into the elevator with three more of them, and I opened my mouth to ask Brooke a question, but she shook her head subtly.

Our room, when we got to it, was *plush*. Like, seriously plush, especially compared to the motels we'd been staying in. It had thick gray carpet and one king bed made up with crisp white linens. The walls were painted the same shade of blue as the receptionist's shirt, and the TV was a flat-screen and mounted to the wall. I'd almost forgotten TVs could be like that.

And we had a *sitting area*.

'They didn't have a twin room?' I asked, forcing myself to be casual as I dumped my bag next to the closet. I didn't want to let my mind skip ahead to thinking about sharing a bed with Brooke.

'I guess not,' she said with a shrug. 'We got the saver rate, though. I don't want to argue with that.'

I wanted to argue, or offer to sleep in the little scoop chair or even on the floor, but I knew Brooke wouldn't let me do any of those things now that we were friends. It was a king bed. There was plenty of space in it.

We'd be fine.

I'd be fine.

'Are you planning on telling me what's going on?' I said, trying to be assertive without being an asshole.

Brooke sat down in the gray armchair and stretched out her legs. She pursed her lips and looked up at me.

'We need more cash,' she said after a moment, her voice strangely neutral.

'And staying in an expensive hotel is going to solve that?' I retorted.

'Jessie . . . How morally opposed are you to a little light theft?'

I sat down on the bed. 'Brooke.'

'Just a little,' she said, holding up her hands. 'You want to tell me those guys downstairs can't afford to lose the contents of their wallets?'

She was so frustrating I wanted to strangle her. And also kiss that smug expression right off her face. But mostly strangle her.

'How?' I asked wearily.

'I'm going to put on my ugly St. Catherine's shoes, white shirt and black skirt and pretend to be staff.' She made it sound so easy.

'And then what?'

'Start in the coat-check area next to the ballroom, or wherever they're having dinner tonight. I need you to work the lobby bar.'

'You want me to *help*?' I couldn't stop the sudden rush of panic and my fingers curled into fists around the comforter. 'Oh no, Brooke. That's really not a good idea.'

'You look like the most innocent person who's ever existed. You're gonna be great.'

'I can't,' I said quickly. 'I'm not like you, Brooke. I can't do that.'

'You can,' she said, soothing and reassuring, petting the air in front of me. 'I promise. We'll wait until later, when they're all blind drunk, and it'll be the easiest thing you ever did.'

'You've done this before.'

She nodded. 'Yeah, I used to do it with my cousin for fun.'

For fun.

Spoiled little rich kids who could afford to get caught, who knew their parents would pay the fines and drive them to community service if they were given more than just a slap on the wrist.

The anger was bubbling in my stomach, ready to spill up and out if I let it.

Kids like Brooke and her privileged cousin would never know what people from my side of town had to go through, what would happen to people like me if we were caught lifting wallets. She could do stuff like this for fun, but I couldn't, and, for just a second, I resented her for it.

It wasn't fair.

But then, life wasn't fair.

And maybe this was my chance at righting some of those wrongs. After all, the guys in their designer suits were from Brooke's side of town, not mine.

I shook my head, unable to reconcile my resistance with Brooke's convincing. 'We'll never get away with it.'

'We need cash for when we get to Orlando. We have enough to get down to Florida, but once we're there, motels are going to get really expensive.'

'No one carries cash anymore, Brooke. They pay for stuff with their credit cards.'

'These guys will,' she said. 'Especially at the bar. Especially for tipping.'

'How do you know all this?'

'I'll explain later.'

I flopped back onto the bed, groaning. 'Brooke. Seriously.'

'I will!' she said. 'This was the plan until you came along. I could've maybe rinsed more out of my family's credit card, but I was always planning on, you know, liberating what I needed.'

'Stealing, you mean.'

'If you want out, you can stay up here,' she said. I could tell she was baiting me.

'No,' I said. Then again, with more conviction. 'No, I'm in.'

She grinned, in that cat-like way of hers. 'Excellent.'

It was only early afternoon, so we left the hotel still wearing jeans and T-shirts, and walked the half-block to Target so Brooke could pick up what she needed.

Being back in a big city put me on edge. I was waiting for the moment someone tapped me on the shoulder, a police officer put their hand on my arm, someone in the crowd shouted 'Jessie!' and I'd know I'd been recognized. I felt my anxiety flare every time I met someone's eye by accident, or a police car drove past us, or a sign told us THESE PREMISES ARE MONITORED BY CCTV. It didn't feel anywhere near as safe as those tiny towns in the middle of nowhere.

I wasn't ready to cut this road trip short, to give up the precious freedom that it had given me. The freedom was a gift, one I'd never expected and now never wanted to let go of.

I wasn't ready to let go of Brooke, either. If we ever did end up back in Seattle, I couldn't be sure whether she'd treat me like she did now or like she had before – friendly but cool and distant – and I really didn't want to find out. Despite my restless anxiety, Brooke seemed calm, like this was a regular Friday afternoon shopping trip to pick up hair ties and tights.

'We need to make you look not like you,' she said.

'That shouldn't be difficult.'

Brooke stepped back and assessed me, head to toe. 'I think you could pass as a college freshman.'

'You think?' I was acutely aware that I was often mistaken for being younger than seventeen, rather than older.

'Yeah. Why not?' Brooke grabbed a shirt and thrust it at me. 'Hold this.'

'I'm not sure it's my size.'

She pointedly rolled her eyes at me. 'It's cropped, Jessie. On purpose.'

'Oh. Oh no.' I held the shirt out to her, desperately hoping she'd take it back. 'I can't wear this.'

'Why not? Do you have a giant tattoo on your stomach that no one's allowed to see?'

No tattoos, and my bruises had faded into barely there shadows, so I couldn't even use that to my benefit.

'I am not a cropped-shirt kinda girl.'

'Exactly.' She turned to me and put her hands on her hips.

Shit.

'You're not supposed to be you. You're supposed to be a college student.'

I didn't have a good response to that, and Brooke smiled, knowing she'd won.

'I need to find you some props,' she said and turned on her heel, stalking off into the darker depths of Target. I followed her wearily, still questioning whether this was a good idea.

'Run it again,' Brooke said.

I rolled over to bury my face in the pillow and groaned. 'No.'

We were back in the hotel room, chilling out before the evening, and Brooke was determined to have me repeat our story until it became second nature. No more tripping over my lies.

'Jessie,' she said, her voice stern. She'd started calling me Jessie all the time now, and I was happier about that than I'd ever tell her. 'Run it again. Who are you?'

'Jenna Roberts.' I rolled back over to stare at the ceiling. Coming up with a new last name had been simple – my dad's name was Robert, and Jenna was starting to roll off my tongue easily enough.

'Where are you from?'

'Tacoma. I'm a student at the University of Puget Sound.'

'Go UPS!'

Tipping my head to look at her, I laughed and raised an almost enthusiastic fist-pump. 'Woo-hoo!'

'What are you studying?'

'English Lit and Spanish.'

We were keeping much of the story as close to the truth as we dared, and since I was taking AP English Lit and Spanish, it made lying easier.

'Where are you going?'

'To St. Louis, with my cousin, for a funeral,' I replied quickly. 'Grandpa Jim.'

'Hell of a long journey.'

'I'm scared of flying.'

'Why here? Why this hotel?'

'Needed to stop for the night. Not allowed to stay in motels – it's not safe.'

'Who's paying?'

'My dad,' I said with a cynical smile. I was sure he hadn't paid for anything for me in years.

She nodded. 'You're getting there.'

While she was grilling me, Brooke had been getting ready. Her hair was pulled back in two long, thick braids and pinned into an updo that looked elegant but still practical. She'd put on a lot more makeup than I'd ever seen her wear before, her eyes dark and smoky behind long lashes. It made her look older, more sophisticated, and less like the Brooke who had checked in at the front desk earlier. I didn't know eye makeup could be such a good disguise.

She'd changed, too, into our familiar St. Catherine's uniform. I'd found the silky blue neck scarf the hotel staff wore when I'd gone to use the guest laundry room – a bunch of them had been left in a bag on the counter.

Slipping one into my pocket had been easy. My first theft of the night.

Brooke tied it with a flourish and adjusted it so the knot sat on the side of her neck.

She caught my eye in the mirror and saw me chewing my bottom lip. Stealing the neck scarf had been one thing. I still wasn't convinced about what was coming next, though, and she could clearly sense my hesitation.

'Stop worrying,' she said, and turned around to face me. 'Look, if it doesn't work out, just come back up here and hang out until I'm done.'

'Chicken out, you mean,' I said hotly.

'It's not chickening out, it's being sensible. If you don't think you can make a clean lift, then don't bother. It's better to back out than to be caught.'

'Okay,' I said softly.

'I'm serious, Jessie. Don't get fucking caught.'

I nodded, determined not to let her down, and rolled off the bed. I instinctively tugged at the hem of the T-shirt to make it cover my belly. Which it didn't.

Brooke had already styled my hair for me, pulling it back on the side with clips. She'd bought me a copy of *Pride and Prejudice*, multicolored pens and a pair of oversize tortoiseshell glasses with plain glass in them, since my eyesight was fine. I was allowed to wear my own jeans, thank God.

She'd only made a few tweaks to my appearance, but I was pretty sure my own mother would double-take before she recognized me. That was one small reassurance. I didn't look like me – the old me – so maybe I could step into a new persona and be Jenna for the night. Jenna wasn't Jessie, after all. Jenna was cool and confident and smart.

'I'm going down now,' Brooke said, wriggling in the tight skirt so it sat right on her hips. 'I can't wait around anymore.'

'Break a leg,' I said, too scared to smile.

Brooke grinned and winked at me. 'You too.'

I watched her slip out of the room, her flirty wink leaving me with brand-new butterflies in my stomach.

At nine p.m., the bar was busy.

I'd waited in the room for a while, pacing and practicing my lines and trying to settle my nerves, before heading back down to the lobby. I picked my seat strategically, on the far side of the curved marble bar, which put my back against a wall and gave me a good view across the room.

'What can I get you?' the bartender asked as I hooked the handle of my backpack on the purse hook under the lip of the bar. I took my jacket off, too, and folded it across my lap.

'Could I get a Coke and a bowl of French fries?'

He nodded and set a black square napkin down in front of me.

I took stock of both the layout of the bar and its patrons while the bartender poured my drink. There seemed to be a few people around who were wearing jeans and casual dresses, as well as all the guys in suits. Brooke had already prepped me for that, and how I needed to establish myself in the room before making a move.

I took the paperback and pens out of my backpack and set them on the bar, leaving the bag unzipped at the top. Back in the room we'd given the book a decent beating to make it look like I'd been reading it for a few days already, dog-earing pages and breaking the spine.

Chapter Fifteen.

Mr. Collins was not a sensible man ...

I'd read the book before, so it didn't take long to get into the swing of it, randomly underlining various passages as I went along. The bartender brought me my drink, and I nodded my thanks, and ten minutes later a waiter came over with a decent portion of fries, with condiments on the side in tiny white ramekins.

From my vantage point I could see the clocks on the wall behind the check-in desks, and right when Brooke had said they would, businessmen started appearing at the bar. She had found a program for the convention, so we knew the dinner finished at ten, before the 'casino and dancing' portion of the evening started.

By ten thirty the place was packed with people moving back and forth between the ballroom and the bar.

I kept my head down, scrawling brightly colored notes in the margins of the book, and waiting for someone to get close enough. Getting here early had been good for me. I was still more nervous than I'd ever been in my life – and that was saying something for a person who was perpetually anxious – but I'd claimed my spot and I knew what I was doing. In theory.

'What are you reading?'

Bingo.

The guy was old, older than my mom for sure, with light-brown hair that was going gray at his temples.

I turned the book over and smiled as I held it up to him.

'Ah, Austen. A classic,' he said pretentiously.

'It's an assigned text for my class.'

'Enjoy.'

He'd sized me up now, and, having deemed me too young to make a move on, smiled politely and turned to his friend so I was left staring at the back of his head. His jacket was unbuttoned and hung loose at his waist. All my nerves crept into my throat, making me breathe faster and harder, and my vision blurred around the edges. None of that mattered, though. No one was looking at me.

It was now or never.

I stretched down to scratch my leg and, as my hand moved back up, I reached into his jacket pocket and slowly, carefully, plucked out his wallet.

It was heavy.

Shit.

Shit!

Moving leisurely – people noticed quick movements – I dropped the wallet into my open backpack.

And . . . that was it.

He didn't notice.

Neither did anyone else.

Nothing changed – the noise of dozens of buzzing conversations continued, the bartender kept working the bar, people kept drinking their drinks.

Nothing happened.

In my chest something was happening, though: my heart had worked its way up through my chest to lodge in my throat, and all my blood had redirected to rush in my ears. I forced myself to breathe slowly, calming my nerves and releasing the tension that had gathered in tight knots along my spine.

I flipped a page in my book, having read absolutely nothing.

I sipped my Coke, slurping the last drops from among the ice.

'Another?'

I startled so hard I almost fell off the barstool.

'Sorry,' the bartender said, laughing awkwardly. 'I didn't realize you were so absorbed.'

'No, it's my fault.' I forced myself to smile at him. 'I should pay more attention.'

'Do you want another?' he repeated, gesturing to my empty glass.

'Please.'

I picked at the fries to give me something to do with my hands. They were cold now, as I'd been too nervous to eat before. The man whose wallet I'd stolen moved away with his beer, not even glancing back at me. A few seconds later, his space filled with someone else.

I took three more wallets in the next hour and a half. All

of them from slimy older guys who leered at me, their eyes drinking in my body like they had permission to look. The second one was easier now I knew how it worked. He had slicked-back black hair, smelled like strong cologne and talked too loudly. The third was a man trying to hit on a woman, probably his colleague, who nodded politely while he mansplained at her. I noticed her eyes glazing over, her beautifully manicured nails tapping against the side of her wine glass. She wasn't paying any attention to him.

I was.

He leaned toward her, trying to get her to flirt back, or show any kind of recognition of his self-assured greatness, and I had to wonder if she noticed when I lifted not just his card wallet but a money clip from his pocket, too.

If she did, she didn't say anything. I never even made eye contact with her.

The fourth guy was a real asshole, shouting at the female bartender for getting his order wrong. She was politely apologetic as she remade his fancy bourbon cocktail, and I didn't feel bad at all about sliding his wallet out of his jacket pocket while he was berating her.

Leaving with four wallets didn't feel like chickening out. I signaled to the bartender and paid up, in cash from my own wallet. He might remember me in the morning – the girl who had read *Pride and Prejudice* and tipped decently on a few glasses of soda and French fries – but he would forget me by the weekend.

I stuffed my book and pens back into my backpack, on top of the wallets I didn't dare look at, then zipped it up tightly and wandered slowly back to our room, wanting to keep up my easy-going disguise until I was safely away from wandering eyes.

Brooke wasn't there when I walked in, and I wanted to throw up and scream and dance around the room all at the same time. I wanted to dig into the wallets and count the cash.

I didn't do any of that.

I forced myself to have a shower, letting the hot water soothe my tense muscles. I'd always done a lot of thinking in the shower, since it was a safe space in a way almost nowhere else in my life was. It didn't take long for little tendrils of guilt and shame to start creeping around me. Growing up, we'd never had much, and I was used to not asking for things – money included. Taking it from someone else, even if they could afford to lose it, didn't sit completely right with me.

'Jessie?'

'I'll be out in a second,' I called back, relieved that Brooke had made it to the room safely.

I turned the water off, wrapped myself in a towel and changed into my pajamas before leaving the bathroom.

Brooke was at the mirror, unpicking her complicated hairstyle. 'Well?' she asked.

'You go first,' I said, wanting to surprise her with my haul.

I rubbed the towel over my hair, trying to wring out as much of the water as I could, and sat on the bed to braid it before we went to sleep. Not that I could go to sleep any time soon. I was too hyped up.

Brooke went over to the dresser and pulled out a crisp white pillowcase, laughing as she turned it out and eight, maybe ten, wallets tumbled out of it.

'Easiest thing in the world.'

'Shit, Brooke,' I murmured. 'I only got four.' That seemed almost pathetic now.

I pulled over my backpack and fished them out. 'Oh, and a money clip.'

'That's really good, Jessie. Especially for your first time!'

'What are you going to do with the wallets?' I asked, curious, as Brooke started to sort through them.

'Dump them,' she said. 'I'm just going to take out the cash. Taking the credit cards and using them is a whole other ball game.'

The nerves that had consumed me earlier in the evening now settled in a rock of anticipation in my stomach. I'd be devastated if my wallets didn't bring in much cash. There was no way I could better Brooke's haul, so I wasn't going to aim for equality. But being able to contribute, and being part of whatever this was . . . that had become increasingly important to me.

'Ready?' Brooke asked.

'Absolutely.'

'Pick one.'

I grabbed one of the wallets I'd taken, though I couldn't remember which man it had come from. Dark-brown leather with a snap closure. I flipped it open and went straight for the dollar bills.

'Eighty-five. No – ninety. That's a ten, not a five.'

I set the bills down on the bed and put the wallet to one side.

'Good start. I want to see what's in that fucking money clip.'

I laughed, and Brooke prized it open, tugging free the folded bills.

'Holy shit, Jessie. There's like ... almost three hundred bucks here.'

We kept going, back and forth, tit for tat, until we had eight hundred and twenty-five dollars in front of us.

Brooke fell silent. I looked up at her, and she seemed to sparkle in the artificial hotel room light.

'Holy shit,' she breathed again, and I couldn't hold it in anymore.

I let out a strangled scream and bounced on the bed, displacing all the bills we'd stacked in careful piles.

'Jessie!' Brooke yelled, then she did the same, bouncing on the bed next to me, before collapsing on her side in a fit of giggles.

I laid down next to her. 'Not bad for one night's work.'

'I knew you'd be great,' she said, her face alight with a mix of excitement and satisfaction.

When she reached for me, I let her pull me into a hug, and for a second we tangled together, elbows and knees and wild energy, before we both flopped onto our backs, breathless. She grasped my hand and squeezed it, and didn't let go.

Brooke tipped her head to the side and smiled at me, her cheeks flushed, and my heart stuttered. This didn't feel like a friends thing, it felt different, like we were right on the edge of something *more*.

Brooke swallowed hard and her eyes grew intense, and I didn't dare look away.

Was she going to kiss me?

How would she react if I kissed her?

I looked down at our joined hands, then back at Brooke. Electricity sparkled between us for a second more, before Brooke turned her head and looked up at the ceiling, still smiling.

'I knew it,' she said again, and I let myself bask in the feeling. Brooke believed in me. My heart almost hurt from how good it felt to hear that.

10

The Stranger – Billy Joel

Brooke fell asleep quickly, curling up on the side of the bed closest to the window and throwing her arm over her face. I'd noticed that was how she liked to sleep, hiding her face from the world.

I laid on the other side of the bed, leaving as much space as was humanly possible between us, and tried to calm my still-racing heart.

I couldn't help but run the night over and over in my head, replaying each of the wallets and how I'd lifted them, the men I'd stolen from, the woman with her wine glass and bored expression. I'd been nothing to them – either invisible or not worth paying close attention to – but I'd made sure they would remember what I'd done more than any boring lecture at the convention.

The power felt electric in my veins. They shouldn't have ignored me.

Brooke snored softly from the other side of the bed.

She had looked so pretty and so much older than me

tonight. With red lipstick and her hair pulled back instead of loose around her shoulders, she could easily pass for someone in her early twenties. I liked her more like this – bare-faced and relaxed. This was the version of Brooke I had gotten to know, and I had a feeling it was the purest, most condensed version of her. She was different with me than she was at school. In a good way. Then again, I was different with her, too.

I tried to reason that sharing a bed wasn't a big deal. It was probably something girls who were friends did all the time. It didn't need to mean anything. It didn't mean anything to *Brooke*.

I tried to extinguish the fiery feeling in my belly that wanted to flare bright. I wasn't going to force myself on her, or convince myself that maybe she had feelings for me. She didn't. And that was okay.

It was late before I fell asleep and Brooke had stopped snoring. The peaceful rise and fall of her shoulder, her skin pale in the moonlight, convinced me to let it all go and sleep too.

During the night we must have both moved, because when I woke up the next morning and opened my eyes, Brooke's sleeping face was inches from my own. I startled back, terrified that my subconscious had done something inappropriate in my sleep.

As slowly as I dared, I rolled over and away from her, edging back to my side of the bed.

The bed was huge. This was ridiculous.

Slowly, my heartbeat returned to a normal rhythm, and I decided to get out of bed before Brooke woke up and noticed me being weird. When I was in the bathroom, I heard her moving around the room, and that was a relief. I wanted to let her sleep as long as she liked, but I couldn't read very well in the dark – this fancy hotel had good blackout curtains, unlike the cheap motels we'd been staying in up until now.

Brooke was sitting in the armchair when I came out of the bathroom, her long legs stretched out in front of her.

'Did you sleep well?' she asked me with a smile.

'Yeah,' I lied, and smiled too. Brooke didn't need to know the truth.

While I was getting dressed, Brooke got ready in the bathroom, then I packed up everything and left the pillowcase with the wallets hidden inside by the door, ready to dump them in a trash can when we left.

Brooke came out with a cagey expression on her face. I immediately tensed, wondering what high jinks she was planning next.

'So,' she started, 'how would you feel about catching up with my cousin today?'

It took my brain a second to follow her thoughts – Brooke's cousin, who lived in Denver, because she'd chosen to come here instead of going to college in Utah.

Reaching out to someone who knew either of us sat uneasily in my stomach. Maybe Brooke trusted her cousin wouldn't turn us in, but I didn't know her. What if she decided to join our road trip? I didn't want that at all.

I sat down in the gray chair, and Brooke took the bed opposite me, reversing our positions from yesterday.

'Do you know where she lives?' I asked.

'Yeah, kind of. Me and Julianne visited her last year.'

I chewed on my bottom lip, and Brooke watched me intensely.

'Don't do that,' she said gently, reaching out to squeeze my knee. 'You'll hurt your lips.'

I stopped, startled, and stared at her. Brooke kept talking, apparently unaware of how much her casual touches affected me.

'If we follow the signs for Denver Zoo, I should be able to find her neighborhood from there,' she said.

'Why do you want to see her? Won't she, like, immediately call your parents? Or the cops?'

'Nah,' Brooke drawled. 'Meredith isn't like the rest of them.'

'The rest of who?'

'My family.' Brooke straightened up, combing her fingers through her loose hair.

'I want to go see her because I think she'll help us.'

I sat with that for a moment. 'Do we need help?'

She shrugged. 'She used to live with a bunch of theater performers, and I know at least some of them are interning at theme parks. Meredith almost signed up for the same program. So they might be able to help us when we get to Orlando.'

It hung between us in the air, then, that thing we weren't speaking about.

Running away was one thing.

We'd done that.

We knew where we were going, and we had a plan – sort of – for when we got there.

But it wasn't like we were going to walk right into Disney World and get jobs, not without any experience, and no resumes, no references.

I wanted to shove that unspoken thing out of the room, to go back to planning how to steal from drunk businessmen, because at least that was something tangible. I could see myself pickpocketing much easier than dancing through a theme park wearing a stylized ballgown, even though it would mean dealing with a guilty conscience.

Brooke raised her eyebrow at me, asking a silent question. I was pretty sure if I said no, I didn't want to go see Meredith, she would let it go. There might be a little argument about it, but she wouldn't force me to if I felt strongly about it.

And I wanted to go to Disney World, goddamn it. Brooke had put the idea in my head, and it had grown and gathered speed and turned into my daydream now too.

'Okay,' I said, kicking my legs up in a move that sent my chair spinning. 'Maybe she can help.'

'She's the one who taught me how to . . . you know.'

Pickpocket. Right.

'And the –' she lowered her voice – 'you know, *gun*, is hers.'

'Why do you even have it?' I asked, finally voicing the question I'd been burying.

'She gave it to me.'

There was so much more I needed to know. Why did Meredith think her seventeen-year-old cousin needed a gun? What the hell was Brooke running away from? Was there a possibility that something as bad had happened to her back home . . . someone just as bad as the Creep?

I really didn't think Brooke had killed someone. But then, she probably didn't think I was being chased by the police because *they* thought *I* had killed someone. Most teenage girls didn't run away from a murder charge.

As the moment stretched between us, I knew I could break our original promise not to ask each other what we were running from. If her answer had something to do with the gun, though, would that change what we had now? If she knew about the Creep, would it change things for her?

I wasn't going to ask. Not yet.

'All right,' I said eventually. 'Let's go find Meredith.'

'Great,' Brooke said with a huge sigh, then checked her watch. 'We need to move. Check-out is at eleven.'

'Holy shit, I thought you were dead.'

Brooke's cousin looked a lot like Brooke. They had the same heavy eyebrows and thick dark hair, though Meredith styled hers a lot shorter than Brooke. She had a septum piercing, the silver hoop looping between her nostrils. I found myself staring at it for a moment too long, wondering if it had hurt, and whether the hurt was worth it.

We'd left the hotel without stopping at the front desk, not wanting to give any of the staff the chance to recognize

Brooke from last night. We'd paid in cash, anyway, so it wasn't like they needed to process a credit card payment.

Finding Meredith's apartment had taken slightly longer than we'd anticipated. Brooke kept driving in circles, trying to find somewhere that looked familiar, and I started regretting throwing away our phones. And not having a map.

Not that I knew how to read a map.

She'd eventually found the zoo and drove the couple of blocks to Meredith's neighborhood. We parked the Mustang in a shady spot under a tree before we went to find the apartment block on foot.

'Surprise,' Brooke said, making a little jazz hands gesture.

'Come in,' Meredith replied.

On the front step of her apartment building, wearing a man's shirt and black cycle shorts, and with her toenails painted neon orange, Meredith looked amazing – cooler even than Brooke, and I'd been holding Brooke up as ultimate girl goals. Meredith held the door open and gestured us both inside.

'This is Jessie,' Brooke said.

'Hi.' I gave a little wave.

Meredith's apartment was tiny, which made sense because she was a college student, and she'd hung beads and fairy lights from the ceiling and covered the walls with brightly patterned fabrics. One sad, brown corduroy couch slumped in the corner, behind a low coffee table that was covered with baggies of weed.

'What the hell's going on?' Meredith asked.

She took a seat on a huge beanbag, and I sat down next to Brooke on the couch, trying not to stare as I took in the apartment.

'I needed some space,' Brooke said, and Meredith rubbed her hands over her face and groaned. 'I'm guessing you heard.'

'Your dad called my dad a couple days ago,' Meredith said. She sat upright and reached for a mug that looked like it was hand-made. By a six-year-old. Who only had a vague idea of what a coffee mug was supposed to look like.

'Oh, good,' Brooke muttered.

'Your mom,' Meredith said pointedly, 'is hysterical, thinks you've been kidnapped, raped and/or murdered. Your dad, however, thinks you're throwing a tantrum and will be home by the end of the week.'

She glanced at a calendar taped to the wall. 'Which is tomorrow.'

'I'm not going home tomorrow,' Brooke replied firmly.

'No, I guessed that. No one really thought you'd end up here. I think the only reason I was told was because my dad had to fulfill the insatiable Summer appetite for gossip.'

'Did you really think I was dead?' Brooke asked. She leaned forward, bracing her elbows on her knees.

Meredith shrugged. 'I figured it was the most likely scenario.' She tilted her head to the side. 'Except, your car was gone, so there was always a possibility you hadn't been stolen by human trafficking gangs or eaten by a bear.'

'God, my family is so dramatic.'

'Why are you here? Do you want a drink?' Meredith pushed herself to her feet and took three steps to her left, which put her in a tiny space that might, if I was being generous, have been considered a kitchen.

'Do you have any soda?' Brooke asked.

'Sure. Jessie?'

'Anything. Thanks.'

Meredith brought over two cans of La Croix, set them on the coffee table and swept all the little baggies of weed into a basket.

'I was hoping you could help us,' Brooke said, clearly scoping out Meredith's mood.

'What do you need?' she asked.

Brooke cracked the tab on her can. 'Do you have a spare phone we could borrow? Both ours got stolen.'

'Is that all? I thought you were going to ask for money or drugs or something.'

'No, Mer, we have loads of money and drugs,' she said sarcastically.

Meredith cocked her head, studying us, and I noticed that she had the exact same eyes as Brooke, too: deep brown, with flecks of gold in the iris. Those Summer genes were strong.

'Brooke, you're only seventeen,' she said after a while. 'Your folks are really worried about you. Are you sure you don't want to call them?'

'I'm fine,' Brooke said with a long sigh. 'I just need a break from them, you know?'

This wasn't going how I'd hoped, and when I glanced at Brooke, she seemed annoyed too. This didn't feel like the right time to be asking Meredith for help getting jobs in Orlando.

'Where are you going?' Meredith asked.

'Anywhere. Nowhere. I can't stand my mom hovering over me for one more fucking second. Getting out of Seattle was the most important thing.'

'Well, you know I understand that feeling.' Meredith stretched her feet out to study her toenails. 'You can crash here for a few days if you want.'

I glanced at Brooke but had no idea how to read her expression.

'That could work,' Brooke said casually. She looked over at me, and I tried to keep my expression neutral.

'Could I talk to you for a second?' I asked Brooke.

She looked confused, but nodded, and followed me to the tiny kitchenette area. Meredith was still only six feet away from us.

'We'll be fine,' I said in a low voice that I was certain Meredith could hear. 'If we stay here tonight, we can get moving tomorrow and still be in New York in a couple days.'

Brooke frowned at me for a second, then her eyebrows shot up in understanding.

'Once we're in the city, no one is gonna be able to find us,' Brooke said, a little louder.

'Exactly.'

Meredith stood up, and I stepped away from Brooke, suddenly aware of how close we were huddled together.

'Give me a minute. I'll be right back.'

'Sure,' Brooke said.

I waited until the door had closed behind Meredith before turning back to Brooke.

'Wanna tell me what that was all about?' Brooke asked, leaning back against the counter.

'Sorry. I know we're not going to New York, don't worry. It just doesn't hurt if other people *think* that's where we're headed, you know?'

'You sound really paranoid right now.'

'I know.' I held my hands up. 'If your cousin turns out to be cool, then great. I'll apologize to her another time, when all of this is over. I'm just trying to cover our backs.'

Brooke nodded. 'Okay, I get it. And New York makes sense. My family wouldn't be surprised to hear I was heading that way.'

'Because of your sister?'

'Partly, yeah. I also made a big deal about wanting to spend the past couple summers with Julianne. If Meredith did call my folks, this would all be plausible.'

I let my shoulders slump with relief. 'Good. Are you going to ask about her friends helping us get jobs?'

Brooke shook her head. 'I figure if we borrow a phone, then I can always call and ask her once we're down in Orlando.'

'That makes sense.'

On the counter, Meredith's incense burned out, sending a white curl of smoke to the ceiling. Brooke pulled me into a quick, hard hug. I got over my shock at the affectionate gesture and tentatively wrapped my arms around her back. For a second, just a second, I rested my head on her shoulder.

Brooke's arms tightened around my waist. 'We're going to make this work,' she said confidently as she stepped back and gave me a reassuring smile.

My stomach flipped over, and I decided I could tell her how I was feeling. Well, a small part of how I was feeling.

'Brooke, I don't think we should stay here tonight.'

'But you just said –'

'I know,' I jumped in. 'I know. It would be good not to have to pay for a motel, but just in case someone did recognize us from last night, or if the local cops were called, or if Meredith decides to be responsible and call your parents to tell them where we are . . .'

Brooke sighed heavily and ran her fingers through her hair.

'It might be better to be somewhere else,' she finished for me. 'You're right. It's just, you know, a nine-hour journey to get to Kansas City, and I'm getting really sick of driving through the middle of nowhere.'

'Let's break it down. Stop in the middle of nowhere tonight, get there tomorrow.'

'That's another day, though,' she said, her voice breaking into a whine.

I shrugged. 'I'm not in a rush, Brooke.'

'No, I guess me neither.'

Meredith came back a few minutes later with a paper bag which she emptied out onto the counter. She'd found a couple of phones, chargers, a stack of cash and some ID cards.

'They aren't great,' she said. 'They're old phones I never bothered to throw away. But they work, so you can use them for now.'

They were both iPhones, only one of them in a protective case, and the other with a tiny crack in one corner of the screen. They were old, but just having something to use again was going to make life easier.

'Thank you,' Brooke said. 'That's perfect.'

'Have these, too. I don't need them,' Meredith said, pushing the two cards across the counter. One was her University of Denver student ID card, the other her driver's license. In the photo, she had much longer hair, and it would take someone looking real close to realize it wasn't Brooke. That ID put her age at twenty-one, which could help us out if we ever needed it. 'And the cash. There's two hundred there.'

'Are you sure?' Brooke asked.

Meredith waved it away. 'It's fine. It's my emergency cash. Call it a birthday present or whatever.'

Brooke pulled her into a hug, and Meredith rolled her eyes and patted Brooke's back, and said, 'Yeah, yeah. I'm not giving you weed, though.'

'Ugh.' Brooke pulled out of the hug. 'I don't smoke.'

'Good for you. Don't start. You wanna hang around for a while?'

Brooke looked at me.

'I don't mind,' I said with a shrug.

'Let's go out,' Brooke said decisively. 'I haven't had a chance to catch up with you in forever.'

I personally thought it would be better to keep moving, to get out of the city before anyone started looking at us in connection with the pickpocketing at the convention last night. But Brooke had already agreed not to spend tonight with her cousin, and it was more important to me that she was happy than I eased my own paranoia.

We waited while Meredith pulled on chunky black boots and fished her keys out of another wobbly ceramic bowl-type thing.

'How long have you lived here?' I asked while Meredith locked the front door.

'Three years. I'm going to have to move out in the summer, unless I enroll on an MFA or something.'

'Is that the plan, now?' Brooke asked.

'Eh. Maybe.' Meredith took off at a clip, moving through her neighborhood with the confidence of someone who knew the area well. 'The choice is between staying in school or getting a job, and I don't know if I'm ready to join the rat race.'

Brooke snorted with laughter. 'Like you're going to do some high-flying corporate job.'

'I might,' Meredith said. She tugged at the long feather earring hooked through her left lobe. 'I could.'

'No, you couldn't,' Brooke replied.

'What's your major?' I asked her.

'Ceramics,' she said, and really, I should have seen that coming.

We passed a long row of indie stores selling plants and coffee and a second-hand bookstore that tugged at my belly. Next to the bookstore was a tattoo and piercing place, and I wondered if that was where Meredith had gotten her nose pierced.

The idea sprang into my head fully formed, and I grabbed Brooke's arm to get her to stop.

'What do you think?' I asked, pointing.

She looked into the window. 'You want a *tattoo*?' she squeaked.

That made me laugh. 'No! But I could get my belly button pierced.'

'Oh my God, you have to be kidding.'

In the grand scheme of things, this probably wasn't as big a deal as the haircut. It would be less noticeable to most people. But I couldn't help but want to chase that high from last night – to do something outrageous that the old Jessie would never have considered.

'Do it,' Meredith said. 'I've got mine done. It barely hurts.'

'Why not?' I asked Brooke.

'No, you absolutely should. I just can't believe you're suggesting it.'

I grinned. 'Are you up for it too?'

It didn't escape me: the way Brooke set her jaw before nodding.

The bell above the door tinkled when I pushed it open, and a woman behind the desk looked up, then smiled at us. She was wearing a black tank, showing off the full-sleeve tattoos on both her arms. Her hair was bright, flaming red, and she had piercings in her ears, lip, nose and elsewhere, too, if I could make a guess. If Brooke hadn't been standing right next to me, I would have swooned.

'Hey. Can I help?' she called.

I walked past the drawings of tattoo designs on the walls and leaned on the desk.

'Can someone pierce my belly button?'

'Sure,' she said. 'It's sixty bucks for the piercing, jewelry and all the cleaning solution.'

'Great.' I'd take the money out of my cut from last night.

I glanced over my shoulder at Meredith and Brooke, who had gone a little green.

'You don't have to,' I told her, unable to keep the laugh out of my voice. I wasn't used to being the confident one, and seeing Brooke like this was . . . sweet.

'Maybe I could watch you first?'

'That's fine,' the tattooed lady said. 'You can bring one person back.'

'I'm fine waiting here,' Meredith said, pulling her phone out and taking a seat on a black leather couch. 'You two go ahead.'

'Come on through. I'm Sammy.'

'Jessie,' I said, not wanting Meredith to overhear me giving out a fake name and then ask awkward questions. 'This is Brooke.'

'Nice to meet you both.' She had a broad Boston accent, and I wondered how she'd ended up here. It was probably rude to ask.

Her space was cordoned off from the rest of the shop, where two heavily tattooed guys were adding more tattoos to people who didn't seem at all bothered that they were having needles repeatedly jammed into their skin. The noise from their machines was louder than I had expected – a sharp buzzing that hurt my ears. I could only imagine how it felt for the people getting tattooed. I wasn't sure that I ever wanted a tattoo, but the belly button piercing idea had taken hold in my head.

Sammy had a chair and a bed like the one at my doctor's office, covered in both plastic and a layer of paper. In one corner, she had a glass cabinet full of jewelry – brightly colored gems winking from belly bars, as well as studs for ears and hoops for eyebrows and noses.

'I need you to read and sign this,' she said, handing me a clipboard with a consent form.

I'd gotten my ears pierced at the mall when I was five, and I still remembered the process: holding a teddy bear with pierced ears while a woman jammed the earrings into my earlobes. It had hurt. I remembered that, too, and nerves fluttered in my belly.

It wasn't enough to put me off, though.

The form was straightforward, and I scrawled my name at the bottom, adding a year to my date of birth in case there was a problem with my age. She hadn't asked for ID, and I wasn't going to offer. The second page was a 'How to Care for Your New Piercing' pamphlet, and I took that and folded it so I could shove it into my pocket.

'I'll pierce it with a bar, but you can switch over to a

hoop in about eight weeks if you want. You can come back here or to any piercing shop and they'll help you if you need it.'

'Sounds good, thank you.'

Sammy went to the cabinet and pulled out a tray with the different jewelry options on it. I wasn't into the sparkly ones – I was sure they looked good on some people, but I wanted something a little more discreet.

'How about that one?' I asked, pointing to a plain black bar with a ball at each end.

'Nice. Hop up onto the bed for me.'

Brooke came around and I reached for her hand, more for her sake than for mine. I squeezed it, and she squeezed back, and I fought the urge to squirm.

'You ready?' Brooke asked, teasing.

'Definitely.'

Sammy came back with a silver tray prepped with a long needle in a sealed bag, my black bar in another, a Sharpie, a mirror and a bottle of some kind of clear liquid.

Brooke squeezed my hand again as Sammy explained the procedure, showing me that the needle hadn't been used before and the bar was brand new. I nodded through it all, and nodded again when she put two tiny dots on my belly button to guide where the piercing would go.

'Does it look okay?' I asked Brooke.

'Great.'

She was white as a sheet.

Sammy had me lean back and then snapped on clean gloves.

'Breathe slowly for me,' she said. 'Do you want me to talk you through what I'm doing or shut up until it's over?'

'You can just do it. I don't think I need the details,' I said with a laugh.

'Okie-dokie. Stay still for me. It'll be pretty quick.'

I reached for Brooke's hand again and she threaded our fingers together. Partly I wanted the reassurance . . . mostly I wanted to hold her hand.

I closed my eyes, not needing to see the huge needle go through my flesh. Sammy grabbed my belly fat, swiped it with the alcohol, and then came a bright, sharp pain as she stuck the needle through my skin.

I forced myself to take another slow, deep breath as she manipulated the bar into place.

Brooke's grip on my hand suddenly went slack, and I opened my eyes and lifted my head right as Sammy slapped her hand down on my chest to stop me moving.

'Stay,' she barked at me. She leaped around the bed to catch Brooke as she slid to the floor in a dead faint.

'Oh my God,' I squeaked.

'She's fine,' Sammy said. Then, louder, 'Brian!'

One of the huge tattooed guys looked over then leaned in to say something to his client, before stripping off his gloves and rushing over.

'No, stay there,' he said to me when I shuffled to get up and help.

Between them, Sammy and Brian maneuvered Brooke into a chair, and a few seconds later her eyelids started to flutter.

'Thanks,' Sammy said to Brian. 'I've got her.'

I was glad Brooke had been unconscious for that – I knew she would have been mortified. Brian squeezed Sammy on the shoulder and went back over to his workstation.

'Hey, there you are,' Sammy said in a soft, soothing voice.

'Shit, I'm sorry,' Brooke rasped, covering her face with her hands.

'No need to be sorry. Just stay there for me.'

Sammy walked back around to her station and took a bottle of water out of a mini-fridge.

'Are you okay?' I whispered.

Brooke nodded. Her cheeks were starting to get some color back.

'Here,' Sammy said, passing the water to Brooke. 'Needle phobia?' she asked.

'Apparently. Shit. I'm so embarrassed.'

'Nah, you're all right. You're not even my first fainter this week. Stay put while I fix Jessie up, okay?'

Brooke nodded and opened the water, then took a tiny sip. She caught my eye, then gave me a smile and a little nod. I didn't want to make her feel more embarrassed by asking questions, so I just smiled back.

'Are you all right?' Sammy asked me seriously.

'I'm fine.'

My belly was throbbing with a new pain, hot and aching rather than the sharp sting of the needle, but it hadn't hurt nearly as bad as I'd prepared myself for. I instinctively pressed my tongue to my back tooth, wondering if that still hurt, and found it solid and unmoving. It had healed without me even noticing.

'Great.' Sammy put another pair of gloves on to swipe more alcohol over my new piercing, which *did* sting, and slapped a white bandage on top of it, securing it with tape. She held out her hands to me and I took them so she could swing me around and help me stand up.

'You are golden,' she said. 'Take care of it and you'll be fine. Give me a call if you have any questions. My number is at the bottom of the leaflet I gave you.'

'Thanks,' I said with a smile.

I reached out my hand to Brooke and gently tugged her to her feet, then didn't let go of her hand once she was standing.

'I'm not touching you for at least twenty-four hours, even if you swear to all the goddesses that you're fine,' Sammy said.

'I'm going to use that as my excuse for why I don't currently have a piece of metal shoved through my flesh,' Brooke said.

Now she was standing up, she looked pretty much back to normal. I was still going to stop at the first store we came across and buy her a candy bar, though. She needed sugar.

We followed Sammy back to the front desk, and I added a decent tip to the cost of the piercing for the problems we'd caused her. She gave me a genuine smile when she thanked me.

The whole ordeal had taken less than thirty minutes.

'Are you sure you're okay?' I asked Brooke, brushing my thumb over the back of her hand.

'I'm humiliated,' she said.

'What the hell happened back there?' Meredith asked. She was still sitting on the couch, and I thought she might be laughing at us.

'Brooke fainted,' I said, making sure to keep a totally straight face.

'Shit,' Meredith said, and she did laugh. I guessed it was allowed. They had known each other their whole lives.

'Laugh it up,' Brooke muttered.

Meredith held the door open for us as we filed back outside.

'You should've told me you have a needle phobia,' I said. 'I would never have made you come with me.'

'I didn't know I have a needle phobia.'

Brooke lifted her hand to shield her face from the sun, and I rolled my eyes and reached into my backpack for her sunglasses.

'Well, you learned something about yourself today,' I said, hoping she wouldn't mind me joking with her.

'Thanks,' she said, taking her sunglasses and sliding them on. Then she threw her arm around my shoulders, and I leaned into her side.

'Does it hurt?' Meredith asked.

'Not too bad,' I said. 'It's kind of throbbing right now.' Brooke shuddered, and I laughed.

'Come on,' I said. 'I want to get a snack.'

'No, let's go eat,' Meredith said decisively.

'I'm not going to argue with that,' Brooke said.

Meredith took us to a little Asian restaurant a few streets away from her apartment that only sold vegan food. The walls were covered with a thick green carpet of plants, so many plants it felt like the room was alive. Breathing. Instead of tables, the restaurant had long communal benches with disposable chopsticks stored in terracotta pots.

'Are you allergic to anything?' Meredith asked me.

'Nope.'

'Great. I'll order.'

'Fine by me,' I said.

I watched Meredith tap our order into an iPad on the table and pay with her credit card before I could offer to split the bill.

'You eat the weirdest shit,' Brooke said, tearing open a packet of chopsticks. 'We couldn't just go to McDonald's?'

'Eat a vegetable for once, Brooke,' Meredith fired back. 'It won't kill you, I promise.'

I didn't say anything. Watching the two of them interact reminded me that I'd never really had that relationship with someone – not with a sister or a cousin or a really close friend – before I'd had Brooke. I wanted to be sad, to wallow in regrets, but I forced those feelings into the feelings box so I didn't have to examine them. This wasn't the time for indulging in melancholy.

The food, when it arrived, was better than I'd expected. I couldn't name anything except the big bowl of sticky white rice, but that didn't mean it wasn't good.

'Is this tofu?' I asked, holding up a piece with my chopsticks.

'Gross,' Brooke muttered under her breath.

'Yes, Jessie,' Meredith said pointedly. 'That's tofu.'

'It's pretty good,' I said.

Brooke rolled her eyes.

Despite the unfamiliar food, the restaurant was fairly busy, so we didn't linger after we finished eating. As we walked back to the car, it occurred to me that we might have actually gotten away with what we'd done in the hotel. We hadn't been tracked down by police with sniffer dogs, or a SWAT team, or a man in aviator sunglasses flashing a badge at us before slapping handcuffs on our wrists.

I probably watched too many cop shows.

'I still can't believe you got this thing going,' Meredith said, running her hand over the hood of the car.

'Did you see it before she fixed it up?' I asked her.

Meredith snorted with laughter. 'It was my dad who found it in the first place. He had to tow it back to the garage. Couldn't even get the engine running.'

'It runs now,' Brooke said sweetly.

Meredith pulled Brooke into a tight hug, and surprised me by hugging me too. I hugged her back, grateful for the moment of almost normalcy she'd given us.

'Take care of yourselves, okay? And call me if you need anything.'

'We will,' Brooke promised.

She didn't bother opening the door to get in the car, she just hopped over the top. I wasn't sure I had the upper-body strength to do the same, and I knew she'd laugh at me if I fucked it up. But I did it anyway.

It was kind of wild, throwing myself into the car like that, even if my landing wasn't the most elegant.

'Nice,' Brooke said, and tipped her sunglasses down.

Meredith watched us as Brooke pulled out of her parking space and into the flow of traffic. Brooke wasn't watching the rearview mirror, but I was as Meredith lifted her hand in a wave.

Then she reached into her pocket and pulled out her phone.

11

Goodbye Yellow Brick Road – **Elton John**

We left Denver on a high.

I felt like Brooke had slowly, methodically and completely unpicked everything I knew about myself and the world, and reshaped it. I'd been hiding behind Mouse for years, because other people seemed to know exactly who Mouse was, and I could fit that expectation. It was the easy way out. But Brooke had shoved Mouse to the side, leaving me raw, exposed and completely free. I couldn't decide if that was exhilarating or terrifying or both.

Watching Brooke pass out at the sight of a huge needle had definitely made her feel more real, and her sulk afterward when Meredith had teased her about it just made me fall for her even harder. She was cute when she was grouchy.

The old Brooke was easy to have a crush on. This Brooke was easy to fall in love with.

Her attitude soured as we navigated out of the city and onto the highway that took us to the state border and cut through the wide-open Kansas landscape, and it amused me that I didn't care about her wild moods anymore. Brooke perked up when we were in cities, among crowds, or just talking to other people. She brightened, almost visibly, and it was like I could see her pulling energy from those around us.

I, on the other hand, still loved these endless stretches of nothing. Just me and Brooke, and the Mustang, and the landscape, and the wildlife, and the sky. If I could have this forever and nothing else, I'd take it.

The cassette deck clicked, and I automatically reached for the glove box for the next one.

'Any requests for the DJ?' I asked.

'Something fun,' Brooke replied.

I pulled out a handful of boxes and set them on my lap so I could go through our choices. I had picked my favorites from the collection Brooke had amassed, and we spent enough time in the car that we had cycled through them all regularly.

'Jessie,' Brooke whined, while I took my time picking the next album.

'Hang on.'

I grabbed more boxes and paused when one rattled.

'What's this?' I asked, holding up a box I hadn't seen before. It had a plain white paper insert, no album artwork, and it felt way too light. It must have been buried at the back of the glove box.

'Oh, that's ... You can put that back,' Brooke said quickly.

Brooke was a lot of things, but evasive wasn't one of them.

'Is it drugs?' I asked, shocked.

She snorted with laughter. 'No, it's not drugs. Fine. Open it, if you like.'

'I'm not going to touch your stuff if you don't want me to, Brooke.'

'It's a very small car, Jessie,' she said drily. 'There's no point in me hiding stuff from you.'

I watched her for another second, waiting to see if she'd change her mind, then I pulled the top of the case open with a satisfying click. Inside was one shiny bronze bullet. I didn't touch it.

The game had changed again.

I had been going along with Brooke's suggestions since we'd left Seattle, because it felt like she had things under control, like she knew what she was doing, and I definitely did not. I wanted to be mad at her for keeping me in the dark – about the gun, then the plan to pickpocket, then Meredith, and now the bullet. And I wanted to be frustrated that she still didn't trust me. But mostly I was resigned.

'Just one?' I asked.

Brooke nodded. 'It's . . . insurance.'

'I thought the gun was insurance.'

'It is. Yeah, it is,' she said, quietly confident, and glanced over at me. 'I keep the bullet separate and hidden. I'm not going to do anything stupid with it, and there's no chance of having an accident because I'm not going to even put it in the damn gun.'

A gun on its own wasn't necessarily dangerous, I knew that, and neither was a bullet. I didn't like guns all that much. Having one changed how much trouble we could potentially get in. Shouting at Brooke would be easy, if I wanted to. We could yell at each other for a few miles while we sped down the highway, but at the end of the road there would still be a gun and a bullet in a cassette case, and accepting that now was the easy way out. Brooke had fallen silent after her little rant, and I could feel the tension slowly smothering the car.

'Okay,' I said with a sigh that blew the tension away.

'Really?'

'Yeah. Did Meredith get this for you too?'

Brooke laughed, a little nervously. 'All my sketchy shit comes from Meredith. You must have figured that out by now.'

'You look a lot like her,' I said, putting the bullet cassette back into the glove box.

'I know. I look more like her than either Julianne or Hope. People always used to think she was my sister when we were growing up.'

'I bet.' I stuck a new cassette into the deck. 'How are you related?'

'Her dad and my dad are brothers,' she said, her voice ticking up so I could hear her over the music. 'Meredith's dad is my uncle Tony. He's the black sheep of the family.'

'I can't believe your family is big enough to have black sheep.'

She laughed. 'Yeah. My dad is a family court judge, and his older brother is a surgeon. A pediatric surgeon. Uncle Tony used to race cars.'

'No way!'

'Yeah. He was good at it, too, took a couple NASCAR titles back in the day. My dad always talks shit about him, but Uncle Tony is, like, *loaded*. He made good investments with what he won from racing, and now he sits around and occasionally buys vintage cars to fix up when he gets bored.'

'Is that how you got into cars?' I asked, remembering how Meredith had said her dad had originally bought the Mustang.

Brooke's expression fell. She gave me a fake smile – I could tell it was fake because I knew her real smiles now – and nodded. 'Yep.'

There was clearly something going on there, and I could tell she didn't want me to poke into it. Brooke was either wildly enthusiastic about anything to do with her car or completely shut off, and I could never tell which way her mood would swing or why.

'Can I ask you something?' I tried.

'You can ask,' she said lightly. The 'but I won't answer if I don't want to' was left unspoken.

'Why . . . ?'

'Why cars?'

'Yeah, I guess.'

Brooke tilted her head from side to side, stretching her neck. She glanced over her shoulder, then pulled into the outside lane to overtake a semi-truck before answering me.

'I suppose I realized a year or so ago that I was being groomed for politics.'

I went on high alert at her choice of word – 'groomed' carried a lot of weight, and I wasn't sure exactly what she meant by that.

'It all started to click in place,' she said, looking out the windshield and not at me. 'Daniel will work in law, Julianne is in medicine, Hope will cover off the arts . . . and I didn't have a clear path like they did. I was talking to Meredith when she was home for spring break last year, and she kind of joked that my dad would love to say his kid was a senator or something, and I was like, holy shit, she's right.'

The worst thing was, I could see it. Brooke would be good in politics, with her charm and her debate skills and her good looks. She had the kind of personality that people would rally behind. It wasn't such a stretch to imagine a Mayor Summer one day. A Senator Summer. Even a President Summer.

'I'm guessing that's not what you want,' I said.

'No,' she retorted with a harsh laugh. 'Definitely not. I had already started talking to my uncle Tony about him helping me to buy a car, because he knows everything there is about them. And he pulled up a picture of the Mustang on his phone. He said he was gonna buy it anyway, but if I helped him fix it up, it was mine.'

'I wondered . . .' I said, then trailed off, but Brooke waved a hand at me, encouraging me to continue. 'I wondered if it was, like, some kind of . . . rejection of femininity.'

She laughed again, brighter this time. 'No, not exactly. I just saw it as an opportunity to do something different – to get out of the house for a few hours and go somewhere my parents wouldn't be breathing down my neck.'

'Oh.'

'Not such a big deal.'

Brooke's wildly varying moods around her car were starting to make sense now. It wasn't a girl-boss thing, like I'd thought, but something she'd used to get away from her parents. It was her independence.

'So, when did you start your life of crime?' I said, sensing Brooke wanted to move on to other topics.

I watched as her temperament neatly shifted gears again. She tipped her head back and laughed.

'Oh my God, Jessie, you're fucking hilarious. It's hardly a life of crime.'

'I grew up in the church, remember,' I said. 'Before last night, I'd never even stolen a candy bar.'

'All right. Well, we were kids. Meredith was born in between me and Julianne, and her half-sister, Friday, is six months younger than me.' She glanced over. 'Uncle Tony doesn't have more than one kid with any of his ex-girlfriends.'

'Good for Uncle Tony,' I said mildly.

Brooke cackled, clearly happier now she was back on familiar ground. 'I know, right? Anyway, the four of us used to hang out in the summer, and Meredith was, like, the ringleader. Tony always encouraged her rebellious streak, so she had no problem being a rule-breaker. She would get us shoplifting lip-gloss, candy bars, that kind of thing. She learned how to pickpocket while away at camp.'

'Oh, I did not go to summer camps like that,' I said, reorganizing the cassettes.

'Me neither!'

'We had a lot of nature study and Bible study and singing around campfires.' The first few summers I went to church camp I hated it, but I felt like I had to stick it out since our church had fundraised for the less fortunate kids to go. After a few years, though, it became an escape. No one called me Mouse at camp, and even though it was before the Creep came along, it was good to get away from real life for a few weeks. 'It was better than being at home.'

'I never went,' Brooke said. 'I would've hated it. Anyway, that's where Meredith learned how to lift wallets and stuff. She said they used to practice in their bunks at night until they could all do it without anyone feeling it. And then when she came home, she taught us.'

'Did you do it a lot?'

'No, hardly ever. Julianne learned how to pick locks after reading Nancy Drew books, though. We all thought we were these super-badass middle-school girls.'

'I would've been absolutely terrified of you. And the rest of your girl gang.'

'Ha! Honestly, we thought we were so cool. But I never did much, apart from practicing with the rest of them. There's plenty of places you can learn about it, if you want to. YouTube videos. That kind of thing,' she said.

'And now Meredith deals weed and gives her seventeen-year-old cousin a gun and burner phones and cash and fake IDs.' I didn't want to sound judgmental, but it still came out that way.

'She wouldn't think of it like that,' Brooke said, shaking her head.

'Like what?'

'Like she's doing anything illegal. Anyway, weed is legal in Colorado. But she's looking out for me. Making sure I can protect myself.'

'Do you think she'll tell anyone she's seen you?' I asked. I hadn't forgotten Meredith's expression as we drove out of Denver.

'Maybe.' Brooke tipped her head to the side. 'Probably not for a few more days, though. I expect she'll call Julianne, tell her I stopped by, and say I'm heading toward New York. If Jules calls Mom and Dad, then . . .'

'Would she do that?' I demanded, suddenly worried.

Brooke shrugged. 'I don't know. She probably will, depending on how long I'm missing for.'

'And what will Julianne do?'

'Whatever she's told,' Brooke said softly, and even though her words weren't hard or harsh, I stopped digging. There was clearly a bruise there and I didn't want to poke it.

'So, where exactly did you grow up?' Brooke asked, neatly changing the subject, and I was happy to go along with it.

'All over the place.'

'Like, in Seattle, though?'

'No.' Now the cassettes were in an order I was happy with, I toed off my sneakers and put my feet up on the dash, tipping my face up to the sun. 'All over the place between Washington, Idaho and Oregon. I was born in Portland, and my mom stayed there for a few years when I was little, but we started moving around a lot after my dad left. We never stayed anywhere more than a year or two.'

'Oh, how come?'

This was another thing I felt like I needed to sanitize for Brooke's sake. Our families were obviously different – we'd established that ages ago – but I'd still been careful to only tell her things I didn't mind her knowing. These conversations were nice, though. I wanted her to know stuff about me . . . as long as it was the good parts.

'My mom worked a lot.' I paused, not really knowing where to go next, and Brooke stayed quiet. She seemed to recognize that I needed space to figure out what I wanted to say. 'We lived in a lot of shitty apartments, the type where the landlord doesn't care if the carpet is stained or the hot water doesn't work. When my mom decided she was done with one place, we'd pack everything into the car and skip town.'

'So she didn't have to pay the last month's rent?'

The last couple months' rent, if I was honest, but Brooke didn't need to know that.

'Yeah,' I said. 'We moved to Seattle when I was thirteen because I'd begged my mom to let us stay in one place for high school.'

'And you ended up at St. Catherine's? That's some bad luck.'

I laughed, and the tension leaked out of my shoulders. 'It could've been worse.'

I'd ended up at the same school as Brooke Summer. I couldn't be mad about that.

Living in gross apartments all over three different states meant I knew families whose situations were far worse than mine and my mom's, so I never really thought we were poor. Not when I was a kid, anyway. It was only when we moved to Seattle, and I saw how some of the other kids from school lived, that it really hit me.

I never spoke to any of those kids about how I'd grown up. If anyone asked, I'd mumble something about moving around a lot, and they'd assume I was a military brat, and I was fine with that. I could keep a lid on that conversation by being awkward, and Brooke was happy to let me do it again now.

When it got dark, we stopped for the night in the middle of nowhere. There was a time of night, I'd learned, when noise peaked in motels. TVs weren't on full blast but, even so, I could hear what our neighbors on either side were watching. NBC to the left. *Jeopardy!* to the right. The water clunked in the pipes while someone in the room above us took a shower, and the low hum of traffic in the distance was familiar, almost comforting.

The next morning, we got on the road early to head for Kansas City. The sun blazed as it rose, the haze of early morning quickly burning away to reveal a deep-blue sky and a heat in the air I knew wouldn't fade until much later in the day. By early afternoon, we passed the sign welcoming us to Missouri, and in the passenger seat of the Mustang, it felt like we were flying.

I glanced over at Brooke. She was already looking at me, not the road.

'Don't say it.'

I opened my mouth.

'Don't fucking say it, Jessie,' she said, but I could tell she was trying not to laugh.

I widened my eyes and put my hands on my cheeks. 'I've got a feeling we're not in Kansas anymore, Toto!'

'I hate you so much.'

'I don't think you do,' I sang.

Brooke held her laughter for as long as possible, but my hysterical giggles eventually set her off.

'You're such a fucking dope.'

'So, what's the plan?' I asked once we had finally calmed down.

'We should find somewhere to stay tonight,' Brooke said. 'If you can get online on your phone, could you scope out somewhere that isn't too . . .'

'Gross?' I suggested, making her laugh again.

'Yeah. That would be good.'

'Do you want to go into the city again?'

Brooke hesitated, and I watched her carefully as she stretched in her seat, elegantly twisting her back from side to side. She'd left her hair loose today, so the dark waves curled over the edge of her T-shirt, and I liked watching her push it back behind her ear.

'You can say yes,' I said.

'I kinda do.' She sounded almost guilty.

'I don't mind. We're more likely to find a not-gross motel in the city.'

'That's true. It would be good to get out for a couple hours and walk around, you know? Get some exercise.'

'Yeah,' I said. 'I get it. Let me see what I can find.'

The 3G connection out here was terrible, so it took me forever to find the not-gross motel that had a decent parking lot out back and was walking distance to somewhere we could go eat. This was the longest drive we'd done in one day, and I kept switching out cassettes, purposefully picking the ones that Brooke liked to sing along to. After a few days on the road, I'd started singing along with her, and now we had moved on to figuring out harmonies between us. Singing was cathartic.

When we finally arrived in Kansas City, I was hot and tired from the long drive.

'We need to do laundry,' Brooke groaned, hauling her bag onto one of the beds. This room had two queens, made up with crisp white sheets. A part of me wished there was a reason to share just one.

'I'm sure this place has a laundry room somewhere.'

'I'll go find it,' she offered, leaving with a handful of dollar bills to exchange for quarters, and one of the phones tucked into her back pocket.

I used the time while Brooke was gone to do a quick inventory rundown. We probably needed to replenish the snacks we kept in the trunk, but I was starting to get sick of gas station food. And I never thought I'd say that. I'd lived off junk for years, while my mom was too busy with work to feed me home-cooked meals, and it had never occurred to me to resent her for that.

Right now, though, I was ready for a piece of broccoli and a potato that hadn't been fried.

The motel room had a large window looking out over the walkway and parking lot, and I threw the curtains open to let in more of the natural light. We'd checked in earlier than usual, which gave us a few more hours to get stuff done than those days when we crawled into a room just before midnight and collapsed into bed.

The parking lot was fairly empty, with a few trucks dotted around and a couple of larger vans. Brooke's Mustang stood out, but it stood out everywhere. There wasn't much we could do about that. She drove a beautifully restored vintage car – people noticed it.

I set my trashy romance novel on the nightstand and plugged my phone in to charge, then flopped onto the bed to check out what cable channels this motel had.

A few minutes later, the door clicked open again and Brooke walked in, turning a roll of quarters over between her fingers.

'You hungry?' she asked.

'Not yet. I will be soon. But before you say anything, I really, *really* don't want to eat pizza for dinner.'

Brooke snorted and flopped onto the second bed. 'We don't have to get pizza.'

'Or Chinese food, or sandwiches, or . . .'

'What do *you* want to eat, Jessie?' she asked emphatically.

'Something green.'

'God, you sound like Meredith.'

That made me laugh. 'There are worse things to be.'

'Than a hippie, pottery-making vegan?'

'Definitely.'

Brooke closed her eyes, and I watched her for a few moments. Her hands were resting on her stomach and she breathed slowly, like she was purposefully trying to relax.

I looked at her differently now. I knew she'd noticed me looking, and she was either tolerating it because she wanted to stay friends, or she genuinely didn't mind. A few times I'd caught her looking at me, but I'd convinced myself it didn't mean anything.

I didn't want to make her feel uncomfortable by telling her I liked her. I'd never told anyone I liked them, and I really wasn't sure how another girl would react to that – especially a girl who had been happy to let people assume she was straight.

At school dances she'd never gone with a date, but that wasn't unusual at St. Catherine's. The administration were super strict about things like dating and PDAs, and even kissing in the hallways got people hauled in for detention. Most people went to dances in friend groups, except for senior prom, when everyone was eighteen. And we hadn't gotten to senior prom yet.

There was no point in trying to test the waters while I was still hiding so much from her. I was terrible at lying, but I was doing pretty great at not thinking about the blood and death and pain I was running from, and I didn't need an extensive romantic history to tell me that would be a turn-off for any potential romantic partner.

Not that I gave much of a fuck about future romantic partners. I cared about Brooke.

I wanted us to share a bed again. I wanted her to smile at me, and touch my arm, and, maybe, eventually, kiss me – even though that last one seemed like a far-fetched dream.

'This place reminds me of the first motel we stayed in,' she said suddenly, without opening her eyes. I startled, then reminded myself that she couldn't hear my thoughts. 'It's nicer here, though. The people are nicer,' she said.

'We're also, like, more than halfway across the country from home.'

'Shit. You're right.'

Brooke almost jumped out of her skin when her phone rang.

'Are you gonna answer it?' I asked Brooke, now fully alert.

'It's probably someone wanting Meredith.'

I shrugged. 'I'll get it if you want. I can tell them they have the wrong number.'

'I'm closer,' she said, sounding resigned, and picked up the phone. 'Hello?'

'Brooke?' I could only just hear the voice.

'Meredith?'

'No, it's Julianne.'

Shit.

Brooke put the phone on speaker and set it down on the nightstand, then crawled up on the bed next to me. I put my hand on her knee and squeezed it gently as she leaned into my side.

'Hey,' Brooke said.

'Jesus Christ, you have some nerve. You're going to just *hey* me right now?'

'What do you want me to say?'

'I want you to say, "Julianne, I'm turning my sorry ass around right now and driving back home."'

I couldn't help but think I would like Julianne Summer, if I ever had the chance to meet her. Right now, she was terrifying.

'I'm not going home, Jules,' Brooke said. 'I'm fine, though, if that was what you wanted to know.'

'Oh good, I'm delighted to hear it.'

She didn't sound delighted. She sounded mad as hell.

'Brooke. Where are you?'

Brooke glanced at me. I shrugged. 'Des Moines,' she said.

'Liar,' Julianne snapped.

'Does it matter?' Brooke said with a heavy sigh.

'Yeah, Brooke, it matters.' Julianne's voice softened. 'Where you are and what you're doing and who you're with. It all matters.'

Brooke rubbed her fingertips over her eyelids, like she was trying to dislodge the stress building behind them.

'Brooke?' Julianne said again.

'I don't know who I'm talking to right now,' Brooke said. 'I don't know if you're calling because Mom and

Dad told you to, or if you're doing it because you care about me.'

'I've always cared about you,' Julianne replied, sounding hurt.

'I know.'

'Dad called me,' she admitted. 'He's worried.'

Brooke glanced at me. 'So they don't know where I am?'

'No, Brooke,' Julianne said. 'But there's a girl missing. From your school. Do you know anything about that?'

I shook my head frantically. Brooke might trust her sister, but I didn't. If Julianne knew about me, then she probably knew about the Creep, and I couldn't risk her telling Brooke. Not now. We'd come so far already.

'Who?' Brooke asked.

'Her name is Jessie. Jessie Swift.'

She clenched her jaw. 'I have no idea. She's not with me.'

'Are you sure?' Julianne pressed.

'Yes,' Brooke said, sounding annoyed. 'Seriously, Jules, don't call me again. I'm fine. I'll be home soon.'

'Okay, Brooke,' Julianne said with a sigh. 'So long as you're all right. I love you.'

'I'm all right,' Brooke echoed. 'I love you. Bye.'

She ended the call before Julianne could reply.

'Shit,' I said. 'I'm sorry.'

'It's fine. I was kind of expecting it at some point.' Brooke threw the phone down on the bed. 'My parents always pit us against each other. They've obviously convinced Jules that she needs to play the responsible older sister.'

'Do you think she believes you?'

'I think so.'

'Okay,' I said, not totally convinced. I wondered, not for the first time, what had happened to Brooke back home to make her so determined to run far, far away.

'Jessie, are you sure you don't want to call your mom?' she asked gently. 'Or anyone else?'

I shook my head. 'Not yet, no.'

'If you're sure.'

'I'm sure.'

She sat upright again. 'Do you want to get out and go for a walk? We're only a couple blocks away from an outdoor mall.'

'Sounds good.'

I watched Brooke pack up the few things she needed, then fell into step with her as we walked out of the motel.

It was getting close to sunset, and the heat was finally starting to die down as we wandered through the mall. People were spilling out of a sports bar showing several games on huge screens, or juggling small children and ice cream and strollers.

'There,' I said, pointing to a little deli that caught my eye. 'That's what I want to eat.'

'Works for me,' Brooke said easily.

The cost of bread and olives and a cute little charcuterie box was at least double what we usually spent on an evening meal, but I didn't care at all. We had topped up our stash of cash and there was absolutely nothing fried in the paper bag I carried out of the store and over to one of the colorful picnic tables set up in the square. That felt like a victory. I still couldn't figure out how Brooke had the diet of a three-year-old and managed to stay so slim.

'Metabolism,' she said around a mouthful of bread. 'And soccer.'

'I'm jealous.'

'You could always join a soccer team.'

'I don't think any team would take me. I'm too short for soccer.'

'Have you seen the high-school team?' Brooke stabbed an olive with a tiny fork and popped it into her mouth. 'We have a couple wannabe Megan Rapinoes, but most of us just play for fun.'

I couldn't imagine playing soccer for fun. That sounded like torture to me.

A few other families seemed to have had the same idea as us, and had picked up food from one of the places around the square to eat at the picnic tables. It all seemed very wholesome, like this was exactly the type of thing the city government wanted to encourage. If I looked up an advert for Kansas City, it would include me and Brooke, sitting at this bubblegum-pink picnic table, fighting over the last olive.

Brooke swung her legs off the bench and got up. 'I'm going to use the restroom,' she said. 'There's some right behind you.'

I glanced over my shoulder. 'Okay.'

'I won't be long.'

I nodded, and packed up all the wrappers while Brooke was in the restroom, dumping them in one of the trash cans, then picking another bench to sit and wait at so a family could take over our picnic table. I stretched my legs out and rolled my shoulders.

It had taken us just under a week to get to Kansas City, so Brooke's initial estimation of getting to Disney World in ten days was going to be out by at least a few days. I already knew I wanted to stop in Nashville, and we'd probably need to make an overnight stop in Atlanta, too, before making the final push down to Orlando. That would mean Brooke didn't have to drive too much every day, and we could still enjoy some of the cities along the way.

I saw Brooke walking out of the restroom, so I turned around to shoulder my backpack before she got to me.

A kid over at the picnic tables let loose a high-pitched scream and distracted me for a second – only a second.

When I turned back, she was gone.

12

Jagged Little Pill – Alanis Morissette

I panicked.

My instinct was still to panic, to shout her name, to draw attention to myself until someone else ran over to help. How could she have disappeared into thin air?

I jogged over to the restrooms to check them out, to see if I'd made a mistake and it wasn't Brooke who'd walked out of them a few moments ago. But she wasn't there. Only a woman with a small child were washing their hands, and the stalls were all empty.

Where the hell had she gone?

I grabbed my phone and called her number, and while it rang and rang, I went back outside and looked around again, straining for a glimpse of her ripped jeans and thrift store Giants T-shirt.

We cannot connect your call. Please hang up and try again.

I tried again.

And again.

Then, out of nowhere, a strange detachment settled over me. I'd experienced this feeling only once in my life, the day that I'd seen a dead body for the first time and decided to pack up my shit and get the hell out of Seattle, and feeling it again now was unsettling.

Brooke had either wandered off, or someone had forced her to go somewhere with them. Those were the only two possible options. I made myself go to a bench and sit my sorry ass down. Sit down, breathe, think.

My heart was going crazy, beating so hard against my chest it hurt, and I was grinding my back teeth and couldn't stop.

She's gone. She's gone. She's gone.

I forced that voice down until it was just static noise in my ears. Then a thought hit me – had Brooke left me on purpose?

No. She wouldn't. A few days ago maybe she would've considered it, but not anymore. Not after Denver.

If I went to the cops, I'd have to tell them who I was, why I was in godforsaken Kansas City in the first place, and I wasn't ready to have that conversation. I couldn't. Everything that had happened back at home was two thousand miles and seven whole days away from me, and that was almost, almost enough distance that I could handle it.

On the bench, my fingers curled into fists, and I stretched each of them back out, one at a time, before bunching them up again.

I checked the time on my phone.

Brooke had been gone for twenty minutes.

This wasn't normal.

I called her phone again, and it rang out, eventually switching over to the standard automated voicemail.

There was no getting around it. I was on my own.

When I was absolutely certain Brooke wasn't going to walk out of one of the nearby stores and laugh at me for being ridiculous, I made my way back to the motel. It was getting dark now, and that seemed like both a good idea – finding somewhere safe – and stupidly irresponsible – to leave the area. But what else was I supposed to do? Brooke was *gone*, and I had to figure out what I was going to do about that.

The motel room was cool and quiet, only the whirring of the ceiling fan providing any noise. Everything looked just as we had left it. The keys to the Mustang were on the table. She definitely hadn't left on her own, not without the Mustang.

I sat down on the end of my bed, and cried.

I'd never been much of a crier – I'd become good at bottling up my emotions in the past few years, scared of what would happen if I ever let them out. So I hadn't cried when I was packing to leave Seattle. Or that first night, when I was totally terrified and convinced I was going to get caught. I hadn't cried in those dark moments just before falling asleep, when I remembered everything that had led to me running away in the first place – all the blood and the anger and the gut-deep regret that I had never had the courage to stand up for myself. And that no one had ever stood up for me.

Not until Brooke.

And now she was gone.

I couldn't even find the energy to lay down, or move, or wipe the snot and tears from my face. I was a pathetic, sobbing mess. And I didn't want to be alone. I really, *really* didn't want to be on my own.

I forced myself to pick up the phone and call Brooke one more time, just in case, but she didn't answer. The silence on the other end of the phone was almost enough to tip me over the edge, but I was determined not to start crying again. I got up and went to the bathroom to blow my nose and wash my face, though I couldn't bear to look at myself in the mirror.

What would Brooke do in this situation? Probably not sit around crying over it. She was more of a *get shit done* kind of person.

But I was feeling very Mouse, and not very Jessie, and I had no idea how to flip the switch back.

I wandered over to the window to stare out of it aimlessly, and to check that the Mustang was still where we'd left it. The keys were on the desk, so unless someone had hotwired it, the chances were it hadn't moved.

And it hadn't. Obviously.

Staring out the window, something felt off, a creeping fog of *wrongness*. The parking lot was still a motel parking lot – that hadn't changed. But something had.

I pressed my hands to the cool window, resisting the

temptation to press my nose against it and watch my breath fog the glass.

The parking lot was emptier than it had been earlier, which made sense – people had probably checked out and moved on. A few more family-type vehicles had replaced the big trucks and the utility vans.

The black van was gone.

My whole body went cold.

The black van.

I furiously scanned my memory, trying to figure out if the black van that had been parked two spaces over from the Mustang was the same black van from Salt Lake City.

'Come *on*, Jessie,' I muttered.

I couldn't be sure. Not 100 percent. Not even 20 percent sure. But there had definitely been a black van parked near the Mustang earlier, and now it was gone, and so was Brooke. I couldn't discount that as coincidence.

I wanted to call the police, to report this new nugget of information, but that was still a stupid idea, even if I used a fake name so they wouldn't know who I was. I couldn't tell them about the van without telling them everything, and I didn't have enough evidence to prove my point.

Oh, yes, officer, we ran away from home and drove halfway across the country, and there's people following us, and now my runaway companion has disappeared. Can you check the database for the entire United States for a man named Chris who owns a black van? No, I don't know the make, model or license plate number. Or his last name.

It sounded more ridiculous in my own head than it would to a police officer.

I couldn't even call Meredith or Julianne because their numbers were in the call log of the phone Brooke had had with her when she disappeared, and I hadn't thought it was necessary to add them to mine.

If I could get hold of the CCTV for the motel, I could check. Now I knew what I was looking for, I felt like I'd be able to tell for sure whether it was the same van. If they had a room for that kind of thing, I could sneak in and check the tapes.

I bounced my knee anxiously.

I couldn't do it now, of course. There would be people wandering around for hours yet. I could maybe do it later, though. Or in the middle of the night. I could set an alarm, get up at, like, three in the morning and go downstairs to find the CCTV room.

So, that was the plan.

I didn't sleep in the end.

I couldn't sleep.

Panic-induced adrenaline was pumping through my body, and I curled up under the thin sheet, covering my head with a pillow to block out the noise of my own thoughts.

It had completely settled in that Brooke was gone – like, actually gone – and I was the only person who knew that. Part of me kept expecting her to knock on the door at any second and demand to be let in, but as the minutes stretched into hours, I was still alone. If I was going to find her, I had to be more Jessie than Mouse and do whatever sketchy shit was necessary.

I'd never really been responsible for someone else before. Not like this. I'd always done what I could to help my mom, especially when I was old enough to earn some money and help out around the house, but I wasn't *responsible* for her.

I carefully and very purposefully didn't think about where Brooke could be right now, or what might be happening to her. If I let my thoughts go in that direction, I knew I'd lose it again, and Brooke needed me to pull myself together long enough to figure this out.

In that moment, I realized that nothing hurt right now. All my bruises had healed, and since I'd been gone for seven days with no one hitting me, I didn't have any fresh marks that stung.

Instead of thinking about Brooke, I let myself wonder what would have happened if Jessie, not Mouse, had faced up to the Creep. It was a stupid game, not only because he was dead, but because he would have never let me fight back.

I was starting to think of Mouse as a temporary state. I hadn't been her when I was born, and I wasn't her now. It had been too many years of my life, but what was that in the grand scheme of things? A wasted childhood, for sure. If whatever I did next put Mouse behind me, I could probably live with that.

This trip, and Brooke – mostly Brooke – had let me close the door on that part of my life.

At three in the morning, I put the key card in my back pocket, pulled on my sneakers and slipped out of the room.

The night air was cool but not cold. Even so, the hairs on the back of my arms stood on end – more a reaction to my nerves than the temperature.

Stick to the plan, Jessie.

I'd stuffed a couple of dollar bills in my back pocket, too, so if anyone stopped me and asked where I was going, I could ask for directions to a vending machine. I'd studied pictures of the hotel lobby online, so I had a better idea of the layout. And I had a plan for causing a distraction, if I needed one.

When I reached the lobby, I noticed there was only one receptionist on the night shift and no security guard. The bar was closed, and the shutters were down on the breakfast area. The receptionist was in a little room behind the desk. She was awake, but looking at her phone, with her feet up on a second desk chair.

She didn't notice me.

The reception desk was pretty low, and I caught sight of a folder that was open, its pages spread.

Something clicked in my head.

When we checked into places, they sometimes took the car's license plate number and wrote it in a book, so they knew who had paid for parking.

I mentally shifted my plan to take into account this new information. My fingers curled into a ball, and I forced myself to take a deep breath.

In the hours I'd been lying awake, I'd run through dozens of options for causing a distraction, which I needed now. The receptionist would definitely see me if I just casually walked behind the desk. I didn't want to throw a rock at a car, and too many people ignored car alarms anyway, especially in places like this. They were part of the background noise. I also didn't want to do anything stupid on CCTV and accidentally get the cops breathing down my neck.

In the end, I crossed over to the lobby restrooms, not trying to hide, stuffed most of a roll of toilet paper into a toilet and flushed.

Back in middle school, someone pulled this prank at least once a month, flooding one of the restrooms. Like clockwork, the water rose and spilled over the top of the bowl.

Bingo.

I dashed back out into the lobby and pressed my hands on the desk.

'Sorry, but I think your restroom is flooding,' I said, a little breathless from the lie and the running.

The girl rolled her eyes and set her phone down.

'For fuck's sake,' she muttered, just loud enough for me to hear. 'Gimme a second,' she said, louder this time, and I nodded.

She went into the restroom, and I ducked behind the desk, my breath shallow now from nerves more than exertion. I reached up and pulled the folder off the desk, then sat down on the floor so I was out of view of anyone passing by.

'Come on, come on, come on,' I muttered to myself, running my fingers along the rows of handwritten information.

I found the Mustang:

M Summer, red Mustang, 063 - BBH (WA)

And a few rows underneath that:

C Turner, black Mercedes Vito, AAN 8912 (UT)

Meredith Summer. Red Mustang, Washington plates.

Chris Turner. Black Mercedes van, Utah plates.

I knew it. That bastard had followed us all the way here from Salt Lake City. He wasn't an undercover cop, he wasn't a private investigator ... he was following us because he wanted us for something. Or, more likely, he wanted Brooke.

I slapped my hand down on the folder. I was right about him. I'd been right from the first time he'd given me one of his slimy smiles. I took a deep breath, letting my fury simmer down.

Was there another tracker on the car that we hadn't found at the garage? Had one of the mechanics sold us out and told Chris where we were headed? Or maybe he'd just been close enough on our tail the whole time to follow us all the way here.

Either way, I knew who had taken Brooke.

Now I had to figure out how to get her back.

'What are you doing down there?'

I looked up at the face of a confused receptionist.

'Shit.'

The folder fell off my lap as I scrambled to my feet, the sick feeling of being caught curdling in my stomach.

'Sorry,' I said quickly. 'I didn't mean to –'

I stopped talking before I incriminated myself any farther.

'What?' the receptionist asked.

'Touch your stuff,' I finished lamely.

'Oh-*kay*,' she said. 'Do you want to tell me why you were touching my stuff, or should I call security?'

There was no security, I knew that, but I didn't want to call her bluff. I quickly looked her up and down. She was wearing black skinny jeans and a button-down shirt with the motel's logo embroidered in the top corner. She had a lip ring and dark hair pulled back into a messy ponytail. She looked older than me, but not by a lot.

'Can I trust you?' I asked, letting a little desperation leach into my voice.

'I mean, probably not.' She raised an eyebrow at me when I didn't respond.

'My friend has been kidnapped,' I said in a rush.

'Your friend,' she echoed slowly, 'has been kidnapped.' She didn't say it like a question.

'Yes. I'm trying to get her back.'

'That doesn't explain why you were under my desk.'

'I . . .'

I waited until she pointedly rolled her eyes.

'You can trust me,' she said wearily. 'I'm not going to call the police, unless you do something even weirder than looking through my parking lot folder.'

'I can't make any promises,' I said, trying to make a joke, and she pressed her lips together to hide her smile. 'What's your name?'

'Megan.'

She didn't look like a Megan. 'I'm Jenna.'

I wasn't in the mood to trust a stranger with my real name tonight.

'Okay, Jenna,' she said. 'Tell me about your kidnapped friend.'

I followed Megan back into the room behind the reception desk, which was a small office with no windows and a mini-fridge full of Diet Dr Pepper and Pepsi Max. Someone had terrible taste in soda. She gestured to the second chair, the one she'd had her feet up on earlier, and I sat down, letting my clasped hands fall between my knees.

It wasn't that I didn't trust her. I had to learn to trust people. And she wasn't automatically a bad person just because she was a stranger. And I definitely needed help from someone who wasn't involved in law enforcement. I just had to work up the courage to tell her the right lies, that wouldn't put the police on my tail.

'Br—' I hesitated, reminding myself that Brooke had checked into the hotel with Meredith's ID. '*Meredith* disappeared this afternoon.'

'Maybe she went for a walk, or met up with some friends?' Megan queried.

I shook my head. 'We don't know anyone in the city. We're from Washington.'

'Okay,' Megan said. She didn't look convinced.

'She's not answering her phone, and she hasn't come back to the motel, and there's this guy, Chris, who's been stalking her.'

'Someone has been *stalking* her?' Megan said, looking even less convinced now.

'Yes,' I said emphatically. 'We're heading to St. Louis, and we've run into him a few times on the way, so he's definitely following us. I didn't know he was here until I checked your folder, and you have his van listed as being in your parking lot. And now she's missing and so's Chris's van. I wanted to check your CCTV to see if I could find him.'

Megan stared at me intently, and I noticed that there was a little gray in her green eyes. It was hard to see under all the eyeliner.

'Why don't you call the cops?' she asked after a long moment. I could tell she still wasn't sure about me and that made me even more nervous. I needed her to help me, and I needed her to believe me before she could help.

'Because,' I said, treading very carefully now, 'we didn't exactly tell anyone we were leaving. Or where we're going.'

'So you ran away from home?'

'Yes.' It felt good not to lie.

'And you knew she had a stalker when you ran away?' she asked, clearly judging me.

'No!' I said quickly. 'Not until a few days ago.'

'After you left home.'

'Right.'

'I still don't get why you won't call the cops,' Megan said, exasperated.

'Because . . . because if I do that, they'll ship us back

home. And I'll never see her again,' I said, the words melting into a sob.

Understanding dawned in her eyes. 'Ohhh. So you're running away because you're –'

'Yes.' I didn't bother correcting her.

'And your parents don't want you to be together?'

'No.'

She whistled between her teeth. 'This is some gay *Romeo and Juliet* shit.'

I couldn't help but smile, even though tears were spilling over. 'I know. Can you help me?'

She shrugged. 'What do you want me to do?'

'I don't know. Until I checked your folder, I didn't know for certain that it was Chris who'd taken her.'

'So now you know who she's with, but not where they are,' Megan said, swinging herself back and forth in her chair.

'Right.'

'How long has she been missing?'

I checked the clock above the door and surreptitiously wiped my eyes. 'About eight hours.'

'Shit, girl, they could be anywhere by now,' Megan said, frustrated.

I slumped back in my seat and groaned. She was right. I should have called the police right when Brooke had gone missing. They would have figured out her disappearance was linked to Chris right away, and Brooke would be safe. Even if it had meant both of us being sent home, and me literally never getting to see Brooke again or being arrested and put on trial. Somehow the thought of never setting eyes on Brooke again was worse than the idea of being charged with murder.

My breath started to catch in my throat, and I wasn't sure if I was going to have a panic attack or start crying again. Even when I tried to do the right thing, it turned out wrong, and I'd put Brooke in danger for stupid, selfish reasons.

'Shit, are you all right?' Megan said.

'I'm fine,' I lied. 'I just don't know what to do.'

'Hang on. I've got an idea. If it doesn't work, we can check the CCTV, but this is definitely quicker.'

She spun around in her chair and scooted over to the desk, where an old, bulky desktop computer was set up. She tapped on the mouse until the screen came to life, then typed in a password.

'What are you doing?' I asked.

'I know this place looks like an independent motel, but we're not,' Megan said. 'This guy bought up a bunch of them in Kansas and Missouri about ten years ago and he operates all of them as a chain.'

'Okay...'

Megan looked at me over her shoulder. 'We all share a database,' she said. 'I can look up this stalker of yours with the details he used to check in here.'

I stared at her for a second. 'You can do that?'

'Yeah. If he's in the system, I can find him.'

'Oh my God.'

'Hang on,' Megan said.

I watched, my fingertips twitching with anxiety, as she logged into one system, and then another. The computer seemed to whirr achingly slowly in the early morning silence.

'What's his name?'

'Chris Turner.'

'Okay, I'm checking what info we have on him already.'

Megan pulled a notepad toward herself and started scribbling. I watched, not wanting to interrupt her flow, and tried to translate what I could see on the screen. The system looked ancient.

'I've got his credit card number.'

'Seriously?'

She shot me a grin. 'Yep. He checked in this afternoon and he hasn't checked out. But that's not unusual, as we wouldn't expect him to have left until the morning.'

'Is he still here?' I asked, suddenly frantic.

Maybe Brooke was still here, in the room that Chris had booked. Maybe they had just moved the van. I could get her back right away.

'Hang on,' Megan said, clicking through to another screen. Then she winced. 'Sorry. Both the key cards were turned back in at some point this evening, so the room's been flagged as empty. He wasn't supposed to leave until the morning.'

'So they're gone.'

'It looks that way, yeah. Housekeeping checked it out and cleaned the room. He didn't even use the bed.'

'Is that normal?' I asked.

'Eh,' she said with a shrug. 'You see all kinds of shit working this job.'

Megan switched over to the other system and started tapping away again. My knee started bouncing and I couldn't stop it.

'He's not in the system as having booked anywhere else.'

'Shit.'

My knee fell still.

'But we're talking about a network of, like, eighty motels. The chances that he would randomly pick another one in our network is fairly small.'

'Can you check if he's made a reservation in advance? Like, for tomorrow night?'

'Yeah, I can, actually.'

She turned back to the computer and started scrolling through a long list, like she had to manually search for his details.

I wondered who the hell had bought all these shitty motels and insisted on running them on software from the 1990s.

A few minutes later, Megan looked up at me again.

'I've got him,' she said with a grin.

13

Appetite for Destruction –
Guns N' Roses

It was almost four in the morning, and I was so exhausted I thought I might fall over. I had no idea where Brooke was, but now, thanks to Megan and her magic ancient software system, I knew where they were going.

Tomorrow night – or tonight, now – Chris had made a reservation for a motel east of St. Louis. I had no idea if that meant he had always planned to keep moving east, or whether he had been anticipating that would be our next stop. It almost didn't matter. At least I had time to sleep before I had to work out how I was going to get there.

'Are you okay? You look kinda sick,' Megan said.

I shook my head. 'I'm just tired.'

'I forget not everyone in the world is an insomniac,' she said with a wry smile. 'What are you going to do now?'

'Sleep,' I said. 'I'll wait until the morning to decide what my next move is.'

'I know you wanted to check the CCTV,' she said, 'but

I'm going to be honest with you – it doesn't actually work. And when it does, it only covers the staff parking lot.'

I pressed my fingertips to my eyelids as I processed that. 'I don't think it matters anymore,' I said eventually. 'I know where they're going now.'

'Are you sure she's with him? Like, a hundred percent sure?'

'Nope.' I shook my head and blinked on purpose a few times, trying to dislodge the aching, itchy feeling from my eyes. 'But it can't be a coincidence. This guy has been showing up all over the place and then she disappeared.'

'Okay, I get what you're saying. One more question, then you should go to bed.'

'Go for it.'

'Are you sure you don't want to call the cops and let them deal with it?'

'No,' I said honestly. 'That still might be the first thing I do when I wake up later. But I know more now than I did an hour ago.'

'You could've just asked me for help, you know.'

'I'm sorry,' I said automatically. 'I'm not good at asking for help. Or trusting people.'

'Well, I hope you find her,' Megan said. She turned back to her computer and scribbled something on a Post-it note, then handed it to me. She had written down the address of the motel outside St. Louis with a number circled. 'That's his room number for the Phoenix,' she added.

'Thanks.' Now I knew where Brooke was going, I felt like I could put a plan together. But sleep definitely felt necessary first. I couldn't drive while I was this exhausted, let alone all the way to the other side of St. Louis. 'I hate to ask, after everything you've already done for me, but is there any chance I could get late check-out?'

Megan laughed, low and throaty. 'Sure. I'll fix that for you, don't worry about it.'

'I really appreciate it.'

'Actually, there is something you can do for me. I'm way too nosy not to know how this works out.' She took back the Post-it note and scrawled another number on it.

'Text me,' she said. 'Let me know what happens?'

'I will,' I said, standing so I could tuck the paper into my pocket. 'If this works, I don't know how I can ever repay you.'

'Repay me by telling me you got her back,' she said.

'I'll try.'

I made my way through the silent motel to the staircase that led up to my room. On the horizon, the first few rays of dawn were starting to warm the night sky. I turned away from the daylight and tapped my key card against the reader, then locked and bolted myself into the room and fell down face first onto the bed.

I could make a real plan later. I was going to get Brooke back. She wasn't just the first person I'd ever really cared about – she was the first person who had ever really cared for *me*. I was ready to burn the world down to find her.

Despite my exhaustion, I didn't sleep well, and woke up only semi-rested at eleven – too late to get breakfast at the motel. I still had to repack the bags, settle on a plan and get on the road. It would take around six hours to drive to the motel Chris was staying at tonight, and I'd need to take at least one break.

And I was going to have to drive the Mustang.

In theory, that was okay. I'd passed my driving test the previous summer, and the Mustang had an automatic transmission, so I didn't have to operate a stick shift. In reality, I was terrified to drive Brooke's precious car.

The plan had come to me in between bursts of sleep, when I wasn't sure if I was lucid dreaming or actually awake and thinking about what I needed to do. Maybe it had been both. Driving over to St. Louis was the only thing that made sense. I'd never driven that far before, definitely not on my own, and absolutely not in a car that was both old and beloved.

The thought of getting out of bed was terrifying. I felt like a woman in one of those old paintings with a demon sitting on her chest. Paralyzed, unable to move. If I got up, I had to get dressed and then complete all the next steps of the plan.

One step at a time.

I wasn't expecting my mom's voice to come to me.

Her advice usually came with a sharp edge: *Stop being so quiet, just talk to people – why can't you make an effort? Get up, Jessie, get out into the world. Books aren't friends.*

She wasn't wrong, she could just be mean, and I'd gotten used to that over the years.

But *one step at a time* was one of her favorite phrases when I was being smothered by anxiety about tests or quizzes or presentations. *One step at a time, one question at a time, one slide at a time.* It helped far more than her usual advice.

So, I got out of bed. I took a shower, brushed my teeth, dried my hair and pinned it back from my face so it wouldn't annoy me when I was driving. I put on my cropped T-shirt to be more Jessie and less Mouse, and applied some black eyeliner to be more Megan, who was another badass female I could take some inspiration from.

I picked out an outfit that Mouse would never wear: ripped jeans and Brooke's plaid shirt thrown over the T-shirt. I stared at my exposed stomach in the mirror and ran my fingers over my piercing. Another thing that made me more Jessie and less Mouse.

I put my sunglasses on my head, packed up all our bags and ate frosted blueberry Pop-Tarts for breakfast.

I looked at the gun for a really long time. Then I picked up the keys to the Mustang, went out to put the stuff in the trunk and picked up a handful of cassette tapes to take back to the room, making sure to include that extra-light one. The unmarked box.

I didn't want to have to put the bullet in the gun when I got to the motel. I wanted to be prepared way in advance of that, to do things in the quiet and security of this motel room with no one else watching me.

I'd never put a bullet in a gun before.

I thought it would be simple, that I'd be able to figure it out for myself, but it wasn't obvious, and even though the magazine was empty, I didn't want to mess around with a freaking gun. I felt stupid and sick and scared, like a little girl who didn't know anything at all.

In the end, I pulled up a YouTube video and followed the instructions on how to eject the magazine, load the bullet and reassemble everything.

Now I was traveling with a loaded weapon, and everything had changed.

Everything.

But I was in control.

I double-checked, triple-checked the safety, then put the gun in my backpack so it would be close to me at all times.

The alarm clock on the nightstand told me it was past noon, and I couldn't postpone things much longer. I needed to get moving. I kept wanting to delay the inevitable and try to find Amanda who had taken over from Megan on the day shift and ask her something, anything. Instead, I took one final trip back to check out and grab a bag of chips from the vending machine.

I got into the driver's side of the car for the first time, put the top down and adjusted the seat. My legs were a lot shorter than Brooke's. I already knew which album I wanted to play to get myself in the right frame of mind, so it only took me a moment to get the tape deck set up. I flipped my sunglasses down, turned the engine on and took a deep breath.

'You can do this,' I muttered to myself.

I drove for two hours then stopped for gas and to stretch my legs at a tiny service station. Their restrooms were spotlessly clean, which, after a week on the road, I didn't take for granted. I picked up a bottle of water to make sure I stayed hydrated on the next leg of the journey, and a Coke for the sugar and caffeine.

A cop car pulled into the gas station as I was paying, and I closed my eyes and fought the urge to scream. They couldn't be here for me. They just couldn't. Not now. Even though my instinct was to run away, I knew that would draw attention to myself, and I needed to stay inconspicuous. I forced myself to smile at the guy behind the counter as he handed me my change.

'Have a nice day,' he muttered.

One of the cops held the door for me as I walked out, and I felt dizzy, like I was about to faint. This was my opportunity to tell them everything. To get help. To not be on my own anymore.

'Nice car,' the officer said, nodding to the Mustang, which was the only other car out on the lot.

'Thanks,' I said. My voice rasped, but otherwise I sounded normal enough.

Was that a hint? Did he know who I was, and who the car really belonged to? Or did he really just think it was a nice car?

'Yours?' he asked, pausing to let his colleague catch up, and I forced myself to give him an easy smile.

'I wish,' I said.

'Best not dent it,' the second cop said, his voice a full Southern drawl.

I shoved my hands in my pockets to hide how badly they

were shaking. This felt like a set-up. It was too easy, too friendly, to be a casual encounter, and it took serious effort to act normal. I felt like they were both scrutinizing me, these tall men who towered over me, paying too much attention because of the car or because I was a teenage girl or because they'd seen a bulletin to look out for a Jessie Swift, the runaway murderer from Seattle.

Surely they wouldn't be looking out for a vintage Mustang, though? No one from back home knew I was with Brooke.

'I'll be fine,' I said, paranoid now about my accent, on top of everything else.

'Where are you headed?'

I took a longer look at the cop. He was studying me, too.

'Indianapolis,' I said. Then I realized I'd been giving short answers, which sounded evasive because I *was* being evasive, and they needed something more from me before they'd let me walk away. I took my sunglasses off my head and pushed my fingers through my hair, ruffling it. 'My dad owns a garage. Someone bought the car online and wanted it delivered.'

'What an asshole,' the officer said with a laugh. He looked me over again, then seemed to dismiss me. 'Drive safe.'

The second cop tipped his hat. 'Have a good day, miss.'

'Thank you.' I swallowed hard. 'You too.'

I hesitated for a second, then kept on walking. I wasn't going to hang around to find out if they were watching me leave. My cover story had worked – maybe I'd gotten better at lying in the past couple of days – and I didn't want to leave them with any questions about my identity.

I got back in the car and almost wept with relief.

The Mustang, thankfully, behaved as I tore through Missouri. Heavy rock albums proved to be the perfect tempo to define and refine a plan, so I knew exactly what I needed to do when I reached St. Louis.

Brooke being taken was my fault, and getting her back was on me. If it weren't for me, she would be in Orlando already, or wherever she would have ended up if she hadn't stopped to help me back in Seattle. I should have paid more attention to the van, to Chris . . . I should have insisted on Brooke checking the Mustang more thoroughly for another tracker back in Utah.

All of that didn't matter anymore. I had to put it out of my head and fix things – that was my next and only responsibility.

For someone who had only passed her driving test six months ago, the Mustang was a beast to handle. After driving it for only a few hours I'd learned why Brooke loved it so much. The car didn't just drive, it seemed to fly. But it wasn't weightless, it had some heft to it – a sturdy feeling of security even with the top down and the wind whipping my hair. I'd never noticed anyone else on the road up until now, but driving it was different. People stared. Truck drivers sent long, admiring looks my way, though I wasn't naive enough to imagine they were for me rather than the car. Older men in sensible sedans eyed it up, too.

It made me feel like something. Like somebody.

When I got into the city, I found the neighborhood where the Phoenix Motel was located, then forced myself to drive around a few times to get an idea of how things were laid out. I wanted to know my getaway routes, so I'd have more than one option if something went wrong.

It was a little after seven in the evening and the air was warm, making my hairline break out in tiny beads of sweat. It was too early for me to realistically make a move. There were lots of people milling around, and I knew from experience that at this time of day, motels were busy. It was the time when people decided, *hey, let's stop for the night and find somewhere to sleep, we can make the next jump tomorrow*. People looked for clean, compact motels, ones with pastel-painted walls and good lighting, just like this one.

We'd been doing the same thing for a whole week.

I pulled into the parking lot and shouldered the backpack. It didn't take long to do a quick scan of the area, and I tried not to panic when I couldn't see the black van.

They weren't here.

Shit.

I went back to the car, trying not to stress out. I couldn't wait here – if Chris drove in and spotted the Mustang, he would turn around and drive straight back out again. The car was too distinctive. With no better ideas, I drove a few blocks over to a Walmart, parking it between two giant trucks. Then I sat in silence for a minute, jiggling my knee anxiously.

The plan had been a good one. It had been *great*, in fact. I wasn't ready to give up on the Phoenix Motel. I trusted Megan, and her magic ancient system. Maybe Chris had made a late start this morning and was still on his way here. That was the most likely scenario.

I couldn't sit in the parking lot forever, but I didn't like the idea of taking the backpack and the gun into the store with me, because that seemed like a dick move. At the same time, I didn't want to let the gun out of my sight. It had started to represent something else today – not security, or a power move, like it was to Brooke, but a weapon that I had to get comfortable with the idea of actually using.

Would I shoot Chris if it meant saving Brooke?

A week ago, no way.

Now? Yes.

No hesitation.

And that scared me a little. I'd changed from the girl who'd been desperate to get out of Seattle at all costs, but I hadn't realized I was now someone who was capable of shooting a man.

In the end, I put the backpack in the trunk of the car and locked it. That felt like a good compromise.

The trip to the store wasn't just to kill time – I needed more than one option when I came face to face with Chris. I wanted to be able to protect both of us, me and Brooke, and making sure she got out safely meant being prepared.

I picked up a bag of apples and a jar of peanut butter, another box of Pop-Tarts, since I'd eaten the last of our stash, and a couple bags of chips. Then I went to the kitchen section and bypassed cake tins and cooling racks to pick up a knife.

Insurance. That's all it was.

Back in the car, I wrestled the paring knife out of its packaging and used it to slice chunks of apple to dip into the peanut butter while I watched the clock. I needed the sun to set just a little more, for there to be more shadows for me to lurk in.

Finally, around eight thirty, I drove back over to the motel and parked the Mustang in the clearly marked EMPLOYEES ONLY parking lot. It was risky, because I didn't want someone to call the cops or tow the car for being parked in the wrong place, but leaving the Mustang in one of the guest parking lots was riskier. I didn't want Chris to see it and know I was there.

This motel had pale-yellow tiles on the walls to disguise the poured concrete, and pastel-pink doors to all the rooms. It was only when you got close that you noticed the cracks in the tiles, the split edging around the doors. All the rot underneath the cute exterior.

From a hundred yards away, I spotted the black van with Utah number plates. *8912*. I wouldn't forget that number in a hurry.

Instead of fear, I felt a gut-punch of anger. And vindication. And appreciation for Megan. I turned on my heel, went back to the car, and grabbed the backpack.

With the knife and the gun, I felt far more prepared and protected than I had the very first time we'd seen Chris in

Salt Lake City. On impulse, I sidled over to the black van to get a better look at it.

From the outside, it really was just a plain black van – nothing to suggest anything sordid was going on inside it. But I knew it belonged to Chris and I couldn't contain my sudden burst of fury.

Carefully, and quietly, I pulled the knife out of my pocket and stabbed it into the front tire. I was half expecting it to pop, like a balloon, but the rubber put up some resistance and I had to give the knife a good tug to get it out again. I went around the van and did the same to the other front tire. From behind, no one would be able to tell the tires had been slashed, so there was no chance of Chris noticing.

But if I got Brooke out, they wouldn't be able to follow us.

I tucked the knife safely into my pocket and pulled my shirt out to cover it, then walked around the motel, looking for the room number Megan had given me.

113, 115, 117 . . . There. 119. It was right next to the stairs leading up to the second floor, and as I was watching the door, it opened. I immediately ducked into the shadows under the stairs, my heart pounding.

The blonde lady stepped out, glanced around, then closed the door behind her and walked off at a quick pace in her spiky heels.

It took me a second to compose myself.

This was the most outrageous, most scandalous, atrocious thing I'd ever contemplated doing, and when I checked in with all the emotions thumping through my body, I found I was okay with it.

I glanced around the parking lot again, which was quiet now, and took the gun out of my backpack. I stuck it in my other back pocket, then scurried over to the door the blonde lady had walked out of. After knocking sharply, I stepped to one side and pressed my back to the wall, so I was out of range of the peephole.

My whole body was thrumming with nerves as I waited, as I listened to footsteps coming up to the door. The bugs were chirping in the bushes around the motel, and the hum of air-conditioning units filled the atmosphere with more background noise. Maybe, if I was lucky, the people staying in the rooms either side of this one would be out eating dinner, or, if they were in, have their TVs loud enough that they wouldn't hear me.

I felt someone pause by the door, then they pulled the chain off and opened it. I waited, holding my nerve until the door was open wide enough, then I stepped out of the shadows and into the doorway, meaning Chris couldn't shut it in my face.

'Hi,' I said with a grin. 'Miss me?'

'What the fuck?'

He was uglier than I'd given him credit for back in Salt Lake City. Maybe it was because he wasn't wearing his charming sneer and laughing at Brooke's witty conversation, but up close like this I could smell his overpowering cologne and see all the hairs on his neck he hadn't bothered to shave.

'Give her back,' I said clearly.

Chris lunged for me, and I read in his movement that he was planning to take me too, but I was quicker than him.

I pivoted out of his way and reached for the gun in my back pocket.

Even though my hands were shaking, I aimed it right at his face.

'Give her back,' I repeated, as Chris stumbled away. 'Or I'll shoot your fucking face off.'

'Jessie?'

Chris took another step back into the room, and I saw her then, on the second bed, farthest from the door. She was still wearing her jeans and T-shirt from Kansas City.

'Try me,' I said to Chris. 'Please.'

'Jesus Christ,' he said.

I wasn't a brave person. For years, people had been telling me to be more confident, to take risks, to see in myself the potential that my teachers saw in me. That was easier said than done. While some people were trying to hype me up, others were doing their best to tear me down, and I didn't have enough strength in me to let my cheerleaders win.

It turned out there was an override switch for Mouse – I could turn her off if it meant helping someone I really cared about. It had taken Brooke being in danger for me to fully realize that.

Brooke stumbled inelegantly off the bed and got to her feet, swaying a little.

I pushed down on the safety and pulled the slide back.

Brooke walked unsteadily to the door and Chris put an arm out, like he could keep her away from me. She shoved him, just with one hand, but he hadn't expected that, and she managed to knock him off balance. I grabbed her wrist and tugged her behind me.

'Don't come after us,' I said. 'If I ever see you or the woman again, I'll shoot you first. Do you understand?'

Chris didn't say anything, just curled his lip at me.

Then I made my first mistake.

Brooke was breathing hard, close enough to me that I could feel her warmth, and I glanced over my shoulder to check she was okay.

Chris took the opportunity to lunge toward us again and I didn't think. I couldn't make my thoughts move that quickly even if I wanted to.

Luckily for him, my instinct wasn't to press down on the trigger, but to grab the knife out of my pocket and shove the blade up into the palm of his hand. The knife met resistance, and his mouth dropped open in a silent scream, then I pushed harder, and the tip came through the other side.

His chest contracted, like he was going to throw up, and he stumbled backward.

For a split second, I froze.

I'd never had anyone stab me through the hand, but I knew pain. I knew what it was like to feel powerless and helpless, like Chris was right now, and of all the things I'd thought I was going to feel toward him tonight, empathy wasn't one of them.

I forced myself to shake it off.

'Don't even,' I said, my words trembling a little. 'Don't fucking even.'

Chris finally found his voice and his howl of pain was primal, cutting through the air, loud enough that someone else was going to hear him. I stepped back, slammed the door closed and grabbed Brooke's hand.

'We need to run,' I said seriously, as emotion and adrenaline and my fight-or-flight instinct knotted together and punched me in the gut.

She nodded.

I didn't let go of her hand as we sprinted around the side of the motel, past the service entrance, in the opposite direction to where the blonde lady had gone. We clearly weren't supposed to be back here, but it was the quickest way to get to the staff parking lot and the only route that wasn't likely to take us past anyone else.

'Jessie,' Brooke said, but I shook my head, still pulling her along.

'Not now. We have to get out of here.'

We got to the car, and the SUV on the passenger side was gone. Brooke opened her door to get in, and I threw myself up and over the side into the driver's seat.

It took me three attempts to get my trembling hand to put the key into the ignition, and when the Mustang roared to life, I passed Brooke the gun.

'Can you make this safe, please?'

She nodded.

I couldn't watch her do it. I had to put as much space between us and the motel as humanly possible.

14

Bat Out of Hell – Meat Loaf

I drove on autopilot to the only place I knew how to get to in goddamn St. Louis, which was the Walmart down the road from the motel. Realistically, I should've been trying to get farther away – far, far away – but I was shaking and Brooke was too, and I just needed to stop for a second and make sure she was okay before we kept going.

I pulled into a space near the back of the parking lot, and as soon as I killed the engine, Brooke was hauling herself out of the car.

'Brooke!'

I scrambled after her before I realized she wasn't running away – she was just pacing back and forth. I held up both my hands, approaching her cautiously.

'Brooke?' I asked again.

'Oh my God,' she said, her voice and her whole body trembling. 'Oh my God, Jessie.'

I held my arms out, and she threw herself into them. I wrapped her up tight and squeezed, wanting her to know she was safe now. Brooke clawed at my back, then her hands stilled, pressed hard against my shirt.

'You're okay,' I said, soothing and soft.

For a moment, for a *second*, I got to be the one to hold her, to be the one who said everything was going to be all right, and that meant everything. All I'd wanted was to get her back, and now she was here, with me, and my body was too small to hold all the emotion threatening to spill out of me.

She pulled back a little, enough that I could see that the usual dark-brown circle of her irises had completely disappeared and her pupils were blown wide. She had definitely been drugged. And, to be honest, she didn't smell great. Her hair was a little greasy, and I guessed she'd been living and sleeping in the same set of clothes.

'Oh my God,' she whispered again.

Her hands came up to gently cup my jaw, and then ... she kissed me.

Suddenly, I knew what all those romance novels meant when they talked about fireworks, about electricity, like a million buzzing emotions that I'd never experienced before.

I closed my eyes instinctively and leaned up and into the kiss, chasing the wild feeling that had erupted in my stomach. Our noses brushed together, and Brooke made a tiny noise as our lips caught and moved.

At first, I was too shocked, too scared to do much about it, then I rose up on my toes to meet her lips fully, and my fingers curled around her arms just above her elbows. She was shaking a little, probably because of the escape, and I was too, for more than one reason.

My whole world narrowed down to the two of us, and as long as Brooke was kissing me, nothing else mattered.

So my first kiss was with a girl I really liked, who was high as a freaking kite, in the parking lot of a Walmart in Missouri.

Just what every girl dreams of.

'Come on,' I said, taking Brooke's hand and tugging it to make her move. All I wanted was to stay right here and keep kissing her, but it wasn't safe. 'We have to get out of here.'

'I can drive,' she said.

'No, you can't.' I laughed. 'Absolutely not.'

'It's my car.'

I thought it was probably a good thing that Brooke was feeling so possessive over her damn car, rather than freaking out about everything that had happened.

'You can drive tomorrow,' I promised.

'Fine,' she said with a sigh.

She gave in way too easily, reminding me that she was still out of it.

When she was buckled into the passenger seat, I tipped it back so she could rest, and drove south out of the city.

I should have been tired, after sleeping so terribly the night before, but I was hyped up on adrenaline and Brooke's kiss and I felt like I could drive straight through to Orlando that night without stopping. That wasn't what Brooke needed, though – she needed a decent bed and somewhere safe to sleep. There was so much we had to talk about, but all that could wait until morning.

I drove for an hour and a half to get out of Illinois, getting off the highway as soon as I could and taking back roads instead. Even though it was the middle of the night, I could tell it was a beautiful area, the thick trees close to the road on either side providing a canopy of green.

When I spotted the signs for a hiking and hunting lodge, I followed them, and fifteen minutes later I pulled into a clearing in front of a low, wood-sided building with a wide front porch that held a handful of rocking chairs. It felt cooler out here than it had been in the city. Deep in my gut, I knew this was where we needed to be tonight. Way, way out of the city. In the type of place we hadn't been before. A total change in our routine.

Brooke stirred when I killed the engine. 'Where are we?'

'The middle of nowhere. Do you want to stay here while I check in?'

She nodded.

'Don't go back to sleep,' I told her.

'Okay,' she mumbled blearily.

There was a light on over the porch, and through a large window at the front of the building I could see a woman behind the counter wearing a plaid shirt and jeans. The room seemed to serve as a center of operations, with maps and guides stuck to the bare pine walls, and a few deep leather armchairs and coffee tables for making plans.

'Hey,' she said as I pushed open the door, and she set down her book. 'Can I help?'

'Hi. I was hoping you had a room for tonight.'

'I'm sure we can find you something.'

Her accent was thick and welcoming, and I immediately felt like I'd made the right decision. We were safe out here.

She flicked through a large planner and made a note in one of the columns.

'Twin or king?'

I hesitated for just a second. 'King,' I said, knowing we'd both sleep better if we were close tonight.

'No problem. It'll be ninety dollars for the night, including tax.'

I counted out cash from my wallet and handed it over while she went to the wall and pulled down a key attached to a heavy wooden tag.

'You're in one-oh-six, which is right behind us here,' she said. 'You can leave the car where it is, or drive it around – there are parking spaces outside your block.'

'Thank you.'

'If you need anything, there will be someone at the desk all night. I'm here until midnight, then my son takes over until seven. Breakfast isn't included, but there's a diner right next door that opens at six.'

'Sounds great. Thanks again.'

She nodded. 'Sleep well.'

When I left the front desk, Brooke was waiting for me on the porch, leaning against one of the railings.

'Come on,' I told her, gently rubbing her arm as we walked back to the car.

I decided to drive around to our room, to get the car out of sight, just in case someone happened to come across us.

The motel was made up of maybe ten buildings. All of them were made of wood, thick planks and shiny wooden railings that glinted in the moonlight. Our room was on the first floor, and I gathered Brooke up to take her in before going back for the bags.

'This is nice,' she said as I unlocked the door and nudged her inside.

I agreed. The rustic theme continued in here, with a huge king bed on a wooden frame, paintings of the local landscape on the walls, and heavy plaid fabric curtains to block out the light.

'Do you want a shower?' I asked, hoping she wouldn't take it the wrong way.

'Yes,' Brooke said emphatically.

'Okay. I'm going to go get our stuff.'

She nodded and wandered into the bathroom.

I couldn't get all the bags in fewer than two trips, but I managed to haul everything inside while Brooke was still in the shower, and then I locked and bolted the door behind myself.

Being out here made me feel safe enough that I finally relaxed. I wasn't ready to process what we'd been through in the past few hours yet. I was pretty sure that would lead to a very inelegant breakdown, and I was too tired for that right now. I had to be strong for Brooke, to be what she needed me to be, instead of losing my shit and her having to take care of me.

I grabbed Brooke's toiletries bag out of her backpack and knocked lightly on the bathroom door.

'Brooke? I've got your toothbrush and stuff.'

'Thanks,' she called back, and I left it on the vanity for her.

I hoped the shower would help shake her out of whatever she'd been drugged with, but realistically it would probably take until morning until she felt better. After another minute, the water shut off and I heard her brushing her teeth.

She came out wrapped in a huge, fluffy white towel, and I quickly grabbed my own stuff to go get changed.

I couldn't let myself think about Brooke kissing me. She was clearly both deeply traumatized and drugged to the gills, and I didn't want to take advantage.

When I finished in the bathroom, Brooke was in her pajamas, braiding her long hair.

'Are you okay?' I asked tentatively.

'I'm so tired, Mouse,' she said, her voice slurring, and I couldn't be mad at her for using my old nickname.

I ushered her into bed and shut off all the lights except the two lamps on the nightstands. Brooke took the side farthest from the door, and I let her, guessing that's where she needed to be to feel safe. She curled up in a ball facing away from me.

I got into bed next to her, letting the cool cotton sheets slide over my bare legs. I flipped the switch next to the bed and the room fell into darkness.

For a few moments, she breathed deeply, then she started to shake.

'Hey,' I murmured. 'It's okay.'

It was as though once Brooke had started shaking, she couldn't stop. I decided to reach over to turn on the lights again so I could see her, and when I turned back, she was facing me and there were silent tears streaming down her cheeks.

I gently tugged on her hands until she swung her legs around to sit on the edge of the bed next to me.

'Take a deep breath,' I said, knowing from experience that sitting up like this, instead of hunched over, was a better way to get a panic attack under control.

Brooke shook her head, her eyes still panicky and her shoulders trembling.

'You can do it. I know you can. Come on, deep breath.'

'Cold,' Brooke gasped, though it wasn't really that cold in the room. I took her hands again, which were like ice, and rubbed them to warm her back up.

'Breathe with me,' I told her, and took deep, exaggerated breaths until she started to copy me.

She was still silently crying, and I reached up to swipe the tears off her cheeks with my thumbs.

'You are so fucking brave,' I told her. 'You are the bravest person I've ever met.'

'You *stabbed* someone,' she said incredulously, and she wasn't quite in control of her voice or her breathing yet.

That made me laugh. 'I'd do it again.'

Slowly, Brooke's shaky breaths evened out, and I felt it was safe to dash into the bathroom to grab some tissues for her to blow her nose and dry her tears.

'Are you okay?' I asked.

'Not really.'

'That's all right. You don't have to be. Do you want to talk about it?'

She shook her head. 'I'm so tired.'

'Come on,' I said, nudging her back under the covers.

As soon as I settled on my back, Brooke rolled over toward me and I opened my arms to her so she could settle with her head on my shoulder.

We fell asleep like that.

When I woke up the next morning, Brooke was in the shower again, and I stretched out into the space she'd left behind. I guessed it was pretty late from the angle of the sun pouring in through the gap in the curtains. I'd crashed, and every time I'd woken up during the night, Brooke had been pressed up close to me.

I forced myself not to think about what that could mean.

While Brooke was taking the longest shower of her life, I rolled onto my side and dozed for a while. I felt like I could sleep for hours more, and I couldn't remember what time we needed to check out, and if that was soon. I was also insanely hungry.

Even though we weren't that far from Nashville, I wanted to stay right here. Maybe for a month. Or forever.

We definitely didn't have enough cash to stay for a month. We'd have to go back to a city and find another convention hotel full of careless businessmen who we could steal from, and by that point we'd probably be in Nashville anyway, so it was all moot.

Brooke came out of the bathroom in jean shorts and her wolf-howling-at-the-moon T-shirt, and I forced myself to sit up.

'How are you feeling?' I asked.

'Better. A lot better.' She came over to sit on the edge of the bed.

'Do you remember anything?'

I wouldn't push her into talking about what had happened if she didn't want to, but at the same time I really needed to make sure she was okay. The sensible thing would have been to have taken her straight to a hospital or a police station last night, but I couldn't have done that. It would have been too risky for me personally, and with Brooke having been so out of it, I hadn't wanted to make decisions for her.

She shook her head like she was trying to clear her thoughts. 'I remember snatches of things. They kept giving me bottles of water with the top already off. Jessie ... I think they were giving me drugs.'

She said it so seriously I had to laugh.

'Yeah,' I said, reaching out to take her hand. 'You were definitely on something.'

'Shit,' she drawled. 'I've never done drugs before, and I couldn't even enjoy it my first time.'

I squeezed Brooke's hand, appreciating that she needed to joke about it. I thought she'd probably been given a date rape drug – something that would blur her memories and make her compliant. I wasn't going to say that out loud unless she did, though. I didn't need to make her paranoid.

'Did they say why you? Why us?'

Brooke shook her head and frowned. Her fingers played with the frayed rip in her shorts, and I tried to give her the space to think things through.

'Drugs,' she said angrily.

'What, like, dealing them?' I asked.

She looked up at me. 'He wasn't importing avocados. It was drugs.'

I had a sudden moment of clarity, of what a dangerous person Chris must be if he was importing drugs over the southern border. I couldn't let myself reflect on that, though, or I'd get freaked out all over again.

'That's ... *wild*, Brooke,' I said.

'Yeah,' she replied, like she needed me to confirm that before she could believe it. 'I think they wanted me to be, like ... what's the name of someone who smuggles stuff over the border?'

'A drug mule?'

'Yeah,' she said, pointing at me. 'They wanted me to be a drug mule.'

'Why were they following you specifically, though? I don't get it.'

'The woman ...' Brooke looked down at her shorts again. 'Her name is Ashley. She knew we had run away. She has some way of tracking missing people by listening to bulletins or something. Police reports, maybe?'

I nodded. 'Maybe. How did they follow us after you found the tracker, though?'

'Turns out Luca at the garage is a really bad liar,' she said with a wry smile.

'Oh, shit.'

'It's not his fault. They didn't believe him and one of the other mechanics mentioned something about Denver ... Jessie, I think they've been following us the whole time. They were just waiting for their chance.'

That was genuinely terrifying.

'Why did they want you?' I asked.

'They find runaways and take them down to El Paso and threaten to kill their families unless they take drugs back and forth across the border.'

'Holy crap,' I muttered, pushing down my instinct to be even more terrified by this new information.

Brooke nodded. 'They knew what they were doing. They knew me, anyway.'

'They knew your name?'

'Yeah. And they knew who my dad is. His job.'

'To blackmail him?' I asked.

'No,' she said, her eyes sad and desperate. 'To blackmail *me*.'

I reached out for her hand and squeezed it. 'You're safe now.'

'I don't remember much else, Jessie. Just the drugs, and Ashley saying I would be valuable to them.'

I didn't want to push her. She'd only been with Chris and Ashley for a little more than a day. I had a feeling the last traces of drugs were still working their way out of her system, too.

'How's your head now?' I asked.

'Okay. I'm just really hungry.'

'There's Pop-Tarts in the bag,' I said quickly. 'And the woman on reception last night said there's a diner next door, so we can go get something decent to eat in a minute, once I've had a quick shower.'

'That sounds good.'

I didn't want to leave Brooke alone for too long, so I tried to scrub myself down as quickly as possible. She seemed to be coping incredibly well, even considering her breakdown last night, which was probably the best thing to have happened. I knew from personal experience that holding on to those messy feelings wasn't helpful in the long run.

'Hey,' Brooke said when I stepped out of the bathroom, dressed in underwear and jeans, but without a shirt because I'd forgotten to take one in with me. Her eyes lingered on my belly button, and I wanted to curl up like a bug under her close inspection. 'Does that hurt?'

'Not really,' I said, trying not to scramble for a T-shirt. 'It's starting to scab over.'

She gave a little shudder. 'That's so gross.'

I went to my bag and quickly found a shirt. Since Brooke had kissed me, our whole relationship had changed, and for some reason being undressed around her now was so much scarier than it had been before. Maybe it was because I knew she was looking at me the same way I looked at her.

'Will you braid my hair for me?' I said impulsively. I wanted it off my face in this heat, and styling it up in braids would be quicker than blow-drying it.

'Sure. Sit down.'

Brooke nudged me into the desk chair and finished roughly towel-drying my hair. On the desk was a small white card, the size of a postcard, with useful phone numbers printed on it: the front desk, the takeout number for the diner, the activities line where you could book horseback riding or hire bikes. It finished with a reminder: *Check-out is at noon!* That meant we had time to get breakfast.

I closed my eyes as Brooke efficiently folded my hair back into two short braids that tucked behind my ears and left little tufts bouncing off my shoulders.

'You look super cute.'

I snorted with laughter. 'Thanks.'

She smiled at me in the mirror over the desk, then leaned down to press a kiss to the crown of my head. I closed my eyes and let myself soak in her newfound affection. Responding with a kiss of my own still felt like it could be seen as taking advantage, but my self-control was on the verge of evaporating at any moment.

'Come on,' I murmured. 'I need to feed you.'

Brooke walked outside onto the wide wooden porch and stretched up her arms. I locked the door behind us and took a deep breath of crisp morning air.

'This place is totally your shit,' Brooke said.

I laughed. 'Yeah. It is.'

'Is it bad that I don't remember getting here?'

'No.' I reached out to take her hand, but Brooke was the one to thread our fingers together. 'I think we need to go this way.'

She didn't let go of my hand as we walked back around to the front lobby building, passing a handful of other people all dressed like they were ready to go hiking. The trees offered dappled shade under a perfect blue sky, and I wanted to stay here forever, live here forever, and not see a dirty roadside gas station motel ever again.

I hadn't noticed the diner when we drove in last night, but this morning it stood out like a neon beacon among the trees.

'Wow,' Brooke said.

'I love it.'

The diner had a glowing neon sign above the door, declaring it MOLLY'S in electric pink. I pushed open the door to what felt like a movie set: red leather booths, circular stools at a long bar, an open kitchen at the back and a refrigerator case packed full of pies.

'Pie,' Brooke whimpered from behind me.

'Y'all grab a table,' a waitress called over. 'Wherever you like.'

The waitress was maybe my mom's age, mid-thirties. She wore jeans and a pink polo shirt with a white utility apron tied around her waist.

I let Brooke choose a booth near the window and slid in opposite her.

The diner was clearly winding down from the morning rush, with a few stragglers still eating. A family with two young kids, a couple who I guessed were in their sixties, a pair of men who looked like truckers and who I wanted to think were secret lovers.

I'd definitely been reading too many romance novels.

The waitress came over with a pot of coffee, and Brooke turned our cups over.

'Mornin',' the waitress said, pouring Brooke's coffee, then mine. 'I'm Molly. I'll be looking after you today. Menu's there, but you let me know if you want something that's not on it and we'll do our best to fix you right up.'

'Are you still serving breakfast?' I asked.

'Oh, only up until eleven tonight,' she said with a wink.

'Great, thanks,' I replied with a smile.

'I'll be back in just a tick.'

Brooke doctored her coffee with two creamers and three sugars and drank most of it in one gulp.

'Did you eat the Pop-Tarts?' I asked her.

'No. I decided to save myself.'

I knocked my foot against hers under the table and she smiled at me, making my hungry stomach clench hard.

'Let's stay here another night,' Brooke said quickly, like she was expecting me to say no.

'Really?'

'Yeah. I don't want to go anywhere today. I can't . . .' She shook her head. 'This is nice.'

'I think so too,' I said easily.

Molly came back and topped up Brooke's coffee. I hadn't started mine.

'What can I get ya?' she asked.

Brooke snapped her menu closed. 'Can I get an everything omelet, with extra everything, no mushrooms?'

Molly grinned. 'Sure. You want hash browns?'

'Please. And a slice of pie.'

'What kinda pie?'

'Surprise me.'

'Surprise pie and a double-everything-no-fungus omelet, got it.' Molly turned to me, still chuckling a little after hearing Brooke's giant order.

'Uh, just bacon and eggs, please,' I said, laughing with her.

'You want toast and hash browns, hon?' Molly asked.

'Sure. Thanks.'

'No problem. Give me a holler if you need anything else.'

We both leaned back in the booth, and, for a minute, a comfortable silence settled over us. We'd learned how to be together without having to fill every minute with nervous chatter. It would be a long and incredibly dull journey if I couldn't just sit in Brooke's presence without talking.

'I don't know if I'm remembering this right,' Brooke said slowly, still looking out the wide window at the beautiful forest. 'But did you *stab* Chris last night?'

'Uh . . . that's accurate, yeah,' I said cagily, not sure how she was going to react to that.

'Where did you get a knife from?' Brooke asked. She wasn't giving much away.

'Walmart,' I said simply. I reached for my coffee and cradled it against my chest. It wasn't an iced oat milk caramel latte, but it would do the job. 'I used it to slice up an apple and then left it in my pocket for a couple hours, so hopefully that was enough time for some bacteria to grow on it. Oh, and I used it to slash Chris's tires.' I sipped my coffee. It was almost perfect. 'Maybe his hand will get infected and he'll have to get it amputated.'

Brooke tipped her head back and howled with laughter. One of the trucker guys looked over at her, then turned back to his friend, smiling and shaking his head.

'Holy shit, Jessie. I didn't think you had it in you.'

I shrugged. 'I did what I had to.'

'You never told me how you found me,' she asked, looking at me intently from under her long lashes.

'I will,' I said. 'Not now, though. Let's just enjoy being . . . not there.'

'Okay.' She seemed relieved that I wasn't about to dredge up more memories. 'I definitely remember what happened after the stabbing, though.'

A flashback of Brooke's kiss appeared in vivid Technicolor detail, and I felt the blush climb from my chest up to my throat and bloom over my cheeks.

'Me too.'

'That wasn't an accident, you know,' she said.

'Are you sure?' I asked hesitantly.

'*Very* sure.'

This girl was going to make me lose my *freaking mind*.

Molly came over with our food, saving me from terminal embarrassment.

Brooke's double-everything omelet was enormous, covering more than two-thirds of a dinner plate, and the remaining third was full of potatoes. Molly put the plate down, then mine, before producing a bottle of ketchup from her apron pocket and setting it down between us.

'I'll be right back with your pie,' she said.

'You can hold that for a minute,' I said. 'We might need to get it to go.'

She laughed brightly. 'Sure thing.'

Brooke pouted at me, already slamming the heel of her hand against the bottom of the ketchup bottle to cover her hash browns.

'I want pie,' she said petulantly.

'Finish that and you can have your pie.'

Brooke grinned. 'Challenge accepted.'

15

Let's Stay Together – Al Green

We got the pie to go.

Brooke didn't want to go back to the room on her own, and I couldn't blame her for that. She came with me to the lobby building and sat outside on the porch in one of the rocking chairs, her takeout pie in a box on her lap.

The woman who had checked me in last night wasn't there. Instead an older man with thick hair graying at the temples, wearing a neatly buttoned plaid shirt, was poring over a huge map.

He seemed pleased that we were staying another night, and was effusive in his offer of finding a hiking trail for us to follow if we wanted to get out into the wilderness. I managed to hold back his enthusiasm with an almost-lie about Brooke recovering from being sick, and his expression changed to sympathy.

'Let us know if you need anything. There's a drugstore only ten minutes away, and we can get them to deliver.'

'That's really nice of you. I think she just needs to rest up.'

'All right. Well, you know where we are.'

I thanked him again and went back outside to find Brooke.

'There's hiking trails here, you know,' I said, taking the rocking chair next to hers. 'Or we can rent bikes.'

'Jesus, save me.'

That made me laugh. 'Well, we can stay here until noon tomorrow, so there's plenty of time for you to change your mind.'

'I think I'm good, but if I have a sudden and dramatic change of personality, you'll be the first to know.'

Brooke didn't seem to be in any rush to leave the rocking chairs, and it really was very peaceful out here, so I settled in.

'Did the past forty-eight hours actually happen?' Brooke murmured, staring out at the trees.

I had been trying to figure that out for myself. 'I think so.'

'I was kidnapped.'

'Yeah,' I said softly. 'And then I got you back.'

'Holy shit.'

'If you want to go to the police, we can still do that,' I said.

I'd been wary of mentioning the cops up until now, since we'd been doing everything possible to avoid them. But I also didn't want to push it. I knew you couldn't force someone to talk about their trauma if they weren't ready for it. I let the easy silence be an invitation for Brooke to talk, if she wanted to, or not.

She looked over at me. 'I don't remember much,' she said again, and I wondered if this was how she was protecting herself – by not thinking about it.

'Do you want to remember?' I asked, gently pressing to see if she'd open up.

'No.' She settled back again. 'I do want to know how you found me, though.'

I could tell that story.

Recounting it all reminded me that I needed to text Megan and let her know I'd found Brooke, and I pulled my phone out of my pocket long enough to type out a quick message and send it. Megan didn't need to know the gory details. Within a few minutes, she texted me back: *Thank God!! Good luck, Jenna & Juliet xoxo*

I replied with a *Thank you for everything* and decided to leave it there.

'I can't believe you did all that,' Brooke said, shaking her head. 'Well, I can, but . . .'

'Don't worry – I can't really believe it either.'

She reached out between the rocking chairs and took my hand, squeezing it gently, then twisted her palm so she could link our fingers together for the second time that day.

'Thank you,' she said softly. 'That doesn't sound like enough. But I don't know what else to say.'

'I did what I had to do,' I replied. I couldn't accept the weight of her gratitude when she'd done so much for me since we'd left Seattle. Maybe now we were almost even.

'What do you think will happen to Chris?' Brooke asked, letting go of my hand.

'Well, he's definitely going to have to go to the hospital to get his hand fixed. Hopefully while he's there, they'll run his details and the FBI can come in and stick him in a hole of a jail in the middle of nowhere.'

'That's a nice thought,' Brooke murmured. 'Would you really have shot him in the face?'

I'd forgotten that particular threat.

'I'm glad I didn't have to,' I said, which wasn't really an answer. I'd seen enough gore and death in the past couple of weeks, I didn't need to witness any more. And God knows what kind of trauma flashback that would have triggered. 'It would've made things much more complicated, so it's better that I didn't.'

'I'm sad you didn't.'

I snorted, then turned to look at her again. 'Are you okay, Brooke?'

She seemed to recognize that I didn't mean in the immediate, physical way.

'I'm scared,' she murmured, and my heart clenched.

'Of them coming back?'

'Yeah. I know they're probably in a hospital somewhere right now getting Chris's hand un-stabbed, but they could still follow us.'

I was glad Brooke had been the first one to say it out loud. The thought of being followed by them again was a persistent, nagging voice in my head. 'Do you want to check the car?'

She slumped a little. 'Yes. I know there's probably nothing there, but . . .'

'You'll feel better if you check,' I finished for her. 'We can do that.'

I borrowed a flashlight from the guy at the front desk so Brooke could check for another tracker and watched as she almost pulled the car to pieces, surveying every last inch of it before emerging, dirty and sweaty.

She tossed the flashlight in the air and caught it, flicking the light off neatly.

'There's nothing on it, Jessie.'

'Good.' I took her hand and squeezed it. 'Let's go out. Look around a bit.'

'Ugh. I need to change first. I'm filthy.'

I didn't want to go on a hike – we weren't going to venture out onto one of the trails – but I liked the idea of wandering around the motel and the diner. I'd seen signs for a stables that offered horseback treks, and I wanted to go see the horses.

At noon it was hot outside. While I was waiting for Brooke to clean herself up, I swapped my jeans for shorts. I didn't want to get sweatier than was strictly necessary. We detoured to the front desk to return the flashlight, then headed out around the back of the parking lot.

'Okay, it is nice out here,' Brooke said as we stepped onto one of the wide dirt paths.

'I told you,' I said mildly.

We walked for a few minutes in silence, following the path to the edge of the trees, then around another block of motel rooms.

'You know I said before about my parents deciding on where I'm going to college?' Brooke asked.

'Yeah?'

She didn't say anything for a long time, but I didn't want to push.

'I'm not going to fucking college,' she said eventually. 'I'll fail the entrance exams on purpose.'

'You don't want to go at all?' I asked gently.

She sighed heavily and stretched her arms over her head, exposing her flat belly. Her shirt lifted up, too, far enough that I could see the outline of the gun in her back pocket. I hesitated, not knowing if I wanted to call her out on it. I had no idea if Illinois had open carry laws, but I'd watched her take the bullet out of it last night, so I knew it was safe. I decided that if it made her feel better, I could handle it. We fell back into step alongside each other.

'No. So you know I worked on the car with Tony, my uncle?' I nodded, remembering. 'We put together a business plan. I want to go to trade school, learn how to fix up cars for real. Tony says I've got a talent for it, and, honestly . . . it's the only thing I've ever done that's felt right. Do you know what I mean?'

'Not really.' I looked over at Brooke. 'I don't think I've ever felt like that about anything.'

'I hadn't either. I was just prepared to go along with whatever my parents wanted because it made life easier.'

'Have you always done that?'

Brooke shook her head. 'You don't understand.'

'So tell me,' I insisted.

She sighed and pushed her hands through her hair. 'My parents mapped out my life before I was even born. They picked all my friends from when I was in kindergarten. If I met someone who wasn't the "right" kind of person, I wasn't allowed to be friends with them.'

I knew some parents were controlling, but it was so far from my own experience that it seemed totally alien. I squeezed her hand, encouraging her to go on.

'My parents would do, like, a background search on anyone I got close to. A few times, when I was younger, I refused to give up my friends.' She gave me a sad smile. 'That didn't make any difference. They cut those friends out for me. I wasn't allowed to go to their houses, they weren't allowed to come to mine, I couldn't be anywhere those friends were going to be. It was bullshit. It still is.'

'So you just went along with it?' I couldn't imagine Brooke being willing to let go of anything that easily.

'In the end, yeah.'

I wasn't expecting her to be so honest.

We turned another corner and I spotted a sign for the stables, telling me we were on the right track.

'It was easier,' she murmured, 'to do what they said, rather than fight them on it. It wasn't like I had much time, anyway. I had extracurricular activities most days, and when I wasn't doing something at school, I had a tutor at home. On weekends they got me involved with dance and gymnastics, so I was always at presentations or performances or meets, and then when I said I wanted to join the cheerleading team to, you know, put all those skills to use, they said no. It wasn't the *right* kind of extracurricular activity.' She sighed loudly. 'I don't know if you know what it's like, Jessie, to have every last minute of your life programmed.'

'No, not really. My mom doesn't care about me. Not like that.'

Brooke looked at me. 'Well, I couldn't do it anymore,' she said, and I could hear the tears catching at the back of her throat. 'For seventeen years they've been in control of everything. I'm not allowed an opinion unless they endorse it. They decide what dentist I go to, my doctor ... my fucking gynecologist is one my mom picked for me. I'm not allowed to choose where I go to college or what career I'll end up having, and to tell them no?' She shook her head. 'It's fucking impossible.'

'So you ran away,' I said, finally understanding.

I didn't know what it was like to live under that kind of pressure, but I could understand why it had driven Brooke to run away. Finally escaping her parents' control must have felt like sweet freedom. I was surprised that she was willing to share her secret with me after making me promise not to ask her why she was leaving Seattle, but I was touched that she clearly trusted me now.

'I had a plan,' Brooke said. 'Tony and I worked out how many years I'd need to be at trade school. How I'd take business management classes, too, so when I was done with school, I'd be able to open my own garage. You know, a female-owned garage, one where women feel like they're not going to be ripped off or talked down to because they don't know what's wrong with their car. I'd set up a training program to have other women come and apprentice with me. Uncle Tony was going to back me financially for the first five years, and after that I would've hopefully paid him off.'

'Your parents said no.'

'They didn't say no, Jessie. They laughed at me.'

I took her hand and led her over to the stable block. It looked to me like most of the horses were out, and a small crew was cleaning out the stalls and tending to the tack. I stepped up onto the bottom rung of a fence and draped my arms over the top. Next to me, Brooke did the same.

'They fucking laughed at me,' she murmured. 'Said I was being a silly little girl. That I don't know what the real world is like, and, anyway, they weren't having a daughter of theirs doing a manual job. Like I was a working-class stain on their upper-class sensibilities.'

'That's . . . gross,' I said, not able to find a better word. I was from the sort of family that Brooke's parents wouldn't approve of, and, though I'd never met them, I felt a sudden burst of deep, visceral hatred for them.

'I want to make my own choices.' Brooke breathed deeply. 'Not just because cars are really interesting to me, not just because it's something that I could see myself making a really fucking amazing career out of. I want to make choices for myself, for *once*. For the first time in my freaking life.'

'I get it,' I said.

'They threw my plan in the trash. And it was that

moment that I realized I was totally, completely trapped by them. They frame everything as if they're doing the "best thing" for me, but what that really means is that I will never be able to set a toe outside of their boundaries, or else I'll be punished, for the rest of my life. I'll never be able to get married unless they approve the person ... they'll control my social life, even my kids, if I ever have them. Could you live like that?'

'No,' I said plainly.

'Me neither.'

I wasn't sure what else to say to that. 'I'm sorry' felt pathetic and insincere, even though I *was* sorry. No one should have to live under somebody else's control. Not Brooke with her parents, or me either, having to hide from the Creep in case he decided to lash out at me. It was all so wrong.

I shuffled over and wrapped my arm around her waist, and, after a moment, she tilted her head to kiss my cheek. It felt like the whole world was shifting – the air, the sky, the ground under my feet all moving to accommodate Brooke and what she meant to me. My friend, the girl I liked, the girl who liked me back. It was so much more than I could ever have hoped for.

I didn't want to force Brooke to keep talking about her parents, especially when she was clearly dealing with so much trauma from the whole situation. And it *was* trauma. I could see it: in the way she shrank herself when talking about her parents, about the expectations that had been put on her and the absolute control she'd been forced to live under. I wanted my mom to care about me more, but the Summers took it to such an extreme that I almost felt grateful I hadn't been brought up that way.

We took a meandering route back, even though the afternoon had brought on the kind of heat I really wasn't used to after living in the Pacific Northwest for most of my life. I was going to need a new wardrobe soon.

'Do you want to do anything this afternoon?' I asked as Brooke unlocked the door to our room.

'Honestly? No, not really.'

'Want to watch crappy daytime TV and share your pie with me?'

'Yes and no, in that order,' she said with a laugh.

I shut the door and Brooke doubled back to flip the bolt across. I felt better knowing no one could get in. She left the gun on the dresser, in clear sight of the bed and the door, and I held my tongue again.

'The diner is, like, thirty seconds from here,' I said as she settled back down on our unmade bed. 'We can get more pie later.'

'Fine,' she sighed, and I didn't think she minded really.

The pie was blueberry, with a brown-sugar crust, and it looked and smelled *insanely* good. Brooke handed me one of the wooden forks Molly had given us and pushed the container toward me so I could take the first bite.

'Thanks,' I murmured, breaking off a small piece to try. The taste lived up to the look and smell.

Brooke didn't stand on ceremony and shoveled a huge bite into her mouth.

'We're going back there for dinner tonight, right?' she asked with her mouth full.

'Unless you want to get in the car and drive somewhere?'

'No,' she said emphatically. 'I looked at their dinner menu earlier and they've got burgers and fried chicken.'

'Your two main food groups!'

'Fuck off,' she said, laughing through another mouthful of pie. 'I'm going to order both, and you can split with me.'

'Sounds good,' I said. 'And more pie?'

She nodded. 'They have a chocolate peanut butter pie and I *want that*.'

'Why didn't you order it earlier?'

Brooke pulled a face at me. 'It's not breakfast pie.'

I snorted with laughter. 'Isn't all pie breakfast pie?'

'Absolutely not.' She held up her hand to tick off on her fingers. 'Pumpkin, oatmeal, or any fruit pie can be for breakfast. Chocolate, pecan, anything caramel is dinner pie.'

'Key lime? Or lemon meringue?'

She circled a finger in the air. 'All day long, baby.'

I laughed again, took a final bite of blueberry breakfast pie, and nudged the rest back to her. I was still full from earlier.

'Brooke, where do we go from here?' I pushed myself to ask.

'Nashville?'

'Brooke.'

She took another huge bite of pie – to give herself time, I was sure, to come up with an answer.

'Nashville,' she repeated determinedly. 'Then Atlanta, then Orlando.'

'Then?' I prompted.

'I told you,' Brooke said, scratching off some of the brown sugar from the piecrust and licking it off her fingernail. 'We can call Meredith and she'll help us get jobs as princesses.'

'You really think that, Brooke? Really?'

She sighed heavily and pushed her hands through her hair. 'I have to believe it.'

'I don't think you do,' I countered. 'I think we need a better plan than *let's get jobs as princesses*.'

'That plan got us this far.'

I couldn't argue with that – the Princess Plan had been a big enough dream when we left Seattle to propel us more than halfway across the country. But the closer we got to Orlando, the more outlandish it felt, even with the possibility of Meredith helping us. Everything seemed more *real* since Brooke had been kidnapped. It wasn't that we were blind to the dangers of what we were doing up until now, but we couldn't ignore them anymore. Even if Brooke was happy with the Princess Plan, I needed a Plan B. I wanted to know someone wasn't going to come along and steal away this freedom we'd fought so hard for.

'I looked it up on my phone the other night, Brooke, and we can't afford more than, like, four nights in Orlando before we go broke. Do you know how much hotels cost there? It's insane.'

'So we'll go lifting some more wallets.' She shrugged. 'It worked last time, it'll work again.'

'I know.' I didn't want to be mad at her, but she was so *frustrating*. 'I know, Brooke, but every time we do shit like that, we draw attention to ourselves.'

'Look, I've been to Disney World before,' she said. 'Trust me, there are literally thousands and thousands of people walking around. And none of them are paying attention to anything. They're all too busy looking up at whatever shiny, sparkly thing has caught their eye.'

'So we start stealing from families?' I asked hotly.

'You didn't want to steal from anyone a few days ago. You changed your tune on that quick enough.'

'Are you trying to rile me up on purpose?' I groaned, frustrated.

'No.' She closed the lid on the takeout box and put the leftover pie back in the fridge. Then she turned to me with regret written all over her face. 'I'm sorry.'

'It's okay,' I replied softly. 'I just want to know what happens next.'

'We'll figure it out,' she promised.

'I can't go back,' I whispered to her.

'Will you tell me why?'

It was almost inevitable that I was going to tell her now. She'd told me what she was running from, and so our old deal was off. Before I could go there, though, I had to accept that when she finally knew, she might not be able to get over it. Opening up could potentially be the deal-breaker that shattered what we had right now, and, selfishly, I wasn't prepared to let her go. Not yet.

'Yeah,' I said, full of the inevitability of it. 'But not now.'

She sighed, and I had to look away from her sad eyes, feeling her sense of betrayal like a knife in my gut.

'Okay, Jessie. Okay.'

16

The Great Pretender – Dolly Parton

Later that afternoon, Brooke fell asleep while I was half reading, half watching the TV, and I tried to rearrange my thoughts about the past two days so they fell into some kind of logical order. It didn't work. Any way I looked at it, Brooke should have been having an actual nervous breakdown right now, but apart from being tired, she seemed better.

She was super focused on the road ahead, on getting to Nashville and then Orlando as soon as possible, and even though it was going to take us a few more days and a lot more miles, it was starting to feel like we were running out of road. All the things I didn't want to talk to Brooke about were going to be shaken loose eventually. My job now was to prepare myself for that, and the inevitable fallout.

Having someone I cared about was totally new territory for me, and I was stuck between wanting to tell Brooke everything, so she knew all of it – the good and the bad – and hiding the bad stuff so she didn't decide to ditch me. I didn't really think Brooke would do that, but we hadn't talked about our relationship, about what this was between us. I wanted it to be more than friendship, but I didn't know if it was normal to be that upfront.

I watched as she stirred, and yawned, and blinked awake, my heart impossibly full.

'Hey,' she said sleepily.

'Hey back.'

'I'm hungry.'

That made me chuckle, because if Brooke was hungry, then she was feeling normal.

'Do you want to go back to Molly's?'

She stretched and grinned. 'Definitely.'

'Good, because I do too.'

'Is it time to go for dinner yet?'

I glanced at the alarm clock on the nightstand. 'It's five thirty. By the time we get ready and walk over there, yeah.'

'Okay, good,' she said around a huge yawn.

I reached out and brushed my hand over her hair, and she smiled up at me then touched my hand.

'Are you okay?' Brooke asked. I nodded, but she gave me a *look*. 'Sure?'

I hesitated, then got up off the bed. I was full of nervous energy, and I needed to pace it out. All of a sudden, the flirting and touching and occasional kissing wasn't enough – I needed to *know*, for sure, that I wasn't trying to force something between the two of us that wasn't really there.

'What is this?' I asked, pointing between us and feeling like my chest was being cracked open.

She shrugged. 'Whatever we want it to be, Jessie.'

'That's really easy for you to say,' I said desperately. 'You're not the one with an enormous, cringey crush –'

'I'm not?' she said, interrupting me, and I bulldozed over that, totally unable to process it.

'And I don't want to get myself into something which is only going to hurt more in the long run. I'd rather just pretend that last night never happened if that's the case,' I finished in a rush.

Brooke got up off the bed and came over to me.

'Jessie,' she said, leaning in and taking my face in both her hands so I couldn't escape her intense gaze. 'I don't want to pretend last night never happened.'

'No?' I said pathetically.

Her eyes softened. 'No, I really don't.'

'But –'

'No buts.' She kissed me then, so softly that my toes curled, and hot, static electricity crawled down my spine. Then she brushed her thumbs over my cheeks, and I felt like I was going to crumble into dust.

'But you're you,' I said when she pulled away and put her hands back in her pockets. 'And I'm me.'

'Yeah,' she said, like I was being exceptionally stupid. 'That's what I like about it.'

I fidgeted, fingers tapping my thighs as I rocked back onto my heels, and Brooke laughed and leaned in to kiss me again, which *very much did not help*.

'Is this okay with you?' she asked gently.

I pressed the heel of my hand to my breastbone, trying to calm myself down.

'Because if it's not,' she said, 'we can go back to being friends.'

'I don't want to be friends.'

Brooke's eyes widened.

'No,' I said, rushing to correct myself. 'I want this. This more-than-friends thing.'

'Then we're more than friends,' she said simply. Like it could be that simple.

'Is that what you want?' I asked.

'What I want is to go to Molly's.' And I had to laugh, because of course she did. 'And get a burger and some fried chicken, then sit outside on the porch for a while, then come back here to sleep, and then go to Nashville tomorrow. With you. I want to do all of that with you.'

'Me too.'

She took my hand. 'Then let's go.'

The next day, we rolled into Nashville around two in the afternoon.

I'd already scoped out a hotel online, one that was walking distance to the city's downtown area, and I'd made a point of memorizing directions so I could drive and Brooke could rest. She bitched about it, but the fact that she gave in at all meant she probably wasn't ready to drive yet, even if she wasn't going to admit it.

I thought I might like to do a long road trip like this again at some point. Maybe in an RV, so we wouldn't have to look for cheap motels all the time. I wanted to see more of that lush country we'd come across in Wyoming and

Illinois ... I wanted to go to the Great Smoky Mountains and hike the Appalachian Trail and spend weeks out in the middle of nowhere.

But for now, Nashville felt like a significant stop on our journey, and I was determined to make it count – in a good way.

We found the hotel and I went with Brooke to check in. She paid in cash, running her usual line about her wallet and phone being stolen. I watched, leaning against the counter and admiring her. Brooke noticed and rolled her eyes, suppressing a smile.

With the two of us hauling our belongings from the car, we made it to the room in one trip, and Brooke made sure to lock down the Mustang before we wandered the few streets over to Music Row. The sidewalks were wide here, like they were expecting people to be walking around, and we were only a few blocks from the hotel when Brooke stopped and slapped my arm.

'Look.'

The blackboard sign held elaborate chalk typography: OPEN MIC NIGHT – TONIGHT. $500 PRIZE!

Brooke turned to me and grinned, an expression I was starting to become familiar with.

'No,' I said.

'Why not?' she demanded. 'We've been singing all the way down here.'

'Singing in the car or in a choir with thirty other people and getting on a stage in front of hundreds of strangers are two entirely different activities, Brooke.'

'Not really,' she said. 'Come on. Where's your sense of adventure?'

That almost made me laugh, and I had to turn away from her so she didn't see my expression and think she'd won.

People brushed past us on the sidewalk, and somewhere, a few streets away, a car horn blasted.

'Well, I'm going in,' Brooke said, and strode into the bar like she belonged there.

'Fuck's sake,' I muttered. And followed her.

The bar was brightly lit, with all the work lights on rather than the candles on the tables and the fairy lights that had been strung from the ceiling. A long wooden bar bracketed the left side of the room, with tables in between it and the stage over on the right.

'Can I help?' a guy called from behind the bar. 'We don't open until three.'

Brooke walked right over to him, unafraid and unashamed. I forced myself not to smile and look like an idiot, because I couldn't help but adore her bold, stupid, extroverted ass.

'I was wondering about open mic night?'

He nodded and put a folder down on the bar.

'Sure. Everyone gets to do three songs, maximum of one original song – we get a lot of tourists here. You can use the piano, or there's usually a few guitars floating around and some percussion.'

'How much to enter?'

'Nothing,' he said, smiling. 'You're free entertainment for my paying customers.'

'How many paying customers?' I asked, leaning against the bar, attempting to look as cool and casual as Brooke.

'A couple hundred, on a good night.'

I gulped.

The guy was wearing jeans and a white T-shirt, and he had fiery dark-red hair and freckles on his nose. I'd honed both my bullshit-detector and bastard-sensor since being on this trip, and he hadn't registered on either.

'You want in?' he asked.

'Yes,' Brooke said emphatically.

Oh my God, no, I groaned silently, already knowing that I'd go along with it, though, because it made Brooke happy.

'Great. What's your name?'

Brooke looked at me. 'Uh . . .'

The bartender looked between us. 'A stage name is fine. You guys need a minute?'

'Summer . . . Swift Summer,' Brooke said, a satisfied grin spreading over her face.

'Oh, you think you're so clever,' I muttered, still trying to hide my smile.

She laughed brightly.

The bartender winked. 'Thanks, Swift Summer.' He was flirting with her, just a little, and she didn't seem to mind.

I did.

'I don't suppose you have space where we could, uh . . . rehearse?' Brooke asked.

'Rehearse' was a very nice way of describing *figuring out what the hell we were going to do in front of several hundred people.*

He looked at her a little closer, then shook his head. 'Not here. But if you go three doors down, ask for Liam. Tell him Damien sent you. He's got some space out back.'

'Great, thank you.'

'Be here for eight. We start at eight thirty.'

'We'll be here!' Brooke said cheerily.

'I hate you,' I said as we stepped out into the sunshine.

'No, you don't,' she said with a smirk.

I mumbled under my breath, mocking her, and her smirk turned into a glorious laugh that made my nerves take flight.

Liam's bar was, helpfully, called Liam's Bar. Brooke did a little shimmy and smacked a kiss on my cheek before walking in and working her charm on Liam like she had on Damien. After her breakdown in Illinois, it seemed like she was purposefully working toward being more like the old Brooke: bold and sassy and fun.

Liam had a space behind his stage that could generously be called a recording studio . . . if I was being *very* generous. The room was wood-paneled and had a drum kit set up in one corner, a piano squashed in next to the door and a selection of guitars on the wall. It also had miles of cables, microphones and a tiny, tiny recording desk.

'This is amazing,' Brooke said, turning in a tight circle in the crowded room.

It smelled like wood and sweat and guitar strings and had no natural light.

I thought it was pretty amazing, too.

'My church has a recording room like this. It's a little bigger, though.'

'Really? What do they record?'

'Christian rock, mostly. The pastor's in a band. It's not *good*, but that doesn't stop him collecting donations to make CDs.'

Brooke snorted and walked over to the piano. She pulled up the stool and ran a series of chords, her fingers dancing over the keys.

'I didn't know you played piano,' I said, unable to tear my eyes away from her hands.

'One of my many extracurricular activities,' she said. 'What can you sing?'

'Very little.'

'Oh, come *on*, Jessie,' she huffed. 'You can sing. I've heard you. We've been singing all the way down here.'

'I can't sing in *public*.'

'Of course you can.'

'You have far more confidence in me than I have in myself,' I said, aware that Brooke saw me in a way no one ever had before.

She played another series of chords. '"Piano Man"?'

'Too cliché.'

'True.'

'"Jolene"?' I suggested.

Since she was playing the piano, I went to the wall and picked a Fender acoustic guitar and took a seat on one of the low stools to check its tuning. I didn't know how to play much, but picking up an instrument in the church youth band had been a good excuse to get out of the house and away from my mom's awful choice of boyfriends over the years.

'And that's not cliché?'

'We could do it as a call and response. A duet.' I took out my phone and pulled up the sheet music, then handed it to Brooke so she could scroll through it.

'Huh.' Brooke picked out the tune on the piano. 'That could work. A two-part harmony.'

'Yes. Exactly,' I said, relieved she got where I was going.

We ran 'Jolene' – Brooke taking the alto line with me filling in the soprano over the top – and it worked. I couldn't qualify exactly how, it just worked. Brooke had a richness to her voice that I'd never be able to copy, something sexy and a little husky that worked for this song. She was the narrator, and I, to my utter surprise, was playing Jolene.

'This sounds ah-*mazing*.' Brooke did a little dance on her seat, and I laughed.

'Next?'

'What about . . .' Brooke said, and played an introduction I recognized.

'"Candle in the Wind"?'

'Yeah. I think we could do some fun harmonies with it again.'

'Like a modern spin?'

'No . . . no. I hate those breathy, nasally little-girl singers. Belt it, like Ms Russo is always telling us to.'

'Sing from your stomach! From your guts!' I laughed.

'I don't think anyone has ever wanted to hear anyone sing anything from their guts,' Brooke drawled, and I leaned back, still laughing.

Brooke played most of the first verse without stopping, and my mouth dropped open as her fingers flew over the keys.

'You, like, *know* that,' I said.

She shrugged, and kept playing. 'I always loved this melody.'

I wanted to ask her to elaborate. It was such a sad song, about a woman who had been one thing to the world and something completely different behind closed doors. The more I thought about it, the more I saw how Brooke could relate – the Norma Jeane she wanted to be versus the Marilyn Monroe people viewed her as. The Marilyn her parents forced her to be.

I'd been one of those people, seeing just the Marilyn. There was no point in denying I'd had a crush on Brooke since forever, but I liked all those superficial things about her: her smile, her laugh, her gorgeous hair, her classic-yet-modern clothes that underlined how beautiful she was.

But I'd been too shy to really get to know her, and that was on me. Brooke had to know she was popular – she was always getting asked out, and I'd often heard people gossiping about her. Brooke and Kendall and Madison. I'd never wanted what they had. God knew, I would never have coped under that amount of scrutiny.

Yet it had never occurred to me that Brooke wasn't coping, either.

I pulled up the lyrics on my phone.

'Let's try it,' I said.

After an hour of rehearsing and trying out new songs, Liam stuck his head around the door.

'Everything okay?'

Brooke smiled at him, and I felt another stab of jealousy. 'Yeah. Really good.'

'Don't play "Graceland",' he said, and Brooke's fingers stilled on the keys, where she'd been working out the melody.

'Why not?' she asked with a huff.

'One of the regulars always plays that. Damien won't mind, but doubles of the same song aren't a good idea.'

Brooke sulked.

'Sorry,' he said with a laugh. 'You want drinks or anything? Water?'

'I'd love a water, actually.' I forced myself to stand up and step out of my comfort zone. 'I can come get them.'

'I can come too,' Brooke said quickly, and I shot her a smile, hopefully communicating that I was okay. I could do this.

'It's all right,' I said, and followed Liam back down to the bar.

He had dark hair and eyes and didn't smile quite as easily as Damien. But he was cool, and he didn't seem to have ulterior motives. He went behind the bar and took two bottles of water from a fridge.

'Oh, no charge,' he said when I pulled out a couple of bills from my pocket.

'Are you sure? Thanks,' I said, stuffing the money into the tip jar instead.

'You guys sound good, by the way,' he said as I twisted the top on one of the bottles.

'Yeah?' I asked, surprised.

'Yeah.' He gave me a small smile. 'Don't know if a couple out-of-towners will win at an open mic night, but I'd have you play here, if you ever wanted to.'

I felt something *swoosh* in my stomach – one of those *I can't believe this is happening to me* moments. But in a good way. Which I was really not used to.

'I'm not sure how long we'll be in the city,' I said with real regret.

'You're just passing through?'

'Yeah. It depends on how long we get caught here for, though.'

Liam smiled. 'I arrived here six years ago. Was supposed to stay for a week.'

'I don't think we can stay here for six years,' I said, allowing myself a moment to let the daydream turn from something wispy and distant to an almost-real possibility. 'Even though I'd like that.'

'Well, let me know if you want to sing one night. Like I said, you're welcome any time.'

The corridor back to the rehearsal room was dark, and I suddenly realized I'd left Brooke alone and that really wasn't okay. It stank of beer back here, sour and sweet at the same time, but the sound of her playing the piano drifted to me after a few seconds. I walked quicker, anyway.

She looked up with real relief when I closed the door behind myself.

'I almost came after you,' she joked.

'Sorry. Liam said we could play here one night, if we want,' I said, handing over her water.

'Really? Wow.'

'Yeah. He doesn't seem like a creep, either, which is a bonus.'

'God knows we've had enough creeps on this trip,' she said.

'Tell me about it.'

It took far more messing around on the piano for us to figure out what the third song in our set should be, and then work out the harmonies. By the time we were done, my stomach was growling – we'd missed lunch and it was almost dinnertime.

'Once more,' Brooke said, and I flopped back on the floor, groaning.

'I can't. I need to rest my voice.'

'Hum it, then.'

Liam knocked on the open door and I sat up.

'Sorry to interrupt,' he said. 'I need this room in about twenty minutes.'

I shook my head. 'No problem. We're just leaving.'

'Once we run this one more time,' Brooke said sweetly.

Liam laughed. 'I could hear you arguing all the way down the hall.' He leaned in the doorway and folded his arms. 'Do you sing together often?'

'We're in a choir together, but we don't usually duet,' Brooke said.

'This is all her idea,' I said darkly, and Liam laughed again.

'If you want something to eat, you should try Music City Burgers across the street. Tell them Liam sent you. Best fried pickles in Nashville.'

'We should do that.' I gave Brooke my best pleading eyes, and she stood up with a sigh.

'Okay.' She nodded. 'Thanks again for letting us use the space.'

'Good luck tonight.'

We went to Music City Burgers and Liam was right: their fried pickles were excellent. The food didn't calm the knot in my stomach, though.

'You look like you might actually murder someone this time,' Brooke said lightly, dragging one of her French fries through a puddle of ketchup.

The accusation, and the rich red of the ketchup, forced me back to a place I really didn't want to revisit right now.

'Jessie?' Brooke asked, clearly worried by my sudden shift in mood.

I shook my head. 'I'm fine.'

'Sure?'

'Yeah.' I reached out and stole one of her fries. 'I'm good.'

'Are you ready for later?'

'No,' I said, forcing myself to give her a smile instead of lingering on the intense flashback that was still threatening to smash through my defenses.

'It's only three songs, Jessie. You can do three songs.'

We'd found an acoustic duet version of 'Thunder Road' on YouTube, and I thought it was almost better than the album version – and we'd listened to the album plenty over the past couple of weeks.

'Do you think they'll put a bucket next to the stage for me, in case I need to puke?' I said lightly.

Brooke laughed and kicked me gently under the table. 'You won't puke.'

I pushed my plate away, not wanting to look at the food anymore now that I was feeling sick from thinking about being on stage.

Brooke caught my eyes and smirked, like she knew what was going through my head. She probably did. She knew me better than anyone.

We had time to go back to the hotel and change, and I wanted to touch up my makeup since it had sweated off in the heat of the day. Even though the hotel was only a few blocks' walk from the bar, the humidity in the late-afternoon air had me sweating again.

'I'm not sure I'm built for the South, you know,' I said, blowing my hair off my face.

Brooke laughed. 'Let me choose what you wear tonight?' she asked.

I unlocked the hotel room door and pushed it open, releasing a burst of blessed cool air.

'From what we already have with us, right?' I said cagily, knowing what she was like.

'You're always so suspicious,' she said. 'But, yeah, we don't have time to go out and get something new.'

I didn't own anything particularly outrageous, so at least I knew Brooke couldn't do much damage.

I took a really quick shower and washed my face, put my underwear back on and brushed my teeth. When I went out into the room, the AC made me shiver, and all the hairs on the back of my arms stood up.

Brooke had set out my black dress from Goodwill, a pair of black tights, my black Doc Martens and a black short-sleeved shirt from her own wardrobe.

'It could be worse,' I murmured.

'Trust me,' Brooke said, floating past me to take her turn in the bathroom.

There was a second mirror in the main part of the bedroom, over the desk, so while Brooke fixed whatever needed fixing, I sat down and started on my makeup.

I'd gotten used to the shorter hair now, and the blonde, and I'd figured out how to do my eyeliner with soft flicks at the corner of my eyes. I really didn't look like Mouse anymore. That felt like relief. Like bone-deep relief.

Brooke came out of the bathroom in *tight* black jeans and a black tank that scooped low over her boobs.

My eyes almost bugged out of my head.

'Is that my top?'

She looked down at her chest, then back at me with a wicked smile. 'Oops.'

She was wearing red lipstick, too, deep, dark red that set all the rest of her features into sharp relief. She came up behind me and took the hairspray off the counter to work it through my hair, making it artfully tousled.

I had lost the ability to speak, because Brooke didn't just look gorgeous, she looked gorgeous *and* she was *wearing my clothes*. My brain short-circuited, and despite the cool air I was suddenly hot all over.

When I stood up, Brooke took half a step back, then smiled at me and stepped in close again, but I wanted to be in charge this time, to be the kiss-er, not the kiss-ee. The boots gave me a bit of extra height, and I leaned in to brush my lips over hers.

'You look hot,' she murmured when I pulled away.

'Thanks,' I said, still not used to her saying things like that.

She grabbed the overshirt that she'd left out and passed it to me. I put it on, and she took the ends and tied them into a knot.

'Holy shit, this almost gives the impression that I have boobs.'

Brooke laughed. 'You have boobs.'

'Not like . . .' I gestured at her.

'Eh, we work with what we've got.'

She put on sneakers, which balanced out her outfit slightly. I wasn't sure how I'd cope if she put on heels.

'Come on. We're gonna be late.'

The bar was already busy when we arrived, and Brooke pointed out our names on a list, so we didn't have to join the people waiting to be let in. That wasn't Brooke's style. She skipped the line and held my hand as we weaved our way through the bar.

The other performers were gathered at a few tables to one side of the room, and Damien came over with bottles of water. We were up third out of ten entrants, which seemed like a good place. Not first or last, which were equally bad, or somewhere near the end when people started losing interest.

I drummed my fingers on the table through the first two sets, only stopping when Brooke put her hand on mine. Then I started bouncing my knee instead, and she gave up trying to prevent my fidgeting.

Damien was acting as MC, introducing each act and encouraging people to tip their bartender.

'Hey everyone, our next set is from Swift Summer. They're new in town, and I've heard they're pretty great, so let's give them a big welcome!'

'I'm gonna puke, I'm gonna puke,' I muttered as Brooke grabbed my hand and dragged me up onto the stage.

We'd agreed to run the set in the same order we'd practiced it earlier, which meant I had to get my shit together enough to play guitar for 'Jolene'. I took the tall stool, angling it a little to hide behind the piano, and ran my thumbs over the strings to check the tuning.

Damien came around and adjusted the two mics so one was pointed at the guitar and the other was way too close to my lips.

'You're amazing,' Brooke mouthed at me. Her smile turned my blood electric.

The noise in the bar never dropped completely – the bartenders were still working, and some people kept low conversations going through our songs. That was good. It was *great*, in fact, because it meant not everyone's attention was on me, and I was much more okay with that.

The stage was lit with a couple dozen lights, so I couldn't really see more than a few rows into the audience. But when Brooke started playing, I couldn't keep my eyes off her.

She was in her element.

Not just because she was the center of attention, but because she was being her most authentic self.

I knew I loved her then.

It had been on the cards for a while.

She was bright and beautiful and, sure, I could have a crush on the way she looked, but that wasn't it anymore. I knew the quiet girl, the funny girl, the talented girl. The girl who had protected me, who had looked to me to protect her, too. The Brooke who had made me Jessie, instead of Mouse, and how could I do anything but love her after that? She'd rewritten me. Remade me.

I set the guitar down for our last song, 'Thunder Road'. This was Brooke, all Brooke, and I just provided harmony. Her sexy, soft, deeper voice worked perfectly for this, and I felt us connect across the stage: my voice and hers.

It was a cliché to say I was startled by the applause at the end of our set, but for a moment I'd totally forgotten we were on stage. Everyone else had stopped mattering.

Brooke came and wrapped me up in a tight hug, too tight, and then she dipped into a little bow for the crowd, and I dropped a curtsey, appreciating the few laughs that drew from my invisible audience.

And then it was over.

I couldn't admit to Brooke that it wasn't as bad as I'd been expecting, because she'd never let me forget that if I did. And if I was being honest with myself, I'd almost enjoyed it. Being on stage with her, feeling that connection, the crowd's reaction to how well our voices blended together, all created a heady mix that I could easily get addicted to. I held her hand tightly as we stepped down off the stage and went back to our seats, accepting congratulations from the other performers.

'You guys were great,' the woman next to me said.

'Thanks,' I replied.

The next band starting up saved me from having to say any more.

I sent the woman a polite smile and turned away, back to the stage, as a guy with a beard and a guitar checked his mic.

It took me half a second into his song to realize that this was the guy Liam had told us about – the one who always performed 'Graceland'. He was good. His voice had that kind of husky tone that was super popular, and he was attractive, too.

Under the table, Brooke put her hand on my thigh. Even though I thought the heat from her palm would burn me, I didn't squirm, and she left it there for the rest of the night.

We didn't win.

That was okay.

From what Liam had told us, I wasn't expecting to, and there were some people playing who were clearly open mic night regulars and objectively better than us. It didn't really matter. Brooke had dragged me into it because of the prize money, and I'd agreed to it because, sure, five hundred bucks would have nicely topped up our funds. But I'd taken more away from the night than the prize money.

When we stepped onto the street, it seemed to have its own atmosphere and buzz, even though it was after midnight on a weeknight. People spilled out of the bars to smoke, and I could hear music from multiple venues.

'You did it,' Brooke said, slinging an arm around my shoulders.

'And I didn't puke!'

She laughed. 'I knew you wouldn't. You were pretty amazing up there, Jessie.'

'You were too.'

I leaned into her side and she squeezed my shoulder, and for the first time since leaving Seattle, I let myself breathe.

17

Dangerous – Michael Jackson

The bathroom was so full of steam I couldn't see myself in the mirror, and when I wiped off a neat square with the edge of my towel, it misted over again quickly. It didn't matter. I could put my pajamas on and brush my teeth without seeing my face.

I was still riding the stomach-clenching high from performing, even though a couple of hours had passed. It didn't really seem possible, or even plausible that I'd actually done it. For years, I'd hidden at the back of our school choir so no one could see me on the stage, and I'd sung for a bar full of people? Mouse could never.

When I went back into the bedroom, Brooke had switched on the TV and was sitting on the couch watching Fox News. Which wasn't like her.

'Sorry, the bathroom's all foggy,' I said, rubbing my hair with a clean towel. 'Give it five minutes and it should clear up.'

Brooke didn't say anything.

'Brooke?'

She was still wearing her black jeans and my top, staring at the TV, gripping the remote so hard her knuckles had turned white. A muscle was twitching in her jaw.

'Brooke?' I asked again, louder.

She turned up the volume on the TV.

'Police in Seattle, Washington, have today confirmed they believe there to be a connection between missing schoolgirl Jessie Swift and the murder of Mitchell Covier in the Greenwood area of the city almost two weeks ago. Swift, who is seventeen, hasn't been seen since the day Covier's body was discovered, and police are concerned for her welfare. Detective O'Sullivan spoke to reporters earlier.'

'We have significant evidence to suggest that Jessie is alive and traveling across the country with person or persons currently unknown. Her mother is distraught and desperate for Jessie to be returned safely. Anyone with any information about Jessie or her whereabouts can contact their local police department.'

'Was Jessie kidnapped?'

'No comment.'

'Is Jessie being treated as a suspect in the murder of Mitchell Covier?'

'No comment.'

I reached over and took the remote out of Brooke's hand, and clicked off the TV.

The silence that enveloped the room was somehow worse.

'What,' she said, 'the actual fuck, Jessie?'

I sat down on the bed so I could face her. My hands were suddenly ice-cold, and I felt sick to my stomach. I couldn't hide this from her anymore. I couldn't protect her anymore, either.

'You said.' My voice came out quieter than I wanted. Mouse-like. 'You said you wouldn't ask me, and I wouldn't ask you.'

'I didn't realize you had killed someone when we made that deal!' she shrieked.

I held my hands out, hoping to calm her down before things escalated.

'I didn't kill anyone. I didn't kill him, Brooke. I swear to God.'

She collapsed back against the ugly orange couch, and it took me a moment to notice that her hands were trembling. She was scared.

Of me.

'This is ridiculous,' she said, shaking her head. 'You're running from the cops? You've been running from them this whole time?'

'What else was I supposed to do?'

'Literally anything else?' she said incredulously. She shook her head. 'I can't believe you kept this from me.'

'I had to,' I said, my voice cracking. 'I couldn't tell you or you would've dumped me in the middle of nowhere.'

'I would never have done that to you.'

'I didn't know that at the time!'

Everything was starting to crumble, and I had no idea what to do next. I didn't know how to fix things with

Brooke, how to apologize, how to keep running when it was clear the cops were hot on our trail. I didn't know how to keep going forward, and I knew, for absolutely certain, that I couldn't go back.

'I didn't kill him,' I said again, more forcefully this time.

'But someone killed him?'

I nodded. 'Someone did, yeah.'

Her big, brown eyes grew hard, and I hated that I was the one who had put that expression in them. 'How do you know that?'

The spiky fingers of fear clawed at my throat, and I shook my head, not knowing what would come out if I opened my mouth.

'For fuck's sake, Mouse.'

'Don't call me that,' I snapped.

Brooke flinched.

I pressed the heels of my hands over my closed eyes and dropped my elbows to rest on my knees.

'What the hell happened, Jessie?' she asked, trying again, and I wanted so badly not to break. I'd been doing so well, keeping it all pressed down, locked up tight so I didn't have to think about it.

'Jessie?' she asked again, and the fear in her voice pried open the box inside me I'd been keeping so carefully closed.

Choir rehearsal had been canceled.

I'd only joined the choir because it kept me out of the house until late on a Monday, and I did anything I could to be out of the house on Mondays, Thursdays and Fridays when my mom worked until eleven, or later.

At the start of the school year, I had looked over the extracurricular activities that were being offered and signed up to whatever sounded the least painful, and choir had seemed like a good option. I could sing with a group – I'd been doing that at church since I was little.

But today choir rehearsal was canceled, and it was Monday, and I didn't want to go home.

I stared at the hastily scrawled note on the choir room door, then turned and went back up the stairs that led to the main lobby of St. Catherine's.

I delayed going home by studying in the library until I got kicked out. The city bus took forever to get back to my neighborhood, now that all the school buses had stopped running. I used to wear headphones and listen to music on the journey, but I'd stopped that a while back, and now just wore headphones so people wouldn't try to talk to me. I preferred being aware of my surroundings when I was alone. That way, no one could sneak up on me.

The bus dropped me off two streets away from home, and I shrugged off my school blazer as I walked. It was getting warmer in the afternoons now.

I headed around the side of the house to let myself in through the kitchen door. We never used the front door at this house. It was for company or the police. Even our Amazon Prime driver knew to drop off parcels on the back deck.

The door was open, just a crack, and I didn't notice at

first. My eyes skimmed over the mess, the disaster, as it took my brain a moment to catch up.

For those few seconds, I literally could not process what I was looking at.

And then it hit me.

Oh, God.

Oh, Jesus.

My breath wheezed out of my lungs, and I gripped the edge of the counter as my knees buckled.

There was blood splattered everywhere.

Over the floor.

Shards of bone scattered around, shiny white covered in sticky black.

Dripping down the walls.

Covering the ceiling.

On the kitchen cabinets.

Clinging to the pretty curtains I'd bought last year. Yellow fabric with daisies on it that matched the color of the cabinets.

The Creep was sprawled on the floor between the kitchen and the living room.

Well, parts of him were.

Other parts were . . . not where they should have been.

A high, pained noise escaped my throat.

The smell of him was thick in the air. Like rotting meat. Which was exactly what he was.

I gagged and stumbled outside, backing away from the sticky, slick gore coating the kitchen, and sank to my knees. The deck was warm from the afternoon sun, and the grooves of the wood pressed into the palms of my hands, leaving red tracks. Time slowed to a trickle, to a drip.

It dawned on me then, way too late, that maybe whoever had done this was still in the house. That maybe they were waiting for me, I was next, and all my senses went on high alert at the same time.

For long seconds, I breathed silently through my mouth, listening as hard as I could for any noise, any hint that there was someone hiding around the corner. But there was nothing. Just a car passing by on the road, a few hundred yards away.

The Creep was dead.

Really, really dead.

Really violently *dead.*

And though I knew the right thing to do would be to call the police – honestly? Fuck the police. The Creep didn't deserve the police.

A calm settled over me like a baptism of cool water. Like blessed relief.

The Creep was dead.

And I had to get out of here. Right now.

The kitchen door was still ajar, and I got to my feet, then nudged it open farther with the toe of my shoe. I edged along the hallway of our single-story house, past his mangled body, to my bedroom, relieved when nothing looked different from how I had left it that morning. My bed was still unmade, my clothes still piled on the floor, the makeup I used to cover up bruises and scars still scattered in front of the mirror.

My duffel bag was at the bottom of my closet, and it didn't take long for me to pack it. Underwear. Socks. A handful of random T-shirts. A couple pairs of jeans. Sneakers. Makeup bag.

What my mom and the Creep didn't know was that I'd been squirreling away money for years now. Since the first time the Creep had squeezed my arm too tight, kicked the back of my knee to make me stumble, backhanded me across the face. He'd left bruises all over my skin.

I stole money from him: ten bucks from his wallet, more if he came home drunk and didn't know how much he'd spent at the bar anyway. It all added up. A little here, a little there. Babysitting money. Working at a coffee shop over the holidays. I kept all the cash locked away in a box in the bottom drawer of my desk, hidden under piles and piles of schoolwork. I knew they would never think to look for it.

The cash was the first thing I put into the duffel bag, hidden inside a pencil case.

I dumped my school stuff out of my backpack to give me space for more underwear, toiletries and a hairbrush. Then I took off my school blazer and hung it in the closet, put on a denim jacket and grabbed my sunglasses.

I went through to the kitchen and pointedly didn't look out into the hall. I didn't need to see that again. I didn't want to look at him.

I could still smell it.

But I ignored that. I had to.

His wallet was on the kitchen counter, where he'd dumped it after walking in the back door, like he always did. I pulled out his credit card and a handful of cash, shoving both in my pocket and leaving the now empty wallet on the counter.

My mind had never been this empty of thoughts.

It was like I knew that if I stopped, if I contemplated what was happening for even one second, I would fall apart. I was going to completely lose my shit, and if I was honest with myself, I'd never done that before. I didn't know what losing my shit would look like, and it probably wasn't the best time to find out.

I took a deep breath, used my sunglasses to push my hair off my face, and walked out the back door.

'And then you picked me up.'

Brooke didn't say anything, just stared at me, wide-eyed.

'I picked you up?'

'Yeah. On Third Avenue.'

'Are you telling me,' she said slowly, 'that instead of calling the police and telling them about the dead body in your house, you got into my car and ran away?'

I thought I'd made that pretty clear.

'Holy shit, Jessie,' she said, putting her face in her hands.

'You said you didn't want to know,' I reminded her. 'We made a deal.'

'I didn't know what had happened!'

'Yeah, that's the point!' I surged to my feet and threw my hands in the air. 'You didn't want to know, and I didn't want to think about it.'

It took a moment, and then everything hit me like a

brick smashing into my face. I dashed to the still-steamy bathroom to throw my guts up.

My knees hit the tiled floor with a sickening crunch, and my fingers clenched around the toilet seat as my stomach heaved. I hadn't let myself go back to the house – back to the Creep – because I'd known this would happen. I'd known my body would betray me. And now the box was open, it was all coming out. After a moment, Brooke came into the bathroom and carefully gathered my hair to the nape of my neck so I didn't get puke on it.

She didn't say anything, just rubbed my back in slow circles as I purged all the poison out of me. When I was done, she got a washcloth and cleaned my face of puke and tears and snot, then handed me my toothbrush and got me to scrub the sour taste from my mouth.

'Come on,' she murmured.

I let her lead me back into the bedroom and tuck me under the covers. I laid there shivering as she shut off the lights and bolted the door and pulled the curtains tightly closed. Then she got into bed behind me and held me close.

I wanted to protect her from all the ugliness that was still swirling inside me. It was too late for that now, though. The cat was out of the bag, and it wasn't going back in. Whatever came next, I had to find a way of living with it.

I fell asleep with her fingers brushing gently through my hair.

It was early morning when I woke, but after the events of last night, I knew I wouldn't be able to fall asleep again.

After my breakdown last night, I'd slept deeply for a few hours with Brooke safely next to me, then I'd woken up and only managed to get little snatches of sleep since. I watched the sky lighten through a crack in the curtain while Brooke breathed slowly next to me, her eyelashes barely fluttering, so I knew she was fast asleep.

I didn't want to wake her, and I really couldn't lay still any longer, so I quietly slipped out of bed. I made a quick pit-stop in the bathroom to wash my face and tie up my hair, then found my jeans, pulled them on and took one of the key cards from the dresser.

I hesitated for a second, then grabbed Brooke's hoodie out of her duffel bag. She'd barely worn it since we'd gotten past Idaho – it had been too warm. It gave me a layer of protection, though, while I was outside. With the hood up, it would be difficult for anyone to see my face.

At the last moment, I paused to scrawl a note on the pad of hotel paper on the desk:

Getting coffee. Be back soon.

The last thing I wanted was for Brooke to think I'd run away.

Ha.

Run away *again*.

It didn't take me long to pick up our regular order from the Starbucks across the street, and when I let myself back into the room, Brooke was just stretching awake.

'Hey,' I said softly. 'I went to get us coffee.'

'Thanks,' she said, reaching to take the cup from me. 'How are you this morning?'

'Fine,' I said.

'Really?'

I forced myself to consider that. 'I'm worried about you.'

Brooke looked taken aback. 'Me? Why?'

'I feel like you think I'm lying. About what happened to the Creep. And maybe you're thinking about calling the cops and turning me in.'

'I don't think that, and I'm not going to call the cops on you.'

Brooke put her hand on the bed, palm up, and I hesitated before laying mine on top. Her fingers curled around it, holding me tight.

'What did he do to you, Jessie?'

I shook my head and took a deep breath. 'It wasn't rape. He wasn't touching me like that.'

I didn't know what to tell her. 'Rape' was a word I knew – it was a word I understood and could contextualize. But what the Creep had done?

Instead of words, I decided to show Brooke. I handed her my drink and she set it on the nightstand so I could get up on my knees and pull off her hoodie and my T-shirt.

'Here,' I said, pointing to the round burns on the inside of my biceps from where he'd put his cigarettes out on my arms. I stretched my hands out to her to show the tiny crisscrossing scars on my palms, my fingers, from being shoved to the floor dozens of times. I turned my hands over to show her the weird bump on the back of my knuckle from where he'd broken my finger, then wouldn't let me go to the hospital to get it fixed. I'd taped it up myself, following instructions online, with a homemade splint made out of popsicle sticks.

'Jessie,' Brooke said in a tiny voice.

I wasn't done.

I pulled my jeans off to show her the marks on my legs, the thick burn from a hot mug of coffee thrown over the top of my bare thigh, my mangled toe from where he'd dropped a skillet on it.

'And this is just what stuck,' I said.

Too many of the marks, the burns, the cuts had healed into nothing. The daily whacks across the back of my head, the punches, the slaps. The words.

Fucking pathetic
Weird bitch
Ugly little rat
Dumb fucking piece of shit
Stupid waste of space
No one's ever gonna want to fuck you
Not a single person likes you
Not even your own fucking mother

'How did no one know?' Brooke asked, clearly shaken up.

I shrugged. 'I guess no one looked.'

'Oh, Jessie,' she sighed, her eyes full of pity, tears ready to spill.

It occurred to me then that I was sitting next to her in pretty much just my underwear, so I scrabbled for my clothes, suddenly self-conscious.

'What was I supposed to say?' I demanded as I zipped up my jeans. 'My mom's boyfriend is mean to me?'

I yanked my shirt back on, working myself up. 'My mom's boyfriend calls me names? It sounds pathetic, Brooke. Everyone would've just thought I was being a whiny kid. No one would've listened to me. No one ever listened to me,' I finished, not sure if I was frustrated or angry or upset.

It wasn't like the Creep went from nothing to breaking my finger overnight. He was charming at first, trying to win me over when he started dating my mom. I knew him from church, but most of the activities were segregated by gender, so I'd never really interacted with him much.

My mom thought he'd hung the goddamn moon.

I made an effort in the early days, mostly for my mom, because she always seemed to end up dating losers, and the Creep was nice to her. He bought her flowers and took her out to nice restaurants, and soon she was dizzy with love.

But once my mom fell for him, he made it clear to me behind her back that he didn't want me around. I was a blot on their otherwise perfect relationship, something he needed to get rid of.

It started with words.

Stay out of the way
No one wants you around
Make some fucking friends, you loser

And then it escalated over the next couple of months to pinches, shoves, kicks, a backhand across my face when I didn't move fast enough for his liking. The first time I was too stunned to say anything back to him, or to my mom, certain that she wouldn't believe her perfect boyfriend could do something like that. The second time he really hurt me, and after that, I was terrified of him.

It only got worse from there.

'So you never told anyone?' Brooke asked, shocked.

It took me a second to gather my vicious, violent rage and contain it.

'I was too scared to tell my mom, but I did tell the girls' youth pastor at our church. She said . . .'

Brooke let me have a moment, then squeezed my hand. 'What?'

'She said it was a serious allegation. And that I should pray about it. And that I needed to think very carefully about what I wanted to happen next, because once I said something officially, I couldn't take it back.'

'Are you fucking kidding me?'

'No,' I said. I extracted my fingers from Brooke's so I could reach for my coffee. I wasn't thirsty, I was furious, and I needed something to do with my hands.

'I told her I wanted to kill him. I wanted him to disappear, to die, to be out of my life forever. I told her, Brooke, that I wanted him dead, and now he's dead.'

I watched as the realization dawned in her eyes.

'Oh, shit.'

'Yeah,' I said. 'Exactly. You see why I had to get out of there?'

'*Fuck*.' She sighed heavily. Then she took hold of my hand again and brushed a kiss across my knuckles. 'You know, I didn't sleep so well last night.'

'I'm sorry.'

'Don't be. I had some good thinking time.'

'What were you thinking about?' I asked cautiously.

'I thought that if he was hurting you, Jessie, then he could've been hurting others as well.'

That felt like a punch to the stomach. I hadn't even thought about that. I hadn't been able to think beyond myself, what was happening to me, and how I could escape.

'Oh, God.' I pulled my knees up and leaned forward to rest my head on them.

'Please don't puke again,' Brooke said with a little laugh that I knew was an attempt to lighten the mood. She reached up to rub gently between my shoulders.

'I won't.' I didn't feel sick, I felt *cold*. 'That bastard was hurting someone else.'

'Maybe,' Brooke said. 'I don't know. It's a possibility. If he was hurting another kid, maybe that kid told someone, and that's who killed him.'

It all clicked together in my head, suddenly making sense.

'Yeah. I could see that.'

'Was he ever, like, left alone with kids from your youth group?'

'All the time.' I turned my head to rest my cheek on my knees and look at her.

'I'm glad someone else killed him,' she said. 'Before I could get my hands on him.'

18

Nevermind – Nirvana

While Brooke was in the shower, I forced myself to do what had become normal – packing up our stuff, moving some cash into our wallets for the day and hiding the rest of it among our bags, checking on what snacks we had left.

I wanted to still be riding the high of the open mic night and being here in Nashville, but the news story had stolen my excitement and filled that space with uneasy foreboding.

'All good?' Brooke asked when she came out of the bathroom. She walked over to me and tucked my hair behind my ear.

I was almost certain that she believed I hadn't killed the Creep, but I also couldn't blame her if she still had some lingering doubts.

'As long as I have you,' I replied.

She smiled and leaned in to kiss my cheek. 'Well, you do have me.'

That felt impossible, and huge, and incredibly precious.

'I really like you, you know,' I blurted, and I felt Brooke's lips stretch into a smile against my skin.

'I like you too,' she said softly.

I opened my eyes and looked at her and my whole body went hot. Brooke was wrapped in just a towel. It wouldn't take much, not much at all, for us to stumble back into bed.

She caught the look in my eyes and hers went dark too.

Then she laughed, a little embarrassed, and stepped back. 'I'll go get dressed,' she murmured.

'Okay,' I croaked.

So she wasn't ready for that. Whatever *that* was. It wasn't out of the question, though. That much was clear.

I was fine with giving her time. To be honest, I needed some myself. I wasn't sure I was ready to take this any farther. Not yet, anyway. But maybe soon.

To distract myself, I reached for the TV remote and flicked it on out of habit, not thinking about what could be waiting for me.

It hit me, like a punch to the solar plexus, when a picture of me stared out from the screen. It wasn't particularly recent – two, maybe three years old, when I'd had bangs and my long hair had covered my face. I looked young. The picture was one my mom had taken the summer before ninth grade, one Saturday when we'd taken a rare trip to the beach.

I wasn't that girl anymore. That was Mouse.

The two hosts were talking about her, not me. I started breathing a little faster, right on the precipice of panic.

'Police have come under fire for not issuing an AMBER Alert for Jessie Swift.'

The screen was still showing my picture, disembodied voices speaking over the top.

'There are a few reasons why that wasn't appropriate in this case. Jessie is seventeen, and there was nothing to suggest she'd been forced to leave the city. The AMBER Alert system is an incredibly valuable tool to inform the public about missing children, but there are specific circumstances for its use.'

The image changed, to one of me and my mom. She had her arm around my shoulder and was beaming at the camera. She looked beautiful, as always, and I looked up at her with a slightly awestruck expression.

That photo had been taken the summer before the Creep, when, despite our rocky relationship, I'd still thought my mom would protect me from anything.

'Why has the information about Jessie been so slow to be released?'

'As her mother's boyfriend was murdered, the initial investigation concentrated on whether Jessie was in any danger, either to herself or someone else, and establishing how she left Seattle.'

'I can't listen to this,' I whispered, turning the TV off again as Brooke walked back into the room. 'Please can we get out of here?'

'Yeah,' she said. 'Of course we can. Just give me ten minutes.'

'Do you think I need, like, a disguise?' I asked, feeling

off-kilter from the news report. Seeing myself on TV was bizarre and disorienting and really, really scary.

'Do you honestly think you still look like the girl in those photos?' she asked, gesturing at the blank screen.

'I don't know.'

Brooke smiled and reached over to ruffle my new streaky blonde hair. 'You look nothing like the girl they're after,' she said. 'But we still have those glasses, from Denver, if you want them.'

'Maybe,' I replied, still unsure.

'Jessie, it's not just the way you dress now, or your hair. They're looking for a shy girl in a baggy T-shirt, and that's not you. Not anymore.'

'I guess.'

'Trust me,' Brooke said confidently, straightening up. 'No one at St. Catherine's would recognize you right now. The police have no chance.'

We checked out of the hotel, packed up the Mustang, and then fell into step with each other as we headed out into the city to explore it one more time before the next leg of our road trip.

'I've been thinking,' Brooke said. Then rushed to add, 'But if you don't want to talk about it, that's totally fine . . .'

'Go on,' I said, wondering what she had to say.

'About your mom.'

I froze, and I could tell Brooke had noticed. 'What do you want to know?'

She brushed her hand down my arm. 'Did she know? About the Creep?'

'No. I don't think so.'

I didn't know how much I could tell Brooke. How she would react.

She took my hand and squeezed it, flooding me with calmness, and in that moment I realized:

Everything.

I could tell her everything.

'Me and my mom aren't that close,' I said. 'She was only sixteen when she had me. Just turned sixteen.'

'Wow, that's really young,' Brooke said sympathetically. 'It must have been hard for her.'

Sixteen and pregnant. It was such a cliché now that I barely gave it much thought, but back when she was a teenager, it was a big deal. She made sure I knew that. My mom thought she was doing the right thing by having me, but the decision hadn't worked out so well for her in the long run. I was pretty sure she resented me a lot of the time, and I was certain she ended up with guys like the Creep because they made her feel like she could relive the youth she'd lost while busy being a single mom.

I didn't know much about my grandparents – my mom's parents – other than that they had encouraged her to give me up for adoption. My mom had left Oregon when I was still a toddler, and I could just about remember going to see my grandparents when I was really little, back before she cut them out for good.

On top of all that, I wasn't like her *at all*. My mom was

bright and sociable, and she loved talking to people – the original extrovert. She was like Brooke in a lot of ways. Pretty and vibrant. The sort of person other people were attracted to because of their looks and personality. I was none of those things. Instead of getting a kid she could take to dance class and sing karaoke with in the kitchen while making dinner, she'd gotten a quiet, mousey child who cried at fireworks because the noise was scary, and who hid behind her mother's legs at the store when someone tried to make conversation. She got frustrated with me when I became shy and introverted, which only made the shyness and introversion worse.

'I think she struggled,' I said. 'We went to church a lot, especially after she stopped all contact with my grandparents. The church has always been like a surrogate family to her.'

'And to you?' Brooke asked.

'I guess.' I didn't know what it was like to have a big, extended family like Brooke's, so I didn't know how different it was to having a church family. 'As soon as we moved to Seattle, my mom found the church we're with now, and that's where she met him.'

'The Creep?' Brooke asked, and I nodded. Her eyes widened. 'Do you think *she* did it? To him?'

I shook my head. 'I don't think she's capable of something like that.'

'Really? You're her kid. And he's the scumbag boyfriend who abused you. I think any mother would do something like that to protect her child if she found out that had been happening.'

'Maybe.' I shook my head. 'But either way, she didn't know what was going on.'

'I'm so sorry, Jessie. This is all so wrong. You should never have ...' Brooke trailed off, lost for words, and I tilted my head so I could kiss her bare shoulder.

'It's okay. Honestly. I feel so much better now that I'm out of there.'

We retraced our steps to the bar from last night, then kept walking with no obvious destination. I felt more relaxed here than I had anywhere else on this trip, except maybe the cabin in Illinois.

'Is there anywhere specific you want to go?' Brooke asked.

I wanted to go to the Country Music Hall of Fame, and the Grand Ole Opry, and explore Music Row, and go to the Johnny Cash Museum and maybe see the replica of the Parthenon. I wanted to stay in Nashville for weeks, not hours, but that wasn't on the cards. The joy of being here, when it had been merely a dream of mine for so long, had been completely destroyed by the news reports. It sucked.

'Let's just walk for a while,' I suggested, hoping to rediscover some magic along the way.

We walked around the city for an hour, stopping to pick up iced coffees but taking them to go. I paused outside the Country Music Hall of Fame and looked up at the giant building with a sour feeling in my stomach that I tried to chase away with coffee.

'We can go in,' Brooke insisted.

I shook my head. 'It's, like, thirty bucks each. It's too expensive.'

'We'll make it work. This is important to you.'

I took her hand and tugged her away. 'I'll go another time. We need food and gas money and motel rooms more than I need to look at Dolly Parton's sparkly stilettos.'

'I'll bring you back here one day,' Brooke said, finally following me. 'I promise.'

'That works for me,' I said with a smile.

She smiled back, and my whole body lit up in response.

'Have you always been into girls?' she asked, seemingly out of nowhere.

She threw her arm around my shoulders and I smiled as I leaned into her side. We'd been this close for a couple of days now, but I still reveled in it, the feeling of her bare arm against mine, the feeling that she'd chosen me.

'I guess,' I said.

'Will you tell me when you figured it out?'

'Oh, wow, you really are curious,' I replied.

'Sue me,' she said cheerfully. 'I don't know anything about this shit. I need guidance.'

'I don't know when I started explicitly labeling it as being attracted to girls,' I replied as we walked up the block on the shady side of the street. 'But I was always super interested in girls, right from middle school. I wanted to be their friend, I wanted to know everything about them. Back then I didn't know what those feelings were, though.'

'Okay, go on,' Brooke said encouragingly.

'It actually took an embarrassingly long time for me to realize that what I was feeling was *romantic*. I used to think I just had these awkward, weird obsessions with girls.'

'When did you *know*, though?' Brooke pressed.

'When I started high school, maybe?'

'Oh.' She sounded disappointed.

'What?' I said, gently prodding her in the side.

'I just feel stupid. I didn't know until, you know ... recently.'

'Brooke, some people don't figure it out until they're, like, thirty. It's not a race.'

'Do you like boys too?' she asked.

'I don't think so.'

Brooke went quiet. 'Does it matter if I do?'

I stopped walking and pulled her into the shade of one of the buildings lining the street. This wasn't an ideal conversation to be having on the sidewalk in freaking Nashville, but we were having it.

'It doesn't matter,' I said gently, squeezing her hand until she looked at me. 'Brooke. You don't have to put a label on it. You don't have to figure it all out right now, or by next week, or even next year. If you like me and I like you –'

'I do,' she said, interrupting me.

'Thanks.' I couldn't help but laugh. 'I like you too. And so that's the most important thing. Okay?'

Brooke gave me a small smile. 'Yeah, okay.'

I wanted to kiss her, but we were in the South, and though Nashville was a big city, and no one had seemed to care about us holding hands last night, I didn't feel like I wanted to be too obvious in the daytime, just in case. Plus, two girls kissing on the street would draw attention to us, and that was definitely something I was trying to avoid.

'It's gonna take three, maybe four hours to drive down to Atlanta,' Brooke said, a hint of regret in her voice. I hadn't made a secret of how much I loved it here. 'But we can stay here a little longer, if you want to. I don't mind getting in late.'

'Let's take a long route back to the hotel and then set off?'

Brooke nodded. 'That works. We can pick up some lunch, too, eat it in the car. That's better than stopping at a drive-thru.'

'I like that plan.'

On the way back to the hotel, we found a place to pick up sandwiches and bags of chips – food that was easy to eat while driving – and I tried to ease the little knot of longing in my chest. I really would have liked to stay here for an extra couple of days, but it was more important to keep moving, especially now my face was being flashed up on the TV.

'I'll take the next leg,' I said as we walked up to the Mustang.

'I'm better now,' she replied.

'Brooke.' I planted my hands on my hips like I'd seen her do.

'Honestly, Jessie. If I need you to take over, I'll let you know. I promise.'

I gave her a long, considering look.

'I just want to be in the driver's seat of my car again,' she said, pleading now, and I gave in.

'Fine, but let me know if you need a break.'

We took the top down and I set everything up in the passenger seat how I liked it, so I had easy access to my backpack, the cassettes and snacks. Brooke had messed up my unofficial glove box filing system, so I worked to get all the cassettes back in order while she drove out of the city.

I let her drive for a couple of hours while we sang along to the stereo, chasing the afternoon that was running away with us. I missed Nashville already, but this was good too: being back in the car, on the road, somewhere no one would be able to recognize me.

'I need to stop for a minute,' Brooke murmured when the song ended. We'd made our way through half of yesterday's album and all of today's already.

'Are you okay?'

'I'm fine.' She signaled and pulled over to the side of the road and into the scrubby grass.

'I can drive if you need me to,' I said as she tipped her face up to the sun.

'I think it's the heat,' she explained, turning her head to look at me. 'I just want to rest for a few minutes without the sun, like, directly on the top of my head.'

'I'll put the top up.'

I was getting better at making decisions. And learning that doing something was most often better than doing nothing.

Brooke tipped her seat back and I worked to put the roof up on the Mustang. We'd done this so many times now I was pretty sure I could do it in my sleep. When I let myself back into the passenger seat, Brooke had her eyes closed and her sunglasses down.

'I'm worried about you,' I said softly, reaching over to take her hand.

This was the first long journey Brooke had made since she'd driven to Kansas City, and I wondered if she had actually fully recovered from everything that had happened. I had a suspicion she hadn't, but I didn't know how to bring it up without pissing her off. She wanted to feel in control, and, God knew, I understood that, so I wasn't about to take that control away from her by suggesting she clearly wasn't okay at all.

'Let me nap for a couple minutes?' she asked. 'If I still feel crummy after that, you can drive.'

'Okay.' I reached up to smooth her hair back from her face and she smiled at me.

The way she'd angled the car meant we were under the shade of some trees. Within a few minutes, Brooke's breathing evened out. I could have taken a nap, too. Instead, I vowed to stay awake and keep an eye on her.

19

There Is Nothing Left to Lose – Foo Fighters

While Brooke napped, I read my book. I only had a couple of chapters left, then I was out of paperbacks. I was sure we could find somewhere in Atlanta for me to pick up a few more – there were bound to be more thrift stores in the city.

It would be an eight-hour drive from Atlanta to Orlando tomorrow, which was longer than we'd driven in one day since leaving Seattle, but I had a feeling that once we were on that last leg of the trip, neither of us would want to stop. At least Brooke had gotten over her refusal to let me drive the Mustang now, so we could take it in turns. Two hours each, then swap. That would give us plenty of opportunities to use rest stops, get something to eat and put gas in the car.

When I finished the book, I pulled my phone out of the glove box and turned it on. It took a minute for it to connect to shaky 3G, but I didn't need a huge amount of bandwidth to check out Orlando. Before I'd started researching the city, I had no idea there were so many corporate conventions held there. Being from the Northwest, I'd always assumed Orlando was a theme park city and nothing more. It made sense, though – they had an international airport and plenty of huge hotels to put people in.

I almost jumped out of my skin when someone knocked lightly on the windshield.

My heart didn't slow down at all when a sheriff's deputy gave me a jaunty wave.

'Brooke,' I murmured, shaking her shoulder.

She startled awake.

'Sorry,' he said, leaning down to the open window. 'Just a welfare check. I was driving past and noticed you had pulled over.'

He seemed friendly enough, but I didn't trust him. I *couldn't* trust him, especially as there was the possibility that he could recognize me at any second. Would the cops be expecting to find me in the middle of nowhere in Georgia, though? If there was ever a time to play it cool, it was now.

He was handsome, with a Southern accent that was starting to sound familiar. His sandy hair was about the same color as the uniform he was wearing, complete with shiny black shoes and aviator sunglasses tucked into the open collar of his shirt.

I scrambled to get out of the car.

'Sorry,' I said as he walked around. 'Didn't mean to worry you.'

'That's okay.' He hooked his thumbs into the pockets of his pants and rocked back on his heels. 'Where are you headed?'

'Atlanta,' I said with a smile that I hoped looked real. 'My friend was feeling a little tired, so we pulled over.'

'This isn't the safest place to stop. There's a gas station with a truck stop about five miles down the road.'

'Okay. We'll head that way.' I silently prayed that would be it. That he would let us go.

'Do you guys have any identification on you?'

My stomach sank. This was it. He was going to call us in.

'I'm really sorry, I lost my driver's license in Nashville,' I said. I tried another smile, like Brooke would, flirting a little to get him on our side. 'I'll pick up a new one next week.'

'How about you?' he asked as Brooke stepped out of the driver's side of the car.

'Sure,' she said easily, taking her wallet out of the back pocket of her jeans. She flicked through her cards and pulled out Meredith's fake ID.

'Meredith Summer,' he said. 'You're a long way from Denver, Ms Summer.'

'I dropped out of college,' Brooke lied with an easy grin.

He handed the fake ID back, then nodded to me. 'And what's your name?'

'Jenna Roberts,' I said, praying that he didn't ask for us to go to the station with him to confirm our identities.

'Okay, Ms Roberts. Why don't I give you both an escort down to the rest stop?'

I couldn't get a read on him to decide if he was trying to follow us because he didn't trust us, or if he was one of those over-eager, concerned types.

I glanced at Brooke.

Brooke turned to the deputy. 'We'll probably head straight on into Atlanta. I feel much better now.'

'No problem, ma'am. Drive safe.'

We made a performance of getting into the car and putting our seatbelts on before heading back onto the road.

The deputy lifted his hand in a wave as we pulled away.

'Shit,' Brooke murmured. 'Shit, shit, shit.' She was drumming her fingers on the steering wheel in a nervous tattoo. 'He's going to run my license plate.'

'You think?'

'Yeah.' Brooke looked back over her shoulder, then glanced ahead at the road. 'I'm going to get off at the next exit. We should take a different route into the city. Maybe bypass Atlanta altogether. Go to Athens, or Birmingham. One or the other, it doesn't matter.'

I hadn't seen Brooke this flustered since . . . ever. But she was right. We had almost got caught, and now it felt like there was a massive spotlight on us.

'I think we need to get out of this car,' I said, still checking the rearview mirror every few seconds. 'It's too recognizable.'

'No,' Brooke said sharply.

'I know it's your car, and you love it, but –'

'No,' she said, cutting me off. 'I'm not selling the car. I can't, Jessie.'

There was something in her voice, the *I can't*, that reminded me that this was more than a car to Brooke. It was her freedom. I didn't know how to balance that against the very real fear that had gripped me.

'Maybe we should drive it to the airport and leave it in a long-term lot, then?' I suggested.

'Someone will steal it,' she said, her voice rising in panic. 'And we don't have enough money to pay to park it and hire another car. We're just going to have to figure out how to fly under the radar.'

'Okay,' I said, taking a breath and trying to think rationally. 'Okay. We'll keep going to Atlanta – it's a big city, right? We can find a hotel with an underground parking lot. Let's get it out of view, at least.'

I glanced in the rearview mirror again, then at Brooke. She was chewing the edge of her thumbnail.

'That could work,' she said. 'As long as they don't follow us into the city.'

'You can drive faster,' I said.

'I can always drive faster,' she replied with a little smile, and I tried to force myself to relax.

Just outside Atlanta we stopped for gas, this time at a rest stop that looked busy. That was better. It was easier to blend in.

'You want anything?' I asked, heading inside to pay.

Brooke shook her head. 'I'm good.'

When I came back outside, she was sitting in the passenger seat. I raised an eyebrow at her.

'You drive,' she said. 'I'm too anxious.'

'Okay. I can do that.'

We hit traffic soon enough, but sitting and waiting for lights to change gave us plenty of time to plan out our next move. In a way, Atlanta was a great place to hide. Big cities had plenty of neighborhoods we could move between, and we blended in with the population, just two more teenage girls in a city full of them. I headed for the downtown area, then looped around the block when Brooke spotted a hotel that advertised its underground parking lot on the sign outside.

She winced as I navigated the turn down a long concrete ramp.

'Don't scrape the car, Jessie.'

She was clearly wound tight. Well, so was I.

'You wanna drive it in?' I snapped back.

Brooke leaned over, grabbed my chin to turn my head, and kissed me hard. 'No. Just don't scrape the paintwork, that's all.'

'You are literally the most difficult woman in the entire world,' I muttered as the barrier rose for us.

'I'm hungry,' she said, craning her neck to look around the lot. The fluorescent lights were harsh down here. 'Where are we going to eat tonight?'

'You're asking me that now?' I demanded. 'While I'm trying to concentrate on getting your precious car into this damn garage?'

Brooke snorted with laughter and ejected the cassette from the stereo to put it back in the case. I tried not to notice that she'd brought the bullet cassette right to the front, so it was easily accessible.

I found a space on the first level underground, which was good because I didn't have to navigate the tight ramps going down, and it also meant we could make a quick escape if we needed to. We put the top back up on the car, grabbed our bags from the trunk, and as we rode the elevator up to the lobby, Brooke put her arm around my waist.

'Take your sunglasses off – you're not a Kardashian,' I murmured.

'Absolutely not.'

She looked hot, so I couldn't argue with her.

The lobby was swarming with people, and we had to wait twenty minutes to check in, which was only annoying because Brooke was fidgety. I could tell she wanted something to eat – she got cranky when she was hungry.

Brooke let me check in this time, and I spun the same story we used at every stop about wallets being stolen and needing to pay in cash. No one working these check-in desks ever seemed to care, other than trying to sign us up to their mailing list or loyalty rewards scheme or whatever. I rattled off a fake email address and smiled through the conversation.

We dumped our bags in the hotel room, and I took a second to brush my hair since it had gotten windswept on the journey down here. When I got out of the bathroom, Brooke was checking over the gun. She noticed me leaning against the doorframe, watching her, and tightened her jaw defiantly before putting it in her backpack to bring with her.

'I'm not arguing with you,' I said lightly.

'Good,' she said.

We headed out to find something for Brooke to eat before her blood sugar dipped any lower. A few blocks from the hotel, Brooke stopped in front of a Five Guys.

'This'll work,' she said.

We spent an hour hanging out, and for just a moment, I felt normal. It was a Thursday afternoon, after school, and I guessed we weren't too far from a high school since everyone here seemed to be around the same age as us. That meant we blended in, and I didn't feel the need to check over my shoulder every few minutes, wondering if someone was following us.

When Brooke wanted a milkshake, I made a point of going to buy one for her. I wasn't sure if this was a date – I'd never been on a date – but I wanted to do it anyway, even though I paid for it from the stack of cash we were sharing. I thought it meant something if I bought it, and the way she smiled at me when I carried it back to our booth made me think it meant something to her, too.

As soon as we walked back outside, a police car raced past us, its lights flashing and siren blaring, and I immediately went back on high alert. I almost wanted to berate myself for relaxing, but we needed to eat, damn it – we couldn't constantly be on the run.

Brooke seemed to sense my nerves and ran her hand down my arm in a sweetly reassuring gesture.

'How are you doing?' I asked as we walked back to the hotel.

Brooke shook her head. 'I don't know. I feel like I'm questioning everything, you know?'

'I know,' I murmured.

'That cop,' she said. 'He was really looking at Meredith's ID. I know we look similar, but we're not freaking twins.'

'He didn't question us, though. He let us go.'

'Yeah. That was good. I just have a bad feeling.'

'About him in particular?' I asked.

'Maybe. I'm trying to put it all together.'

We walked in silence for the next block.

'What if,' Brooke said as we were waiting for the lights to change, 'Meredith told Jules that you're with me.' She nudged my arm to get my attention and we crossed the street together. 'And that I have her ID. Then Jules told the police. Or she told my parents, who called the police.'

'Would she do that?'

'If she saw the same news reports we've seen, then yeah. Maybe.'

'Shit,' I muttered.

'So then if the cops know we're together, and they know I've got Meredith's ID, and that cop runs my license plate . . .'

'It won't take them long to figure it out,' I finished for her.

'We need to get out of here as soon as we can,' Brooke said, glancing over her shoulder. 'First thing in the morning.'

'I'm okay with that.'

'And maybe we skip Orlando altogether.'

That didn't feel right to me. We'd worked so hard to get there – it felt important that we at least saw the city.

'You didn't tell Julianne or Meredith that's where we're headed, though,' I said. 'No one knows where we're going.'

'I know. I really just want to shake things up a little, you know?'

I could hear the anxiety lacing her words, and decided we could have this conversation again in the morning, when she'd calmed down.

Something felt wrong as we turned the corner for the hotel and I noticed two police cars parked outside, their lights flashing.

Brooke looked at me and frowned.

'We need to take a detour,' I said.

Brooke's eyes went wide, frantic. 'How did they find us so fast?'

We got closer to the front door of the hotel, and it became even more obvious that something was going on – the police hadn't set up a barrier, but in the lobby there was definitely more than two police cars' worth of uniformed officers.

'I don't like this, Brooke,' I said. 'I don't like it at all.'

Her eyes went hard, and she shook her head. 'This is really not good,' she said.

'Listen, I know we might be paranoid right now, but –'

'No, you're right.' She grabbed my arm, and we moved toward the street entrance of the parking garage. Our footsteps echoed on the cool cement, putting me more on edge. 'We should go check the car.'

I felt Brooke tense as we walked up to the Mustang.

'That's not –' she started, and a rage settled over her.

'What?'

'Someone messed with the roof,' she said, stalking over to it. 'It's been put back wrong. They've been in my car.'

'Let's go,' I said immediately. 'Brooke. We need to go.'

'I know,' she said, glancing at me, and I could see my panic reflected in her eyes.

I jogged over to the passenger door and let myself in. By the time I was done buckling my seatbelt, Brooke was pulling out of the space.

'We left our bags in the room,' she said suddenly as she pulled out into downtown traffic. 'With all the cash in them.'

'We can find a public lot and park the car, then come back for the bags later when the police have left,' I said. My heart was hammering in a way it hadn't since St. Louis. I felt the tension crackling between us, nervous energy being shared back and forth.

'Shit, Jessie,' Brooke said, slamming her hands down on the steering wheel. 'We're so fucking close.'

'I know, Brooke,' I said. 'I know.'

We were half a block away from the hotel when the sirens started.

20

Ready to Die – The Notorious B.I.G.

Brooke drove too fast, weaving through traffic, erratic enough that I was sure someone would have called the cops even if there weren't already two police cars on our tail.

She banked quickly as she turned to go down a side street, the whole car leaning into the bend.

'Fuck!' Brooke exclaimed.

A car was blocking our exit, its hazard lights blinking pathetically. A few seconds later, the police blocked the street behind us. With high brick walls on either side of us, there was nowhere to go.

We were trapped.

'Oh my God, Brooke,' I whimpered.

She dropped her head, and I watched as her hands, still gripping the steering wheel, went white-knuckled. When she looked up at me, she had a haunted look in her eyes and a determined tightness to her jaw.

'Do you trust me?' she demanded.

'Yes, of course.'

'I need you to play along. There's no time to explain, but just go along with what I'm saying, okay?'

'Yeah.' I nodded. 'Yes. I can do that.'

'Okay. Get out and come around to this side of the car. Slowly. Please.' Her voice broke on the 'please'.

I didn't know what Brooke was planning, but she clearly had something in mind, and I trusted her – more than anyone, more than *myself*. I was shaking, and she noticed. She leaned in and kissed me hard, once, on the lips.

'Go!'

I nodded and unbuckled my seatbelt with trembling fingers. Brooke started reaching into the glove box and my confused brain tried to figure out what she needed a cassette tape for right now. I swung myself out of the car, slammed the door closed and forced myself to look at the people who had been chasing us since we left Seattle.

'Jessie Swift!'

'Hands up!'

I instinctively listened, scared – no, *terrified*. You can be sure I put my goddamn hands up.

'What's going on?' I called out, desperate to come across unaware.

I couldn't count the number of police officers at the other end of the street. There must have been at least three cars, their lights flashing out of sync with each other. I walked around the back of the Mustang, trying to make it look like I was walking toward them when I wasn't. I needed to get back to Brooke, and her plan. A small part of me still believed we'd get out of this, and I was clinging to that thought as hard as I could.

Both my knees and my bladder felt weak, and I was way past the point of *thinking* I was going to throw up – I could taste the acid stinging the back of my throat. But out of nowhere, a fierce rage settled over me. How *dare* the cops corner us now? After everything we'd done? After all we'd been through? They hadn't been there for me back in Seattle, they hadn't done anything when Brooke went missing, and now they wanted us? In a stinking alley in downtown Atlanta. Of all the fucking places.

The next chorus of *hands up* rang out as Brooke got out of the car and took two quick steps toward me. She wrapped an arm around my waist to bring me in tight.

A few police officers had dashed forward, their guns pointed straight at us, and my head started to swim. I felt so trapped, so crushed. The walls of the buildings on either side felt like they were pressing in, and the heat of the street seemed to crawl up my legs and glue me to the spot.

'It's gonna be all right,' Brooke murmured.

Get down, get down, get down.

'Brooke,' I said. I felt light-headed, black spots dancing at the edge of my vision.

'Do you trust me?' she asked again.

I nodded. I was starting to go numb. I couldn't feel my lips.

Brooke reached behind her and pulled the gun out of her back pocket, then in one swift move she shoved me in front of her to shield her body, wrapped one arm around my neck and pressed the barrel of the gun to my forehead.

I was glad of the arm around my neck because my knees gave out. Brooke held me up.

The noise in the street doubled and bounced off the walls – I couldn't hear what any of the cops were shouting even if I'd wanted to. Brooke probably couldn't either.

'Let us go,' she said, her voice cracking. Then again, louder. 'Let us go!'

Hands up, hands up, hands up.

'Let us go,' she repeated. 'Or I'll shoot her.'

Everything went eerily quiet. No one seemed to dare move, and time crept forward slowly, wispy and fuzzy, like we were in a dream.

My breath came in snatched gasps as I stared at the shocked police officers. Then tears filled my eyes, blurring their faces.

Brooke was playing a dangerous game now, banking on the police wanting us alive more than they wanted us in custody. I wasn't so sure that was the case. She still had the upper hand, though – they didn't know about the one and only cassette bullet. They didn't know the gun wasn't fully loaded and that she wouldn't start shooting them after she shot me.

I'd promised to trust her, and I did. I did.

But we'd run out of road, run out of options, and I couldn't go back. Not to Seattle. Not to Mouse. All I wanted was to be with Brooke, and I had no idea how she was going to get us out of this.

The noise ratcheted up again as police crept in. I dared

a glance over my shoulder and more cops had blocked the other end of the alley, too. We were surrounded on all sides.

'Don't move!' Brooke screamed. 'I'll shoot!'

Then, much quieter, so only I could hear, she whispered, 'No, no. God, no.'

I could feel how badly she was shaking as well, and as I stared down the barrels of a dozen police-issued revolvers, I realized the same thing as Brooke. She knew they weren't going to let us go. They weren't going to let her take me 'hostage'. They'd shoot us before they let us escape.

I tipped my head back and she was tall enough that the little movement meant I could kiss her one final time. Kiss her goodbye, in case this really was my last chance.

'Thank you,' I whispered. 'For everything.'

Brooke nodded, and I could taste the tears on her lips.

The metal of the gun against my skin had heated up now. It wasn't so cold when she pressed it harder against my temple.

I closed my eyes.

The noise faded.

And then she dropped the gun.

She dropped the gun.

21

Closing Time – Tom Waits

The police swarmed us, cold metal and scratchy black fabric and hands moving my arms forcefully, but surprisingly carefully, behind my back. Lights flashed, red and blue, red and blue, and the dank smell of standing water from last night's rainstorm wafted up from the ground.

People were shouting, but I felt myself drifting away. It didn't matter anymore. My mind was blank and my body was numb, and it didn't matter.

I turned my head, and Brooke was bent over the trunk of the Mustang while another police officer put handcuffs on her. Like the ones on me. Our eyes met, and she grinned. Cat-like. Shark-like.

Brooke-like.

'I love you, Norma Jeane!' I yelled. This was it. I might never get another chance to tell her. I couldn't let them take us away without saying it. 'I love you!'

'I love you too, Jolene!' she screamed over the noise of everything going on around us.

Brooke turned her face so her forehead was pressed to the red paint on the car, and I saw her shoulders were shaking with laughter.

Or maybe not laughter. Maybe something else.

I stopped paying attention to everything after that.

You have the right

To be silent

I love

To a lawyer

You have the right to

Used against you

I love you

Silent

You have the right to remain

A lawyer

Questions, now

I love you too

You have

You have the right

You have the right to remain . . .

*

I was put in the back of a cop car and taken to an Atlanta police station. They didn't bother taking my photo or fingerprints, which confused me, but multiple people asked for my name and date of birth, and whether I had any identification on me.

I didn't, but I recited my name and birthday every time I was asked.

The officer who had driven me to the station led me to an interview room and took off my handcuffs.

'Wait here,' he said gruffly.

I was panicking now, desperate to know where Brooke was, what was happening to her, if she was getting the same treatment I was or if it was worse for her because of the gun. Or if it was worse for me because of the murder charge. Something lurched in my stomach and I thought I was going to throw up. It was definitely going to be worse for me.

I paced back and forth across the worn carpet, glancing up at the clock on the wall every minute as the second hand made its slow, relentless circle. After fifteen minutes, a harried-looking woman came into the room.

'Jessie Swift?' she asked, and I nodded. 'I'm Claire Morris. I'm with the judicial service. I look after minors when their parent or guardian isn't available to represent them.'

She was short, though still taller than me, with reddish hair pulled back into a braid, wisps of it coming loose around her face. Wearing jeans and a white shirt, and carrying a tan leather backpack, she had the smart-casual vibe nailed. I wanted to trust her, but it was impossible to trust anyone right now.

'Law enforcement have contacted your mother to let her know you've been found safe. We can wait for her to get here if you want,' she said in a rush, 'but we'd have to put you in a foster home until she arrives in Atlanta.'

'I don't want to wait,' I said quickly. 'Where's Brooke?'

'I don't know. I'm sorry,' Claire replied.

'Can I see her?'

'Not right now, Jessie. Please sit down,' she said, gesturing to one of the chairs. She settled into the other one and pulled a notepad from her leather backpack.

'I'm good.' Walking was better. I was full of nervous energy, and I needed to get it out somehow. I drummed my fingers on my thighs as I moved. 'Are you, like, a lawyer?'

'No,' she said with a sharp laugh. 'I'm a social worker.'

'Do I need a lawyer?'

She looked up at me, not laughing anymore. 'I don't know. Do you?'

I shrugged.

Before I could say anything else, there was a quick knock on the door and it swung open. The police officer who walked in was a woman who wore her hair in long, thick braids past her shoulders. She wasn't wearing a uniform, just jeans and a T-shirt, with a blazer covering her weapon harness. She looked calm and elegant and totally in control. I immediately envied her. I wanted to be calm and elegant and in control, and instead I was a snotty, splotchy, terrified mess.

'Take a seat, Jessie,' she said, putting a folder down on the table.

I finally stopped my pacing and sat down on the edge of the chair, clasping my hands between my knees.

'I'm Detective Audrey Beaufort. I've just got a few questions for you.'

'Okay,' I rasped.

Detective Beaufort checked one of the pieces of paper in her file and didn't look at me.

'I didn't do it,' I said in a rush.

'Didn't do what?' she asked, raising her eyebrows a little.

'I didn't kill him.'

From next to me, I heard Claire sigh. I glanced at her, and she had her eyes shut, her fingers pinching the bridge of her nose. 'Do you want a lawyer, Jessie?' she asked.

'No,' I said. I was sure I was making the wrong decision, but I couldn't stand the idea of having to wait to get this conversation over with.

'Who didn't you kill, Jessie?' Detective Beaufort asked calmly, finally turning to look at me. Her dark-brown eyes were piercing, and I felt myself shrinking under her attention.

'Mitchell,' I whispered.

'Mitchell . . . ?' she prompted me.

'Mitchell Covier. He's . . . He *was* my mom's boyfriend. He's dead now.'

A moment of fear gripped me, because – No, I'd seen his body, he was definitely dead.

'He's dead, right?' I asked desperately.

'Yes,' she replied, her expression totally unreadable. 'How do you know that?'

'It was on the news,' I said. 'And ... I saw his body. Before I ran away.'

She nodded slowly. 'When was this? When you saw Mitchell's body, I mean.'

'Right before I left Seattle. On the Monday afternoon.'

'What time did you get home from school, Jessie?'

'About five thirty, I guess. Choir was canceled.'

Detective Beaufort kept asking questions, guiding me through what I'd seen, what the kitchen looked like, where Mitchell's body was. My stomach was heaving, my fingertips were icy cold, and the back of my neck and my face hurt from clenching my jaw so hard. My body was reacting to the stress, but my mind was shockingly clear.

It was almost, *almost*, a relief to finally tell someone all the details. For it all to be over.

The detective picked up another piece of paper from her folder.

'Why didn't you call the police when you found Mitchell's body?' she asked, and even though I knew that question was coming, I didn't know how to answer it.

I looked desperately at Claire.

'Do you need a minute, Jessie?' she said softly.

'No,' I murmured. 'I thought you – the police – would think I'd killed him.'

'Did you kill him?'

'No,' I said as clearly as I could.

'Did you want to kill him?' Detective Beaufort asked.

'I wanted him to stop hurting me.' That wasn't an answer to her question. We both seemed to know that.

'He was hurting you?' she asked, her tone a little more gentle now.

I nodded.

'Did he rape you?'

'No,' I whispered.

'But he was physically abusive,' she clarified.

'Yes.'

'You don't have to tell me about it now, if you don't want to,' she said, leaning forward a little. 'But I'm here to listen if you do.'

I shook my head. 'I don't know if I can.'

'That's okay. I have a few more questions. Can we keep going?'

'Sure,' I croaked.

'Did you tell anyone about the abuse? Did you maybe ask someone to kill him for you?' Detective Beaufort asked.

I wondered where Brooke was. What they were asking her. I wondered if her parents were already on a flight down to Atlanta to pick her up, and what would happen to her then. My breath hitched, and I could feel the clawing panic creeping over my chest.

'Jessie?' Detective Beaufort prompted, shaking me out of my downward spiral.

'No,' I said again. 'No, I didn't kill him, I didn't ask anyone to kill him for me and I don't know who killed him. I don't. I'm sorry.'

'Okay, Jessie,' she said. 'We're going to arrange for you to be sent back to Seattle. Seattle PD will want to talk to you since this is their case.'

'I'm not . . .' I'd already been arrested. 'Being charged?'

'We're not detaining you, no. Since you're a minor, we'll make sure you get home safely.'

I wanted to scream. This was all wrong, so wrong, and I didn't know how to tell them that going back to Seattle and my mom was worse than anything they could do to me.

I looked desperately at Claire. 'Is Brooke coming too?'

'I'm sorry – as I said, I can't tell you anything about Brooke.' She'd put her notebook away in her leather backpack and it looked like she was getting ready to go. I couldn't understand how the conversation could be over already.

'But . . . but . . .'

This didn't feel right at all. The panic rose up inside me again, clutching at my throat.

'I don't understand,' I said, my voice catching and breaking.

Detective Beaufort put her papers back in the folder and caught me with her intense gaze.

'You haven't been charged with a crime, Jessie,' she said, and maybe it was my imagination, but she sounded a little kinder now. 'Seattle PD have been looking for you because you disappeared after a man close to you was found dead, and no one knew where you were.'

'They thought I killed him, though . . .' I said desperately.

'Did they?' she asked.

'They must have.' I couldn't comprehend any other reality.

Detective Beaufort leaned forward a little. 'Jessie, listen to me,' she said clearly. 'You say you didn't kill him. My colleagues in Seattle don't think you killed him.'

Claire jumped in. 'You were brought into custody partly to make sure you were safe, to ensure no one was making you do something you didn't want to do, and partly so the police could ask some questions for the investigation into Mitchell's death. We've established all of that now. So you can go home.'

'Do I have to go back to my mom?' I asked, hating how pathetic my voice sounded.

The two women exchanged glances.

'Not necessarily,' Claire said.

'I still don't get it. The police were chasing us . . .'

'Chasing you?' Detective Beaufort asked. 'I don't think so, Jessie. There has been an alert out for you since you went missing, because you're only seventeen and because of the circumstances. We've been keeping a lookout for you, but no one was chasing you.'

I wanted to push her for more answers, to ask about the sheriff's deputy who had stopped us outside Atlanta and the cops who had followed us in Salt Lake City and the child protection people just outside Portland, but all that felt like I was giving too much away.

Without warning, ice-cold realization crept down my spine as Detective Beaufort's words settled in.

You say you didn't kill him.

We don't think you killed him.

I had never needed to run away.

No one had thought I'd torn the Creep to pieces and left him bleeding on the floor.

There was no reason the past two weeks had ever needed to happen. I could have stayed at home, in Seattle.

And if I'd never gotten into Brooke's Mustang, she wouldn't have met Chris and he wouldn't have kidnapped her. Drugged her. Traumatized her.

My heart started to beat faster, and my breath turned shaky. I had to get back to her right away, to explain, to make sure she was okay. I collapsed in on myself and a high, painful whine escaped my throat.

'Jessie?' Claire said, rushing over and grabbing my shoulder.

'What's wrong?' Detective Beaufort demanded. 'Are you hurt?'

I shook my head and wrapped my arms around my waist, trying to physically hold myself together.

'Are you in pain?' Claire called out, and I had no idea how to answer that.

They'd just torn everything I knew to be true apart and scattered the pieces. Now I had to rebuild the truth – the actual truth, not just my fears – based on what I'd been told. Guilt seeped into my pores. Would Brooke ever forgive me?

Claire couldn't come with me back to Seattle because she had another kid she was representing the next morning. She said goodbye to me and wished me luck and I tried to tell her *thank you*, but the words stuck in my throat. She smiled at me, though, and I think she knew I was grateful even though I couldn't speak it out loud.

I was assigned another liaison and shipped unceremoniously back to Seattle. Sea-Tac airport was cold and dark when we arrived, and surprisingly quiet. I glanced at a huge clock on the wall – it was just after midnight. It took me a moment to remember that we'd crossed three time zones over the past couple of weeks. I'd barely noticed.

Being back in Seattle didn't change how I felt. I was still completely numb, not able to really process anything. What Detective Beaufort had told me was such a contradiction to everything I thought I knew that my brain didn't know how to handle it. No one had been chasing us. Except Chris, who the police didn't know anything about. No one thought I'd killed the Creep. I was free to leave. They had sent me home.

My liaison took me to a hotel and told me to get some sleep, that she would be in the next room if I needed anything, and I nodded and wondered where my bags had gone. I had nothing – no toothbrush, no pajamas, no Brooke, and I wanted to cry. But it was like my body no longer knew how to produce tears.

In the end, it didn't matter. I couldn't sleep anyway.

I replayed the moment in the alley over and over again, trying to figure out if I could have done something different – if I *should* have done something else that would have led to a different outcome, one where I wasn't alone in a hotel room, back in a city I couldn't stand.

I wondered where Brooke was now. Who she was with. We hadn't been put on the same flight home – I knew that much. I wanted to know if she was thinking about me, too, wherever she was.

The next day I was taken to an ugly office building in Bitter Lake, a neighborhood north of my old home in Greenwood. The liaison – I hadn't bothered to remember her name – dropped me off and promptly disappeared. I should have been mad at her about that, but I couldn't find the energy.

I really had no idea what was going on, and everyone who worked here looked so busy, rushing from one room to another with laptops tucked under their arms. I was left in a waiting area with a couch and a TV showing the Food Network, and I curled up into a ball and tried to make myself invisible.

After a couple of hours, someone came over.

'Jessie?'

I looked up at him. He was youngish, brown hair, glasses.

'Sorry to keep you,' he said. 'Someone will be here to get you soon, okay?'

I nodded and turned my attention back to the TV. He didn't say anything else, just rushed off to his next meeting.

It took another hour, and I didn't move except to press my hand to my stomach to stop it growling. I'd caught enough snippets of conversation to figure out this was an agency, for fostering, which worked with local Child Protective Services. Brooke wasn't going to be somewhere like this. By now she'd be back with her family, and, underneath all the numbness, I was scared for her, and scared for what she might do. She might run away again, and if she did, I'd have no way of finding her. I had no idea how her parents would punish her for what we'd done. She could be in trouble, because of the gun. She could be still in Atlanta, waiting to be charged with all sorts of crimes. She could be back in Seattle, or in New York with Julianne, or anywhere in between. But I knew for sure she wouldn't be somewhere like this.

My attention flitted between the TV and the main office opposite my waiting area as another woman came in, briefly spoke to someone, then sat down on the other end of my couch. I was expecting my mom to come and get me, even though I'd told Detective Beaufort and Claire I didn't want that, so I thought she was likely another social worker here to ask me more questions.

'Jessie? I'm Lena.'

I tried to assess her, but she wasn't giving much away. On the one hand, she was wearing a long floral skirt and Birkenstocks, so she looked like someone's hippy aunt. On the other, there was a sharpness in her eyes, behind her wire-framed glasses, that gave the impression she wouldn't take any bullshit.

'I foster young people. I've been told you don't want to go back to your parents?'

I scrambled to sit up, straightening out of my slouch.

'Seriously?'

She nodded and tucked her sandy-colored hair behind her ear. It was long and wavy, and the ends were dyed pale pink.

'I was only called an hour ago, so I don't know the whole situation. But you can come with me.'

'Yes,' I said. 'Please.'

'Okay. Where's your stuff?'

I shrugged, and she sighed.

'Don't worry. Let's get out of here.'

I knew I would have to face my mom eventually, especially now that I was back in Seattle. I had no idea how she had reacted to what had happened. In the news report, they'd said she was distraught, but that was the kind of thing people said when kids went missing. It didn't mean it was true.

Going with Lena was scary because I had no idea what would happen next, but that was nothing compared to the real fear I had of seeing my own mother again. Our relationship was complex and messy, and I was starting to build some real rage deep down inside me because she hadn't seen what the Creep had been doing to me. I was running away all over again, and I was aware of the irony.

'Are you hungry?' Lena asked as we walked out of the building and to her car – a bright-yellow VW Beetle.

'Yeah,' I said.

'Let's grab something to eat, then. Any preferences?'

My mind flicked back to all the junk Brooke and I had eaten over the past couple of weeks, and my stomach, still feeling delicate from all the gut-deep fear, roiled.

'Could we just get, like, a salad?'

Lena laughed and opened the car door so I could climb in.

'Sure. That's not a request I get very often.'

'I need to eat a vegetable right now,' I said.

Eat a vegetable for once, Brooke.

Meredith's voice came back to me clearly, and a little knot in my chest loosened. Everything was still a mess. Actually, everything was even more of a mess now than when I had left Seattle, much worse, but also so much better. I'd learned over the past couple of weeks that I could trust my instincts. I could make the right decisions. I could take charge, and make things happen. I could fall in love and kiss the girl I liked, and it could maybe, one day, work out.

'I know a place that does great salads,' Lena said, and I startled and looked over at her. She'd gotten into the driver's seat without me noticing. 'I'll take you there.'

She pulled out of the parking lot, and I stared out onto the road, wondering what lay ahead.

22

Graceland – Paul Simon

Lena's house was a beautiful old Tacoma home with a wrap-around porch out front and a huge yard out back where she grew flowers and fruit trees and kept fish in a pond. Inside, she'd painted murals on every single wall, as well as some of the floors, and most of the ceilings. It was like being in a fairy-tale book.

She let me explore in a sort of stunned silence while she sat in her kitchen and drank tea that she'd made in a copper pot. She didn't seem in a rush to ask me anything, and I wasn't in the mood to talk, and it suited us both just fine.

When I finally made my way back to the kitchen, she was working on an iPad and looked up at me with a smile.

'All good?' she asked, and I nodded and settled on one of the kitchen chairs.

She told me that she used to teach grade school and now taught music, and when I said I played guitar, she pulled one out of a closet under the stairs. She had a pale-green piano in the living room with scarred and battered keys, and she said she would get me practicing scales and chords because music was good discipline, and good healing.

My bedroom was on the second floor, and it was the only room in the house not decorated in Lena's signature style. I liked her murals, but I guessed if she took foster kids in, they might find it overwhelming. One wall of the bedroom was painted light blue and the other three were cream. I had a dresser, a walk-in closet and a queen-size bed, and the bathroom across the hall was just for me. It all felt like luxury, and I was grateful, so grateful, that I'd ended up somewhere that was nice. Not just safe, but nice, too.

Later that afternoon, we went out to a mall to pick up some clothes and essentials, since I didn't have any of my stuff and I had no idea where it was. Still in Atlanta, probably. I wanted my clothes, and my black dress from Goodwill, and my makeup bag which had grown with items Brooke had bought or stolen for me. And my cropped T-shirt from Target, and my trashy paperbacks, and Brooke. The grief for what had been taken from me swelled in my chest, and I picked up more black dresses and tights and band T-shirts and cutoff jean shorts, determined not to go back to being Mouse. Lena hummed with approval at all my choices and waved away my questions about who would pay for it, mentioning a stipend without offering any details.

That night, I laid awake wondering about Brooke, alternating between fear and anger and deep, aching longing. There was a very real possibility her parents wouldn't ever let her see me again. Or that the authorities would stop us from seeing each other. Or that she would choose to move to New York to be with her sister and closer to her brother, instead of coming back to her parents. Or, worst of all, that she would come back to Seattle, decide she didn't want to be with me anymore, and go back to her old life.

I didn't think that last one was likely, but I couldn't shift the feeling that we'd created something unique and special when we were alone, just the two of us, in the Mustang, with the whole world laid out for us to explore. Would she even want me now life was getting back to normal? Would she still care about me when she learned that it had all been in my imagination – that the police hadn't been chasing us, and therefore it was my fault she'd been kidnapped?

I fell asleep when the sun started to peek around the edges of my curtains.

Which meant I woke up late, of course. I figured out how to use the shower and washed my hair with shampoo that smelled wrong, finger-combing out the tangles. I didn't bother putting makeup on. I had no one to impress and no bruises to cover up.

I stumbled downstairs in one of my new outfits to find Lena at the kitchen table with her iPad again.

'Good morning,' Lena said with a warm smile. 'Do you want tea? Coffee?'

'Coffee would be great.'

She nodded her chin at the counter. 'There's some in the pot. Help yourself.'

Being in someone else's house – especially living there – was weird. Lena seemed to know this, though, and was trying to make it easier on me.

'I've been reading your notes,' she said as I moved around the kitchen.

I was surprised by her honesty, and shocked that I had notes for her to look at.

'Yeah?'

I missed drinking iced coffee with Brooke. Drinking it hot now felt wrong. I leaned back against the counter, cradling the mug to my chest all the same, and Lena twisted around to look at me.

'You want to see them?' she offered.

'Am I allowed?'

'They're your notes, Jessie.'

I thought about that for a second, sipping my coffee. 'I don't think I do. I was there, I know what happened.'

'That's fair. Do you have any questions for me?'

I had so many questions that I didn't know where to start. But one in particular had been nagging me.

'How did they find us?'

Lena glanced down at her iPad. 'I think you were stopped by police in Georgia?'

'Yeah,' I murmured, thinking of the super-friendly cop who had spent too long looking at Meredith's ID.

'He connected the two of you to the missing persons' report and alerted Atlanta PD.' She gave me a sad little smile. 'Brooke's car is very distinctive. They spotted you pretty quickly.'

'Oh.' I sighed, and stared down into my coffee. So, Brooke had been right. We *should* have detoured to another city.

'Anything else?' Lena asked, and I shook my head. I had so many more questions but they could wait for later. 'Okay. There are a few things we should probably talk about.'

I went and sat down at the table, preparing myself for the worst.

I had been kicked out of St. Catherine's.

I could still finish the school year being home-schooled if I wanted.

My mom wanted to see me.

My dad had written me a letter.

I had been asked to go to another police interview, with Seattle PD this time.

'Do I have to?' I asked, and Lena made a face.

'You kinda do. Sorry.' I thought she meant it, too.

I made a face back at her. 'When?'

'Today, I expect.'

I told myself it was better to get it all out of the way, rather than having the prospect of another police station hanging over me like a dark cloud. Despite what Detective Beaufort had said, I wasn't completely convinced that Seattle PD were going to drop everything and let me go.

Lena opened her mouth, then closed it again, and I knew there was something she wasn't telling me.

'What else?' I pressed.

'You asked to be put in foster care instead of being sent back to your mom,' Lena said cagily.

It took me a second to understand what she was implying.

'I told the police in Atlanta that my mom's boyfriend was abusive.'

Lena nodded. 'They'll want to make sure wherever you go next is a safe place for you.'

I realized that was why I'd been carted off to a hotel, then to social services, before someone had picked me up. They wanted to make sure my mom wasn't abusing me too. She hadn't, and she wouldn't, but I still wasn't ready to face her again.

Lena made some phone calls while I brushed my teeth and blow-dried my hair. Despite what everyone had told me – that I wasn't going to be thrown in jail for murder – it was hard to accept. Going back to a police station felt like I was being led to my execution.

When we arrived at the station, I expected to be taken to an interrogation room, one like I'd seen in cop procedural shows, but the room was more like someone's living room, with a couple of comfy couches and a coffee table and a big window that let in a lot of natural light. It wasn't modern, or particularly nice, but it looked like someone had made an effort.

Lena went straight to a couch and sat down. 'You don't have to be nervous,' she said.

'You don't know me very well. I'm nervous about everything.'

That made her laugh. She pulled out a bottle of pale-blue nail polish from her enormous purse and started painting her nails. If anyone else had done that, it would have annoyed me, given the circumstances, but I was starting to realize Lena was incredibly astute underneath her hippy, floral-skirt, kindergarten-teacher exterior.

The door to the room opened, and my heart started to thunder in my chest.

The policewoman introduced herself as Officer Gale. She had silver-gray hair, cut super short, and piercing blue eyes.

Like Detective Beaufort, she wasn't wearing a uniform. But it felt like a carefully staged scene to not freak me out. Which obviously freaked me the fuck out. I didn't know what angle they were trying to take. Was I still a suspect, or did they just want information from me? Or both?

'Do you know why you're here today, Jessie?'

'No,' I said. I was pretty sure there was something in the constitution about not having to incriminate yourself, but I hadn't paid close enough attention in Social Studies class to know the exact details. Besides, it wasn't a lie. There were plenty of things that had happened in the past couple of weeks that they could be charging me for, and I wasn't going to confess to anything until I had an idea of what they knew and what they didn't.

'Let's start at the beginning. Why don't you tell me why you ran away?' Officer Gale asked.

I glanced at Lena, wondering exactly what I should say. I needed to dance on a line between telling the truth and protecting Brooke from getting in any more trouble than we were potentially in. I'd already told the police in Atlanta about the Creep, but they had no idea what we'd done since leaving Seattle: stealing hundreds of dollars at the convention, Brooke being kidnapped, stabbing Chris through the hand. Plus, Brooke's illegal gun that she'd been threatening to shoot me with. I couldn't tell them about any of that.

'Will you tell me the truth if I ask you something?' I replied instead of answering her question.

'Probably,' she said easily.

'Did you think I killed Mitchell?' I said, almost tripping over my words as they rushed out of me. 'Because the cop in Atlanta, she said you didn't – you don't – think I killed him.'

'I don't think you killed Mitchell Covier,' she replied. Her eyes didn't leave mine. She wasn't lying.

'What about before, though?' I pressed, aware that I was in dangerous territory now. The police wanted to interrogate me, not the other way around.

'You were a person of interest, Jessie, but so were a lot of people,' Officer Gale said, leaning forward a little. 'Your mom was a person of interest. So were her ex-boyfriends. Mitchell's colleagues were, too. Do you understand?'

I nodded. Then forced myself to unclench my jaw.

'Let's talk about something else,' she said. 'When did you and Brooke first plan to run away together?'

I frowned at her. 'We didn't plan it,' I said.

'Oh?'

'I left the house with my stuff, and then when I was on my way to the bus station, she pulled over and asked me if I wanted a ride.'

Get to the bus station. Get on a bus. Go.

That felt like years ago now, not just a couple of weeks. It had been a good plan. I was so pleased I hadn't followed it.

'So it was a total coincidence that Brooke was also leaving the city at the same time?' Officer Gale prompted.

'Yes.'

She looked down at her paperwork, and I knew she didn't believe me.

'Jessie, could Brooke have killed Mitchell Covier?'

'What?' I said, startled, and almost tempted to laugh. 'No.'

'You know that for sure?'

'Yes,' I said emphatically. 'The timelines don't add up, and I barely knew her back then. It doesn't make sense.' I shook my head. It was absurd. 'Brooke didn't know anything about the Cr– I mean, Mitchell.'

Office Gale pounced. 'What do you call him?'

I sighed. 'The Creep. I don't think that needs much unpacking, do you?'

She gave me a long, easy look. 'Since his death, there have been some allegations of inappropriate behavior leveled against Mitchell Covier. Do you have any thoughts on that, Jessie?'

My heart sank. 'I don't know if he was hurting anyone else. That's God's honest truth.'

I knew they would want me to go into it at some point – how it had started, what exactly had happened to me, where and when. They were going to want to know why I hadn't gone to my mom, or one of my teachers, or the police, and I didn't know how I was going to explain any of that.

It was hard for me to look back at the girl I'd been when I found the Creep's body and decided to run. That was classic fight-or-flight instinct kicking in, and I'd never had it in me to fight anyone.

Not then, anyway. Now, I knew what I was capable of.

I wondered if Officer Gale knew about Chris. About what I'd done. About what I'd been forced to do to get Brooke back – the knife through Chris's hand. I was almost tempted to tell her. To brag. She knew what had happened with the Creep – or she thought she did – and that gave her an impression of me. One that was wrong. Telling her about Chris would get me in trouble, though, and, more than that, I'd have to explain what had happened to Brooke. She hadn't wanted to go to the police before, and I wasn't going to make that decision for her now.

'He was hurting you, though?' Officer Gale said.

'Yes.'

I had an overwhelming desire to strip off and force her to look at all my scars, the same way I'd showed them to Brooke. I wanted her to face them, face the reality of what the Creep had done to me.

'Do you want to see?' I asked.

I'd gotten a lot worse at controlling my impulses recently.

'We'll get it documented,' Lena said, stepping in. 'Through the proper channels.'

'I can do it now.' I was already getting up and stripping off my shirt.

This was my body, and they were my scars that he'd given me. The man whose death Officer Gale was investigating. She deserved to know what type of man he was.

'This,' I said, yanking my T-shirt aside, 'is where he used to grab my arm and put out his cigarettes on my skin. I learned not to scream when he did it because that just made him laugh.'

I stepped up onto the low coffee table, so I was looming over her, and thrust my hand toward her face.

'This is from when he swung a beer bottle at my head, and I put my hand up to stop him and the bottle broke my finger.'

I shoved my shorts down to my knees, exposing the ugly red scar at the top of my thigh. 'This is from when I didn't make him a coffee one morning, so he took mine and threw it at me.'

Lena got up and gathered me in her arms, a brief, tight hug, then gently set my clothes straight again like I was a little kid.

'I didn't kill him,' I said to Officer Gale while Lena buttoned my shirt, carefully, since her nails were still drying. 'He was a sadistic psychopath, though, and I don't blame whoever did.'

'Did you tell anyone about what he was doing to you?' Officer Gale asked, and I flinched hard. I'd known this would come back to haunt me.

'I spoke to my youth pastor,' I replied. 'I said I wished he was dead. So she knew about it, but I don't know if she told anyone else.'

Officer Gale nodded, and I realized she already knew that. She was testing me, to see if I'd tell the truth.

'How about anyone else?' she pressed. 'Your mom?'

'No,' I said, feeling exhausted all of a sudden.

I sat back down on the couch. Lena pulled a bottle of water out of her purse and handed it to me. It was a silent message to calm down, though I got the impression it came from a good place – she wasn't scolding me.

Officer Gale caught my eye again, looking deadly serious this time.

'Jessie, who's Norma Jeane?'

I cracked.

It was so ridiculous – this mix of what the police knew and what they didn't. Of all the things they could ask me about, of all the things they should have figured out by now, the one point they were most curious about was *that*?

I howled with laughter.

Lena and Officer Gale exchanged a look.

'Norma Jeane was Marilyn Monroe's real name,' I said.

'Is it some kind of . . . code?' she pressed.

'No,' I said, slumping back in my chair. She was just like Brooke: a girl who everyone misunderstood. 'She was just a girl. Just a girl . . .'

Time moved quickly over the next week. I decided that I wouldn't go back to regular high school – not for the rest of this semester, at least. Lena home-schooled me, and she seemed pretty confident that she could catch me up on the work I'd missed. After all, I'd only been gone for two weeks.

I had to keep reminding myself of that. It felt like I'd been gone for years. Long enough to completely transform who I was.

I still had to decide where I was going to spend my senior year, and Lena was letting me find excuses to delay making the choice. She probably knew that I wanted to know where Brooke was going before I agreed to anything, but she didn't call me out on it. I'd been putting off asking what had happened to Brooke, scared that I wouldn't like the answer. At first, being stuck in limbo was a relief, because I didn't have to face the truth, and then it turned into painful, silent torture.

'Can I see Brooke?' I asked one night over dinner when my resolve finally cracked.

'I don't know,' Lena said. She didn't bullshit me, and I liked that about her. 'I'll find out, if you want?'

'Yes. Please.'

We'd talked about Brooke a few times. She obviously featured in some of my notes – the ones that Lena had read – and I'd been fairly honest about who Brooke was to me without specifically using the word 'girlfriend'. It didn't feel right to call Brooke my girlfriend when we hadn't even had the chance to talk about it yet, but Lena was astute. She knew what I wasn't saying.

I had to go back to the police station to have more interviews with Officer Gale, but the tone of them had changed. She wanted to know more about the Creep now, what he'd done to me, what I knew about his relationships with other people. His relationship with my mom. Whether or not my mom had known about how he was hurting me.

I told them she hadn't known. I asked if the Creep had been hurting my mom. Officer Gale said she didn't know.

Lena took me to other interviews, too, with the foster care people, which was awkward. We had to go all the way back to the ugly office building in Bitter Lake, which meant driving through my old neighborhood. Lena always made a point of taking a route that didn't go past my mom's house, so I didn't have to look at it. I was grateful to her for that.

We stopped at Starbucks on our way home, and Lena handed me her credit card to pay for our orders while she found a booth. I got an iced oat milk caramel latte, because the taste took me back to a place and a person I ached with missing, and Lena wanted some green matcha thing that I was definitely not adventurous enough to try.

When I sat down, she had pulled her iPad out of her purse and her expression had changed.

'Thanks,' she murmured as I handed her the mug.

'Did you hear from Brooke?' I asked.

Lena shook her head and locked the screen. 'I'm working on it, Jessie, I promise.'

'Thank you,' I said.

'I have got an update for you, though.'

I guessed it was something big.

'Oh.' I sipped my iced coffee. 'Do they know who killed the Creep?'

Lena looked me dead in the eye. 'Yes. They do. A man called Thomas Dederich has been charged with second-degree murder.'

'I know him,' I said. I pushed my drink away, not sure I could stomach it anymore. 'He goes to our church.'

Lena looked at me, waiting in an increasingly tense silence to make sure I was okay. I nodded for her to keep going.

'Mitchell was physically abusing Dederich's son, and potentially a few other children in the youth program he was responsible for. I can't tell you much more than that, because there's a court case pending, but that's the information that's going to be publicly released.'

'Everyone's going to know?' I asked, not liking how small my voice came out.

'They're going to know Mitchell Covier has been accused of abusing children in the youth program, and that Thomas Dederich has been charged with second-degree murder,' she said. 'Your name won't be mentioned.'

I reached for my coffee again, needing some time to put my thoughts in order.

'I'm not sorry he's dead,' I said.

'I really don't blame you for feeling that way,' Lena replied.

'Mr Dederich ... he's not a bad person. If they need someone to give, like, a statement or something ...'

'You'd do that?' Lena asked.

'Yeah. If he wants that.' The thought of speaking to the police voluntarily, or even getting up in court and telling a judge and jury what the Creep had done to me, made me feel sick, but it was the right thing to do. 'Mr Dederich was just a parent trying to protect his kid.'

'I'll make sure that gets passed on to his lawyer. You're a brave young woman, Jessie.'

I huffed a laugh. 'Not really.'

'I think so.'

'If I was, I would've said something a long time ago.' The guilt would eat at me for a long time to come.

'You can't change that. Or anything else that happened. But it seems like you're making very mature decisions now.'

I wasn't so sure about that, either. Brooke and I had made a whole bunch of stupid decisions alongside the really good ones, and I could guess why people weren't exactly jumping at the idea of us being allowed to see each other again.

My heart hurt.

I was desperate for Brooke and that wild freedom we'd found together, and even though I knew real life wasn't like that, I missed it. I wanted to be in the Mustang again, with the wind in our hair, half singing, half screaming the lyrics of some eighties rock band.

Being back in Seattle with the prospect of facing my demons – and my mom – was harder than I'd thought it would be. Even though I had Lena and her endless patience backing me up, I knew the hard part was still to come. Sooner or later, I'd have to do the mature stuff she thought I was capable of and face the music.

'One step at a time,' I murmured, remembering my mom's instructions.

Lena nodded. 'You don't have to handle all of this at once,' she said, like she was reading my mind.

'Thank you,' I said. 'For . . .' I waved my hand around, hoping to capture everything she was doing for me.

'Any time,' she said. 'You know, there's an awful lot that's not in those notes, Jessie. If you ever feel like telling me what you got up to on that road trip, I'm all ears.'

I laughed. 'Maybe one day.'

She sipped her vividly green drink. 'I'll hold you to that,' she said, grinning at me over the rim of the cup.

It turned out I wasn't allowed to see Brooke on my own – we had to have a chaperone, as per the agreement between Lena, my social worker and Brooke's parents. I guessed that was because the last time anyone had seen the two of us together, she had been holding a gun to my head. I couldn't blame them for being apprehensive, even if it was annoying.

Brooke came to Lena's house, and Lena sat in an armchair in her living room, with her fat ginger cat on her lap, reading a book, and generally trying to make herself invisible.

I answered the door and stared at her for what felt like forever.

'Hi.'

'Hey.'

I opened my mouth, then closed it again. 'I wasn't sure if you'd want to see me,' I said eventually.

'Jessie, I've been asking to see you every day since I got back.'

'You have?' I said as my stomach did an impressive somersault. I pressed my hand to my belly, hoping to quiet my nerves.

'Yeah,' Brooke said with a tentative smile.

'Me too.'

Brooke was wearing black jeans that were ripped at the knees and a baggy black tank and white sneakers. Her hair was loose around her shoulders, and I could tell she was wearing a little mascara. She was perfect, like always.

Her eyes asked me a question, and I answered by stepping forward, then stumbling into her arms. She wrapped me up in safety and security and I put my head on her shoulder and let myself *breathe*.

'I really fucking missed you,' she murmured into my hair.

It had been three weeks, meaning we'd been apart longer than we had been on the road together, and something about that just didn't add up in my brain. The road trip had been such a turning point in my life. It still didn't feel real that it was over.

'I missed you too,' I said, taking another second to hold her before I pulled away. 'You better come inside.'

'This place is beautiful,' Brooke said as she kicked off her sneakers and followed me into the living room.

'This is Lena,' I said. 'She painted pretty much everything.'

'Pretty much,' Lena echoed. 'Nice to meet you, Brooke.'

'Thanks for letting me come over.'

We curled up in the love seat underneath the window, facing each other with our feet tucked up so we could get in close.

It took me a moment of just looking at her before I found my words.

'What happened? Are you okay?'

The question was way too big and way too vague, but I didn't know what else to ask.

'I'm living with my uncle Tony,' she said with a shy smile.

My eyes widened. 'Really?'

'Yeah. I spoke with my parents, and they agreed it was probably for the best. Over the summer, at least, while we figure it all out.'

'They just agreed to it, no arguments?'

'No,' Brooke said. I reached for her hand and smoothed my thumb over the inside of her wrist. 'There was a lot of shouting. As soon as Tony found out I was back, he came over to the house and then he yelled at my dad for a really long time. Then he came upstairs and told me to pack a bag.'

'I think I like Uncle Tony,' I murmured.

'I do too,' she said with a little laugh. 'He's a lot more easy-going than my parents. He's going to get me working on cars again.'

That was probably going to help her heal just as much as any other type of therapy, and I felt another rush of gratefulness that Brooke had an uncle Tony to help her get through this.

'That's good,' I said. 'It'll be good for you.'

'I think so too.'

Brooke turned her hand over, and I started drawing little patterns across her palm with my fingertip.

'What happened,' she started hesitantly, 'after they split us up? In Atlanta?'

I swallowed, taking a second before I answered her.

'I had to tell the police what had happened. To the Creep.'

'God, Jessie.'

I'd thought a lot about whether I should be honest with her, if I ever had the chance. In the end, I'd decided lying to her wouldn't be good for us in the long run.

'They said I was only ever a person of interest,' I said, not looking up to meet her eyes. 'They never actually thought I did it.'

'That's good,' she said gently.

'It is?' I asked.

She used her knuckle to tilt my chin up. Her big, brown eyes were filled with empathy.

'Yes,' she said simply. 'I'm glad that whole chapter is over.'

'You don't ... blame me? For everything you went through?'

I didn't know how else to say it – to try to encapsulate all that had happened in those eleven days we were together in the Mustang, and how it had all ended.

'No. I thought you'd blame me.'

'What for?' I exclaimed.

'Taking you out of the city,' she said with a wince. 'When you could've stayed here and cleared everything up really quickly.'

'That wasn't your fault,' I said, shaking my head.

'And what happened wasn't your fault, either.'

I couldn't quite wrap my head around that. Brooke hadn't done anything wrong. And she didn't blame me, either. All of a sudden, a huge weight lifted from my shoulders. I turned my hand over again and squeezed hers, hoping to communicate all the gratitude I felt.

'Oh, so, guess what I found out?' Brooke asked, easily changing the subject.

'What?' I replied.

'You remember Chris and Ashley?'

'Yes. They haunt my nightmares, actually.' I could joke about it, but it was true. I'd woken up in a cold sweat more than once, dreaming that they were still chasing us.

'The FBI caught up with them. They were charged with abduction, drug trafficking, possession of stolen goods, the fucking motherload.'

'Oh my God. How do you know that?'

'I called Daniel,' she said. 'I thought he was going to yell at me, too, but he said he'd been really worried, and that if Tony hadn't come to get me, he would've taken me in himself.'

'Your brother?' I asked. Brooke had barely mentioned him, apart from the fact he was studying Law at Harvard.

'He's a good guy,' she said, watching the movement of my thumb across her skin. 'Anyway, he dug into it for me and found out what had happened to them.'

'Wow.' It took me a second to process. 'How . . . are you feeling about all of that?'

'Good. Fucking elated, actually. They're not getting out, Jessie. They won't get away with it.'

'Thank God.'

'I know. And, I got a therapist.'

I squeezed her hand. 'A good one?'

'A really good one,' she said with a sweet smile. She reached up and tucked my hair behind my ear. 'I'm doing better.'

'I'm really glad,' I murmured.

I thought Brooke might kiss me then, but Lena was still pretending to read her book, so she didn't.

'I bought you something,' I said, and reached behind the couch to grab the brown paper bag.

I let myself study her expression for a second before handing it over.

Lena didn't let me go out by myself that much, and, besides, her neighborhood wasn't that well connected by bus routes. She didn't mind taking me places, though, as long as she didn't have a piano student coming over.

Going back to Goodwill and thrift stores felt comforting in a way I'd probably have to explain to my own therapist at some point. I'd figured out the magic formula to how things were arranged in thrift stores, and even though I only got a tiny allowance, being a foster kid and all, I liked being able to pick whatever I wanted and know I could probably afford it.

I had found *Graceland* when we'd driven into Seattle for the day. It was hidden in a stack of eclectic cassettes and had cost me three dollars and fifty cents, and even though I didn't know if I'd ever be able to see Brooke again, I'd bought it anyway.

'Oh my God, Jessie.' She laughed when she pulled it out of the bag. Then her eyes started watering.

'Don't cry,' I said immediately.

'I'm not crying.' She pushed the tears away from her eyes before they smudged her mascara. 'You're the sweetest person I've ever met, I swear.'

After so long thinking Brooke would never even *look* in my direction, her reaction made me want to cry too. Girls like me never got the girl they had a crush on, except I did, and I really didn't know how to feel except so grateful, and so in love with her.

I let Brooke pull me into an awkward hug – we couldn't get close enough on the love seat with elbows and knees between us. She reached for my hand as I pulled away and linked our fingers together loosely.

'I haven't got the Mustang back yet,' she said.

I frowned. 'Where is it?'

'Still in Atlanta.'

'Why?' I said hotly. 'They can't just keep it.'

Brooke laughed. 'I agree. We've been trying to get it shipped back, but there's some bureaucracy holding it up. Tony keeps calling them, so hopefully it won't be long.'

'You'll have to find a Walkman or something. To listen to the tape.'

'I'm sure Tony has one somewhere. That sounds like the kind of thing he'd hang on to.' She squeezed my hand. 'Thank you,' she whispered.

I thought there was something poetic about Brooke searching for a land where she'd find grace. That had made me even more determined to get the cassette tape for her – I'd wanted to be the one who helped her find it. A few years ago, I'd underlined a passage on grace in one of the books I'd been given at church: it was the divine strength to endure trial and resist temptation.

We'd done a lot of enduring and not a lot of resisting while we'd been together, and despite everything we'd been through, I was sure I'd come closer to finding grace with Brooke than I ever had before.

Promises for the future were hard when everyone was scrutinizing us from every angle, waiting for us to rebel and detonate like fireworks. They treated us gently, carefully, like we were explosive. I knew I'd see Brooke again, though. After everything that had happened, they couldn't keep us apart.

She kissed me goodbye on Lena's front porch, wrapped in the thick scent of magnolia blossoms carried to us on humid air. I watched her climb into a taxi to go back to her uncle's house, the paper bag with the cassette clutched safe in her hand, and Lena found me there much later, still leaning against the railing with the front door wide open.

I stayed on the porch to watch the sun set, the pinks and oranges bleeding into the night sky, until the stars blinked out and I was ready to go back inside.

Acknowledgements

Does anyone know why the acknowledgements are more difficult to write than the entire book?! I feel like this is my Oscars acceptance speech moment, and I'm sure I'm going to mess it up. I'll try to get this over with before they start playing music to usher me off stage.

The first person I have to mention is my mum, who has supported every single hare-brained scheme I've ever had with a love and warmth that's hard to put into words. I live every day trying to make you proud of me, and it makes me a better person. Thank you for being my mum. I love you.

To the rest of my family: Mr B, Dad and Carolyn, Emily and Joe – having you behind me means I can dream my dreams even bigger. You taught me to 'Aim for the moon, and you might land among the stars.' The landing has been pretty incredible.

I'm still not sure if I believe in fate, but if it does exist, it put this book in the hands of my editor, Amina Parchment-Youssef, at exactly the right moment. Thank you for believing in me and for helping me craft the best possible version of this story.

To go back to the very beginning, the existence of this book is owed to Lucy Cuthew, who was such a generous and encouraging mentor. To say I couldn't have written this book without you is a massive understatement. Thank you again.

To my wonderful agents: Beth Ferguson, who was the first to take a chance on me, and Saskia Leach, who picked up the torch – thank you both for your guidance and support and endless patience.

Finally, I get to be a writer today thanks to more than just a little help from my friends. Andy, Kirsty and Carrie-Anne, who have listened to my anxious chatter about this book for – let's face it – years at this point. You're all amazing. To Fabi and Sarah, thank you for supporting me as this dream took flight. To all the other Brave New Words writers, I'm so proud to have learned and written and grown alongside you.

Want to know more about the writing of *Run Away With Me*?

Read on for a Q&A with author J. L. Simmonds!

1. What inspired you to write *Run Away With Me*?

A few things, actually! I spent some time reading about the escapades of Bonnie and Clyde, which was my initial spark of inspiration – I really wanted to set that vibe in the context of a YA novel. I also had the movie *Thelma & Louise* in the back of my mind, as well as the 1993 music video for 'Crazy' by Aerosmith. If we could go back in time thirty years I would totally cast Alicia Silverstone and Liv Tyler as Jessie and Brooke in the movie version of *Run Away With Me*!

2. Which character are you more like – Jessie or Brooke?

I don't know that I'm very much like either of them, though elements of things I love definitely snuck into both of their personalities, like Jessie's love of trashy romance novels and the thrill Brooke gets from being on stage (I am a rare extroverted author!).

3. Do you have a favourite scene in the book?

This might sound strange, but the end might be my favourite scene. Jessie goes through a LOT in this book, and at the end of the story she's wrested back control over her life and is making good decisions about what's going to happen to her. The book ends in such a hopeful place, and I love that.

4. Music features heavily in the story. Are you a music lover?
Yes, absolutely, and the chapter headings are pretty much a rundown of some of my favourite albums of all time. 2024 was a great live music year for me – I got to see Stevie Nicks live at Hyde Park, and Kings of Leon (who are probably my favourite band who didn't get a shout out in a chapter) in my hometown of Bristol, which was incredibly special. Watching the sun set over Ashton Gate while they played 'Fans' was a real core memory moment.

5. How do you see Jessie and Brooke's lives panning out in the future?
I'd love to think that Brooke achieves her goal of setting up her own garage and I could see her becoming an expert in restoring vintage cars. By the end of the book Jessie has changed so much, but she needs to figure out who she is when she's not living in fear of the Creep. She would definitely go back to Nashville at some point, and I could see her having a career that has something to do with music.

6. If you could go on a 'life-changing road trip', where would it take you?

I'd love to do a long-distance train journey one day – like the Orient Express that runs from London to Vienna, or the glass-roof train that runs through the Rocky Mountains. Long train journeys seem so romantic to me.

7. What is the best thing about being an author?

I've been writing for a very long time – since I was about fifteen – so seeing one of my stories reach bookshops will be a 'pinch me' moment. It feels very surreal that people are going to be reading my book!

8. Can we expect more books from you?

Yes! I have a few more projects that are currently in progress, but my next book will be out in summer 2026. If you liked reading about teenage girls making bad decisions and getting into a whole bunch of trouble in *Run Away With Me*, you will like the next one as well ;)

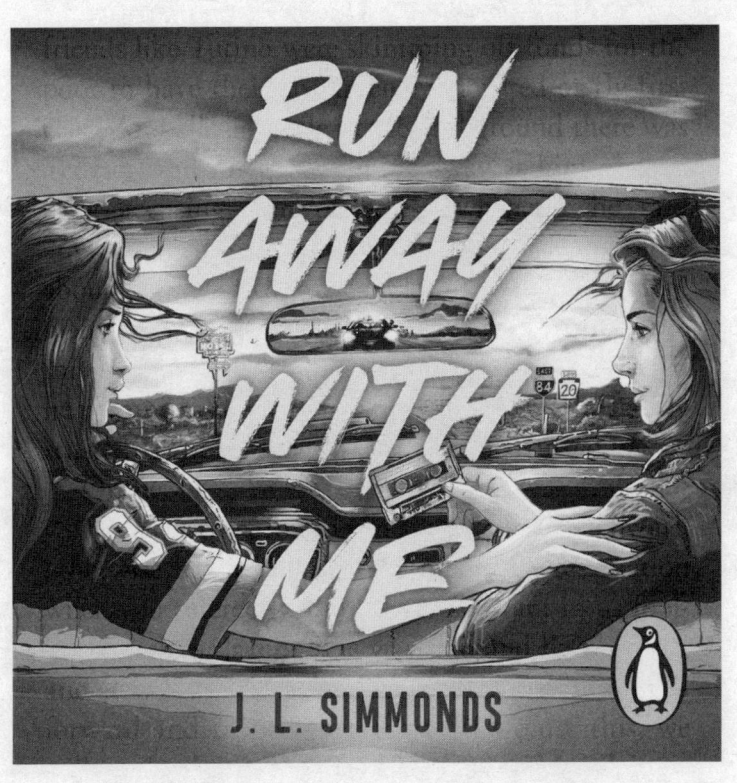

ALSO AVAILABLE TO LISTEN TO IN AUDIOBOOK!

J. L. SIMMONDS grew up by the seaside but now lives in Bristol. She studied English Literature and worked in marketing and communications for ten years before returning to Bath Spa for her MA in Writing for Young People. She writes joyful LGBTQ+ YA, bad poetry and text messages with too many emojis. *Run Away With Me* is her debut novel.